THE 6th HEAVEN

A NOVEL

MONICA BROUSSARD

ACORN PUBLISHING

Helping talented writers publish exceptional books.

www.AcornPublishingLLC.com

For information, address:
Acorn Publishing, LLC
3943 Irvine Blvd. Ste. 218
Irvine, CA 92602

The 6th Heaven

AUTHOR'S NOTE

The Amazon jungle is captivating. Venturing into its depths is like exploring the hidden corners of the mind. The jungle hosts an array of remarkable creatures, including the mighty jaguar, the massive green anaconda, shocking electric eels, and flesh-eating piranhas. Just as travelers must remain vigilant and highly aware of their surroundings, we ourselves must be alert when exploring the concealed areas of our minds, where our deep personal thoughts and emotions reside. Like the jungle, it will reveal its secrets.

DEDICATION

I would like to express my appreciation and gratitude to those whose efforts and inspiration have brought my manuscript to life, as well as to all those who offered me heartfelt words of encouragement when I needed them most. I genuinely thank those who have helped me turn my dream into reality. To my friends who supported me, to my editor who refined my words to perfection, to the designers who brought my book to life with its appearance and essence, and to my family, whose patience and unwavering support were invaluable. To all my unsung heroes who have championed my endeavors. This is my opportunity to express my deep gratitude and acknowledge the vital role you all have played in my journey from concept to publication.

Chapter 1

When Kendal moved into the L.A. penthouse after she and Derek got married, the first thing she did was redecorate the master bedroom. The bones of the apartment were great—spacious rooms with high ceilings and intricate crown moldings—but it felt soulless, like a showroom rather than a place where real human beings lived.

Kendal painted the stately walls a soft green to bring peace and tranquility. She hung elegant artwork depicting natural landscapes, adding to the overall serene atmosphere. Derek had trouble sleeping so she installed heavy blackout curtains and blinds over the massive picture windows.

Yet amid all this luxury, there were signs of neglect. Discarded clothing strewn about and empty bottles of sleep aids on the nightstand. It was clear that the opulent setting held a profound sadness within its walls.

On this particular morning, Derek was buried underneath the plush down comforter, his once-handsome features now marred by tired eyes. A stubbled, unshaven head and face covered in tattoos could barely be seen poking out from the rumpled bedding. He lay there in the darkness, unable to find the motivation to get up and face the day. The curtains and blinds were closed, casting the room into an even deeper darkness despite the bright sunlight outside.

Kendal, overwhelmed with the duties of running their office and plastic surgery clinic, could find little time to focus on the spiral happening with Derek at home. She had moved out of the bedroom the night before, unable to change the sheets or stand the musty smell of body odor and sweat.

Kendal had warned Derek that extended periods of staying in bed and a lack of motivation to face the day could be a sign of decline. His struggles with fatigue and the desire to withdraw from daily activities were clear indications that he was battling depression.

His problems threatened to pull her down, too. Feeling drained, she crawled into bed in the spare room next door, overwhelmed and unsure how to aid him—or if he even desired assistance. For now, all she could do was immerse herself in the myriad responsibilities she had inherited at work, hoping that Derek would eventually find his way back to her. She drifted to sleep with one final thought—she would give him a little more time to recover from whatever darkness consumed him.

Derek burrowed deeper underneath the comforter, drifting in and out of awareness. He was well into his second day of staying in bed.

At the rational level, he knew that his depression could cause a range of problems. At the irrational level, an early morning volcanic eruption had spewed out a debilitating flow of childhood memories, emotions, and sensations buried deep within the recesses of his hippocampus.

The childhood trauma of almost being beaten to death by a rogue gang on his way home from high school had been buried deep within his subconscious for years, surfacing at his most vulnerable moments. It periodically stifled his ability to cope with life. Such was the case during his latest session with his therapist, Dr. Cole, an astute woman with a soft voice and kind eyes who seemed to see right through him. It had crept back like a sly predator silently stalking its prey.

Just a short while before, Derek had been a solitary man. By day, he performed reconstructive surgeries. He lived in a luxurious penthouse near the beach, content to spend his evenings in quiet contemplation.

He had dedicated all his energy to his work as a world-renowned plastic surgeon, immersing himself in this specialized field of reconstructive medicine. Restoring and altering the human body was his passion. All connections to childhood emotional trauma had been buried deep within his subconscious.

But then, one morning, the tattoos appeared after he had a vivid nightmare of a swirling spiderweb that seemed to move and change as he tried to escape. He had awoken with a start, his heart racing and his body drenched in sweat. He remembered every detail—the grotesque spider with its sharp, black legs and beady eyes, looming over him as he struggled to free himself from its web. In his dream, he had been half-paralyzed with fear, unable to escape the creature's grasp as it taunted and tortured him.

Now, as he lay in his bed, still trembling from the intensity of the recurring dream, he realized that the spider was not just a figment of his imagination. It was a manifestation of his deepest fears and insecurities, a symbol of the overwhelming challenges and struggles he faced in his waking life.

The tattoos covered his body from head to toe—even his face.

He had tried to subconsciously resist the spine-chilling transformation, to hide by going back into a deep, fitful sleep that night, hoping it was only a nightmare. But the tattoos seemed to have a mind of their own, and soon, his entire body was covered in a symphony of ink, intricate and detailed, each telling a story he could not understand.

Derek became a spectacle, a mystery, and a work of art. People would point and gawk at his tattoos. He nearly lost his medical practice.

He could not explain the disturbing dichotomy, but he felt an intense connection to these markings. He intuitively realized they were a part of him and he would never be alone again.

After experiencing the vicious beating when he was a teenager that almost took his life, Derek struggled with feelings of unworthiness, believing that he somehow deserved what had happened to him. He had been selfish that day, not listening to his mother and not wanting to visit with his grandmother. Then she died suddenly; he never saw his grandmother again. It felt like there must have been something inherently wrong with him if the universe was willing to use its power against him in such cruel ways.

As a prominent plastic surgeon, he performed each reconstructive procedure with as much focus and precision as if working on his own body. His attention to detail and excellence in each procedure were an extension of the reconstructive surgeries performed by Dr. Christopher Casey on him as a child.

When he performed craniofacial surgery, it was, in his mind, a repetition of the one performed on his face so many years before. A reconstructive microsurgery on the delicate bones of a hand that might someday perform life-altering procedures.

In his dreams, he relived moments of profound regret and insecurity. He had told himself it was for the best when Kendal had left him for a short time before they married. He was protecting himself from the disappointment and hurt that inevitably came with a relationship's dissolution. He had been able to rehabilitate himself in her eyes.

But now, in this vivid dream, he gripped the steering wheel of his parked Bentley and felt the familiar explosion go off in his head. He could not deny the truth any longer. He was a lonely and lost man. The realization was like a punch in the gut, and he could not help but feel a wave of sadness for what might have been.

Still burrowed deep underneath the covers in this realistic dream, he could feel the cool air blowing from the Bentley's dash vents as he tried to calm his breathing. He thought about the old shaman woman he had encountered. She'd grabbed his arm, and Derek accidentally pushed her to the ground. He now understood that she'd seen right through him, into his soul.

He sat in his car, taking deep breaths and trying to prepare himself for whatever was to come next. Finally, he exited the safe capsule of the Bentley and approached the motel with his heart thudding.

Derek could intuitively sense he was stepping into a transformative world where matter could be molded like putty. When he entered her motel room, he was greeted by the scent of incense and sage and the old shaman woman squatting in the middle. Sitting back on the heels of her bare feet, knees drawn tightly to her chest, she reached for a large tibia bone adorned with beads. The other hand delved into her skirt pocket for a small chicken bone she had salvaged from the motel dumpster the night before. Grinding it slowly in a tiny stone bowl, she began a soft chant.

She was unaware of his presence. He seemed to be invisible as he stood observing the ceremony performed in front of him.

He watched as she pulled out a powder-filled pouch and emptied its herbal contents. Using the jagged edge of the sharp tibia bone, she cut her finger and let the blood drip onto the pile of powder. She placed the bone against her thin brown lips. A whistle quavered across the room. Alternating between rhythmic chanting and clicking her beads, the old woman circled the bowl.

As she passed the dresser, she grabbed a water bottle, took a sip, and spat the liquid into the powder. The tibia bone that had once connected flesh and sinew and contained the essence of physical life was now used to stir the roux of her potion. Dipping her first two fingers into the concoction, she scooped up a dab of paste and smeared it along her tattooed forehead. It would disguise her face from evil spirits.

Her finger proceeded down the bridge of her nose, sweeping to the outside perimeter, then down to the chin. She did this first to one side, then to the other. Dipping her fingers in the paste once again, she crossed her arms. Starting at her shoulders, she ran the tips of her two fingers down her arms, all the while continuing her chanting.

Derek understood that the shaman woman was a keeper of sacred knowledge. She restored harmony in the world by dispelling toxic, negative energy, keeping the balance between man and nature through ritual laws of wisdom that extended beyond time and space.

His heart beat faster as powerful forces gathered around her. It was as if Derek saw through her eyes. She pierced the veil of earthly reality, and an electromagnetic field sizzled around the old woman's body. Spirits collided. Lightning flashed, followed by a long roll of thunder.

It shattered her trance. She collapsed to the floor. Before her head struck the corner of the dresser, she saw Derek's face rushing toward her, and she knew he was the man who would save her granddaughter.

His body trembled as he slowly lowered himself to the floor next to the old shaman's body. He clasped her head in his hands. The physical connection ignited an explosion of knowledge.

Derek's eyes flew open.

He sprang up from his bed, full of new energy. He now knew what he had to do.

Chapter 2

"I don't want you to go!" Kendal pleaded. "It's not safe! We just got married."

Derek could hear the anguish in her voice as he packed his duffle bag. It killed him, but in his heart, he knew he had no choice. He shoved another piece of clothing into his pack.

He had had brief moments of happiness since they were married. But more often now, he felt a loss of security and self-esteem. He could barely function. He had no interest in work or even routine activities. Feelings of hopelessness and worthlessness had invaded every corner of his life.

Still covered in tattoos, he no longer talked to clients. He avoided people, places, and things that used to bring him happiness, preferring to isolate himself. Most days, he stayed under the bedcovers, ruminating in his misery.

Kendal stood before him with her hands on her hips. The white tank top and blue jeans hugged her athletic body. Her auburn hair was pulled up in a bun, with strands cascading down each side of her face. With a stern look, she asked him, "When did you ever have the choice? You may think taking this kind of risk will get you the answers you want, but I am sure all it will do is bring more trouble." Her eyes, a piercing emerald-green with flecks of gold, bored into his.

He forced a blink to break her stare. He was determined to find a way to make it work. "I'd find the answers here if I could," Derek said in a reasonable tone, "but Father Mike is coming with me. He knows someone at a mission who can help us until we reach the jungle."

Derek crammed a balled-up t-shirt into the pack. Even though he hated to see Kendal so upset, he was feeling hopeful and enthusiastic about the journey ahead. The risk of danger was high, but he did not mention that to her.

Kendal's chin jutted forward in the stubborn way she had. "Do you hear what you're saying? You're going into the jungle. How can you think this is *not* going to be dangerous?"

"It probably will be, but as I see it, I have no choice." Now Derek's voice was stern, too. He stayed focused on the task, his freshly shaved tattooed head bowed in concentration as he rolled another piece of clothing and stuffed it in the backpack.

His only salvation was to discover why and how these mysterious illustrations on his skin had come about. An inkling of intuition had told him what some of the tattoos meant. But it made little difference if he could not reverse them.

The stakes were high. His sanity depended on it.

"Then what about Tyler? He still needs you, too."

"He'll be on break soon," Derek said, returning to the closet to grab another item.

Tyler was in his first year of college, and Derek had been instrumental in ensuring he started on the right foot. Derek intended to continue mentoring Tyler as he initially promised when he came to live with him after a fiasco with his younger brother. But with his depression and after having the lucid dream with the shaman woman, he knew he wouldn't be good to anyone if he didn't take advantage of the opportunity to take this trip with Father Mike.

Kendal stood in place, listening to his muffled voice drifting from the closet. "I'm sure he'll be just fine," he said between the sound of drawers opening and closing.

Derek returned to the bedroom. "He'll have six weeks before he starts back to school," he said as he stuffed another item into his bag. "This is a perfect time to go—it won't affect him at all."

"It might be a perfect time for him, but what about you? Doesn't the rainy weather start in the Amazon around this time of year?" Kendal asked.

"It will just be the beginning of the rainy season. We should be able to get in and out of the jungle before the actual rainfall and flooding is in full effect."

His focus now was on his current dilemma. His heavily tattooed body made people recoil in fear before he even spoke a word. Former patients wanted nothing to do with him. It felt like a knife was being twisted in his gut every single day.

He was told tattoos were once associated with criminals and sailors but were now widely accepted. That had not been the case for him. These tattoos had not given him the usual swagger most guys projected when illustrated. Nor had it given him the acceptance that would come with such a bold move as to convert his body into a living tapestry. His identity and lifestyle as a plastic surgeon did not mesh with a tattoo collector.

All the years of plastic surgery, physical exercise, and maintenance invested in his body had vanished. It felt like he was deliberately defacing it, like a form of desecration. It would have been different if he had willingly chosen to do this to himself, but that was not the case.

He had not picked these tattoos. They did not commemorate a special moment or memory. There was not a tattoo on him that was a tribute to a transitioned loved one. Some tattoos were reminders of significant moments in his life—mostly bad. Lately, there did not seem to be a positive connection that he could find in the symbols.

He knew Kendal could not understand the profound grief he felt from the loss of his previous life. He had tried to explain it to her. People looked at the tattoos; they did not look at him. They could not see past the tapestry that blanketed his entire being. Derek was not the person they perceived him to be.

The average person who got a tattoo probably believed it would improve their self-esteem by expressing something externally to the world. But his tattoos did not solve any underlying issues—they exacerbated the problem. The difficulties of having tattoos had shaken his confidence and decimated his world. He felt disfigured.

The fact was that being inked hurt his professional and personal relationships. The tattoos had destroyed his body image and liquified his identity. His dull sadness turned grief into anger, making his emotions unpredictable.

Now his marriage was being affected. They'd been happy for a while. The first few months seemed to go by in a blur. He and Kendal were swamped with business decisions. Then, slowly but surely, the tattoos began to reappear.

Then, one day, he went to the market to buy something. The police pulled him over. He sat in his Bentley with both hands on the wheel and waited as the police officer approached. He was asked for his driver's license. He was cautious and respectful when he pulled the license from his wallet, which still had his tattooless picture with his name, Dr. Derek Hollinger.

The police officer looked at the bald man covered in tattoos inside the vehicle and had him step out. He made him put his inked hands on the hood as he patted him down. He then sat him on the curb like a common criminal while he ran the plates. The car did not come back stolen, and the driver's license matched the name on the registration, but the police officer was not satisfied. The officer, still suspicious, felt this might be an identity theft situation. He towed the Bentley to the impound yard and took Derek into the precinct on a possible stolen vehicle charge. The police station had called Kendal to come to identify him since there were no previous fingerprints to match.

Derek had been mortified and degraded by the experience. He was a well-known plastic surgeon being treated like an ordinary criminal. The only way he would be able to cope now was to find the granddaughter of the shaman woman who had done this to him.

He needed answers. *Real answers.*

Father Mike's spiritual counseling had not provided the ones he sought.

The lack of control in his life was becoming a theme. He became wary of venturing outdoors. He tossed and turned at night, consumed with anxious thoughts, and when he finally drifted off to sleep, nightmares came parading into his consciousness. He was sleep-deprived, which had now led to a myriad of other issues.

All he could think about was that he had been branded like a piece of meat, inked like a pig carcass. The face paint had now begun to feel like acid. His fog of misery had turned into self-deprecation.

The soul-crushing ache inside him lightened ever so slightly when

Father Michael told him he would travel with him to the Amazon jungle. He could feel the tears welling up, and the lump in his throat started to loosen.

Derek had been gobsmacked when he found out that the young girl taken hostage by a mobster named ZhiZhu was the shaman woman's granddaughter. He'd hoped to get answers from the shaman herself, but she passed away before he had the chance—another devastating blow.

Her granddaughter had survived her kidnapping by human traffickers because Derek had helped her to flee her captors. Surely, she would want to help him after what he had done for her.

Her miraculous escape proved to him that she must have supernatural powers like her grandmother. She'd not only vanished from the morgue without going through a door, but she had taken her grandmother's body with her. How could one do that?

The phone buzzed in Derek's pocket. He pulled it out, looked at the caller ID, and then glanced at Kendal. "I need to take this." He turned his back to her. "Father Mike, I was just telling Kendal about our trip," he said in an uplifted voice as he left the room.

"Since we don't have a visa to enter Venezuela, we will have to enter through Colombia and make our way over to the Orinoco basin," the priest said. "Right now, it's almost the end of their winter season. We'll have to hurry so we do not get caught in the seasonal flooding of the wetlands. I've spoken to the bishop. One of my longtime friends from the mission will meet us at the airport." Father Mike hesitated. "Did you get your vaccinations?"

"Yes, I got my vaccinations last week." Derek glided his fingers over his tapestried head.

"Only pack what you need. You'll have to carry your dry sack everywhere and need it to be as light as possible. Two sets of clothes, one for day and one for night, and a couple of T-shirts to change into when you become soaked. No bright colors to attract insects. A medical kit and mosquito net—that's it. I'll arrange for the rest of the supplies."

"I was just working on that when you called," Derek said.

"Then I'll see you the day after tomorrow. I will text you the itinerary. We can meet at the airport. My friend at the mission hired one of the local trackers to take us into the jungle to find the village."

The stars were aligning. "That sounds perfect. Thanks, see you soon." Pushing the button on his phone, Derek floated back to his room to continue packing.

Kendal stood next to the bed. "Don't forget this," she said, handing him an EpiPen. "You're going into the jungle and you're allergic to bees. What could possibly go wrong?" She gave him a disgusted look and left the room.

Derek felt her anger like a physical slap. Any negative emotion tossed his way seemed to tighten the shackles around his identity.

He held onto the thought that, if nothing else, this trip could give fresh significance to his tattoos. This journey into the jungle filled him with a newfound sense of purpose and determination. He knew in his heart that this unique situation involving adventure and danger had to have meaning. He prayed to God that it was for good and not evil.

Despite understanding that God's ultimate power could change everything, Derek still struggled with doubts and fears. His faith had yet to materialize. He had been just a regular person and couldn't imagine why he had been the recipient of this tapestry of ink.

Father Mike had told him that the human psyche is fragile and delicate, often molded by past experiences. He had explained that he ran into troubled homeless people every day. It was clear to him that for those people who had endured traumatic events during their formative years, the impact had been catastrophic, propelling them out into the streets.

Father Mike had told Derek that he believed this journey into the Amazon jungle was a divine intervention and that he must guide Derek on this path.

Derek placed the EpiPen in the corner pocket of the bag.

Father Mike, a man in his forties with intense blue eyes and dark hair, always greeted his parishioners with a warm smile as they filed out of the small church. His features were tanned, a hint of his Spanish heritage. When he stood at the church door, he always wore his black pants and shirt with a clerical collar, a symbol of his role as a priest without the formality of the vestments.

As he stood outside the church, Father Mike scrubbed a hand across the day-old stubble on his jaw. He had been so busy with his duties that he hadn't had time to shave, but he didn't mind. It added to his rugged appearance and made him seem more approachable.

His thoughts were interrupted by a call from Kendal, who confided that Derek was struggling. Father Mike was saddened by the news but not surprised. He had just read a study conducted by the National Institute of Mental Health saying that individuals who had suffered severe childhood trauma were at a significantly higher risk of developing a mental health disorder, with a three-fold likelihood for any condition and a fifteen-fold likelihood for borderline personality disorder.

Whether it be abuse, neglect, or witnessing violence, these experiences often had detrimental effects on both interpersonal relationships and cognitive functioning in the brain. The scars ran deep and manifested in self-destructive behaviors, volatile emotions, and an inability to trust others.

To Father Mike, it seemed a miracle that Dr. Derek Hollinger had achieved so much in his disheveled life. It showed that for those who have survived traumatic experiences, the healing journey was a long and arduous one. Father Mike was determined to help Derek get on the right path. With the proper support and resources, there was still hope for a future free from the shackles of his past.

The trauma Derek had endured as a teen when he was almost beaten to death on the street by a group of wayward young men had been a deeply distressing and disturbing experience that had now overwhelmed his ability to cope. Father Mike had watched it manifest itself in various forms.

That violent experience could have a profound impact on a young person's developing brain, leading to changes in neural pathways and disrupting the normal functioning of the body's stress.

Reassuring Kendal that he would check in on Derek, he put his cellphone back in his pocket and stepped back into the little church to do some housekeeping.

Father Mike paused in the aisle of the empty church, fixated on the way the sunbeams caressed the altar, almost as if in reverence. The intricate patterns on the pews, carved with such precision and care. He could still feel the warm embrace of the community, all gathered together in this sacred space, their voices raised in praise and worship.

Father Mike believed that God had made it abundantly clear that He did not want His children to fumble in the darkness, searching for His will like a blind man searching for a light switch. Instead, He wanted them to walk confidently, relying on His plans and purposes. He wanted them to find peace even in uncertainty, trusting He held the future in His hands.

As he picked up the missalettes strewn about the pews, he knew that convincing Derek of this was another matter. It had been a terribly slow process. He had seen Derek's decline in recent weeks and was growing more concerned for his mental health and soul.

Later that day, despite Father Mike's efforts to find peace through prayer while studying the Bible in his quiet office, he could not shake the persistent anxiety that weighed on him. A foreboding feeling had crept into his soul. As he searched for God's plan for his next actions to help Derek on his spiritual journey, a dark veil of doubt and fear kept creeping in, making it difficult to make a clear decision.

Father Mike perceived other elements at play, small signs of grace that may go unnoticed to most but not to those who were attuned to them. He looked around the dimly lit room, where sunlight gently passed through stained-glass windows, casting a blurry spectrum of colors on the walls. The distant sounds of bustling life on the streets outside could be heard, blending with the gentle singing of the choir practicing that floated over from the small church next door. A cooing dove perched on the windowsill.

They all created a serene spiritual atmosphere, the small details that made him feel like he'd caught a glimpse of Heaven on earth. It was a sign of grace, a reminder that even in the midst of chaos and noise, there was still beauty and love to be found. But then why had there been no sign from Heaven?

"Lord, why can't I discern your will?" Father Mike cried out. "Why do I feel so lost and uncertain?"

A gentle whisper floated in a breeze through the room in response. "Be still and know that I am God."

Father Mike closed his eyes and breathed deeply, allowing those words to sink into his soul. He did not need to strive and struggle to find God's will; he needed to be still and trust that God was in control. And as the choir continued to sing, their voices rising and falling in perfect harmony, the whole room filled with peace and joy.

With a newfound sense of purpose, he knew what he had to do. Father Mike closed his Bible and picked up his cell phone to call Derek.

Chapter 3

Derek's tattoos had appeared one morning like a sudden, irrevocable spell had been cast upon his skin. How they got there, what they meant, and how to get rid of them were all questions that harassed him every moment of every day since.

Father Mike had been cautious in his discussions with Derek. His advice for the current dilemma was based on studies of a disrupted life.

Derek had explained to Father Mike that after a day of profound sickness and two turbulent nights filled with nightmares and vomiting, Derek had woken up in his luxurious penthouse with the first rays of the sun streaming through the window, signaling the start of a new day. But he noticed something peculiar as he rubbed the sleep from his eyes and stretched his arms. Black ink etched into his skin in intricate designs and symbols covered every inch of exposed flesh.

This had seemed farfetched the first time Father Mike had heard his story. Derek said that at first, he thought it was just a nightmare. But as he tried to rub the tattoos away, he realized they were permanent. They had been carefully and deliberately etched into his skin, each line and curve telling a story he could not decipher.

Father Mike had never encountered a phenomenon such as this, and he had no idea of its origins. What he did know is that it was not from God. God had made us in His image, and this was not His image.

Derek explained that panic set in as he remembered the stories of cursed tattoos and spells cast upon unsuspecting victims. He frantically searched his memory for clues as to how they got there but came up empty-handed.

Father Mike had tried to be instrumental in his search for answers. He had delved into the Bible looking for hints.

Now, after everything that had happened, Derek had decided there was only one way to find answers. He had to go to the village where the mysterious old woman had lived. She had held the key to his tattoos' secrets and mysteries.

Father Mike had prayed, and now he felt led by the Holy Spirit to assist Derek in this journey to the Amazon.

Since the shaman woman had perished, they had decided together that they only had one recourse: to make the journey to her home village deep in the Amazon rainforest. Derek could not shake the feeling that the tattoos held a darker and more sinister purpose, and he wondered if he could ever rid himself of them.

But Father Mike knew that the tattoos were leading them on a Divine mission to find God.

The commercial jet landed in Bogota, Colombia, where the two men boarded a smaller plane—one of two flights a day that flew into Inirida.

The landing on the small airstrip at the foot of the mountains in Inirida proved to be nerve-wracking. The air traffic control tower was a tiny wooden building on stilts, the runway was frighteningly short, and turbulence created a roller coaster-like experience with sudden updrafts and downdrafts.

When Derek and Father Mike deplaned, the sweltering heat of the muggy air hit their faces like a furnace blast. Derek made the mistake of grabbing the extremely hot and sticky handrail. He yanked his hand off quickly. It felt like he had grabbed a hot poker.

Anxiety began to creep into his mind as they descended the stairs onto the scorching hot tarmac. He grabbed his pack off the trolley, and Father Mike removed a broad-brimmed khaki hat from his case. Derek reached into his backpack and retrieved his red baseball cap and sunglasses. They proceeded through a metal-roofed portico into the brilliant sunlight. A van pulled up straight away and out hopped a stout man with thick curly hair, glasses, and a drenched shirt. He beamed and embraced Father Mike in an immense bear hug.

Father Mike had shed the vestments prescribed by Catholic Church regulations. Today he looked like any other ordinary man. The priest, only a few years older than Derek, shaded his piercing blue eyes with the hat. His facial hair always looked stubbly as if he had not shaved for a day. Today, he wore khaki pants and a safari-style shirt.

A broad smile crossed Father Mike's face. "I was hoping you were going to be the one to meet us!" he exclaimed.

"How could I miss picking up one of my oldest and dearest friends?" the man chuckled.

Father Mike patted his back, looking over to Derek. "This is my longtime friend, Alejandro. He helps run the mission." He moved his hand to his shoulder. "I'm amazed that you were able to get away to come over here to pick us up."

"I had to insist. They really . . ." His voice faded. "Had no choice."

His eyes locked on the tattooed face under the baseball cap and sunglasses.

"This is Dr. Derek Hollinger, also a friend," Father Mike said with a smile, putting his hand on his shoulder.

Derek removed his sunglasses and reached out to shake his hand.

Alejandro had seen some of the Indigenous people's tattooed faces, but he had never seen a white man wholly covered in ink. He glanced at the extended ink-covered hand. He chose not to ask any questions so as not to seem judgmental.

The men shook hands.

"Let's get you loaded up and get moving. It's too hot to stand here." Alejandro took a cloth from his back pocket and wiped his brow as he watched Derek put his bag in the back of the van.

The cool air in the vehicle felt good. They adjusted the vents to blow directly on them.

Alejandro told Derek to reach and open the small ice chest on the floor to get them cold water.

The distance between towns was not too far apart, but the gravel road's poor quality meant it would take several hours to drive from one place to the other. Alejandro looked at Father Mike in the passenger seat and then at Derek in the rearview mirror. Over the vibration, he called out, "How was your trip?"

"It wasn't too bad," Father Mike shouted back. "We only had to change planes once. The layover was short. Coming around to land was a real experience." He laughed. "We flew over the mountain range and dropped into the valley at a hundred-and-eighty-degree angle when we came in for the landing. I didn't know a plane that size could maneuver like that. It was quite thrilling!" He smiled.

Alejandro had thought further on the subject and decided he needed to know. He called over his shoulder to the back, "If you don't mind me asking, Dr. Hollinger, what is the story on all the tattoos?"

"Derek, call me Derek. That is why I am here." Derek leaned forward to project his voice, "To find out *how and why* I have these tattoos."

"Really?" He glanced in the rearview. "What do you mean?"

"Well, I believe an old shaman woman used to live out here in the jungle. She passed away, but her granddaughter might be living out here now. I believe her granddaughter may know how and why I got these tattoos. I'm hoping she can help me find a way to eliminate them."

"I've never heard of such a thing." Alejandro reached over to the cup holder, grabbed his water bottle, and sipped.

Derek sat back in his seat, "Yeah, neither have I."

"What do you think she can do for you?" He glanced over at Father Mike.

Derek's brow wrinkled as he gazed out the window. "Well, I believe the old shaman woman put a curse on me and that maybe her granddaughter can reverse it." His voice amplified back from the surrounding barrage of rattling metal.

After months of internal turmoil, he finally spoke his belief aloud. It had been eating away at him; now it was out in the open.

Outside, the sun started to disappear behind a mountain, casting a warm hue on the horizon and scattered trees.

Derek turned back to look at the driver, a man he had just met. He could sense his skepticism, but he didn't care. He needed answers and was willing to believe in something as fantastical as the redemption of a shaman's curse to find them.

Alejandro shifted in his seat, his face a mask of doubt and discomfort. Finally, he spoke. "Do you really think the granddaughter can reverse it?"

Derek nodded, his eyes never leaving the window. "I have to believe it. I can't live like this anymore."

Alejandro sighed, shook his head, and warned Derek, "Sometimes the truth is more painful than the curse." His round-cheeked face turned to Father Mike. "Do you agree, Father?"

"No, I don't," he said, staring straight ahead. He put one hand out to brace against the dashboard.

It was unsettling to Alejandro when Father Mike avoided eye contact.

The van rocked due to the road's condition. Alejandro used both hands to guide the wheel, which jumped intermittently from potholes the size of minor lakes. "Then why are you here with him?"

"To guide him through the spiritual part of this journey." Father Mike rocked back and forth in the seat as he held his grip on the dash. "To help him see that he has the power to do this, but only God can heal."

"How do you feel about that?" Alejandro yelled back at Derek.

Derek leaned forward again to project his voice. "I believe he could be right. But until I get some answers . . ." He sat back in his seat. He just wanted to avoid the conversation.

Alejandro blurted out his conjecture. "So, it's a lack of faith." His conclusion was made clear from his own experience.

Father Mike interjected. "He must explore the darkness to get to know the infinite power of the light."

Father Mike's dual-purpose statement reminded Alejandro of

when he had come to the church in search of answers after losing his wife and children to dengue fever. He had sat in a pew across from Father Mike, a man known for his wisdom and compassion, and laid out his troubles with a trembling voice. His grief-stricken words seemed to fall from his lips like ripe fruit from a tree.

The pain in his heart felt like his spirit was being crushed by an overwhelming, immobilizing grief. The question foremost on his mind was why a benevolent deity, God, would permit such agony. The numb sorrow had spiraled into disbelief and rage.

Father Mike, a man of quiet faith with a gentle aura and warm smile, had been counseling Alejandro on the nature of grief. With tears streaming down his face, the young man sought solace in the priest's presence. Father Mike listened patiently, allowing his words to come slowly and with careful consideration.

"Grief is a personal experience," he had said. "For each person, it manifests differently. We cannot understand what lies beyond this unknown void, but we can find comfort in knowing that God exists beyond it. He represents all that has been, all that is, and all that will be."

Alejandro had nodded, his expression still filled with sorrow. Father Mike had placed a hand on his shoulder, offering a small gesture of comfort. "I know it's hard, Alejandro. But remember, you are not alone in your grief. God is with you, and so am I."

The young man looked up at the priest, his eyes glistening with emotion. In that moment, Father Mike knew that Alejandro would find his way through this difficult time with the help of his faith and the support of those around him. He would continue to offer his guidance and support for as long as it was needed.

This time was different. The manifestation of the tattoos had been something other than out of the realm of grief. Father Mike's intent in counseling and accompanying Derek was to help him escape his emotional state—to get him beyond the emotions. He knew it could not be through lectures and sermons. It had to be something that would jar him, something that would help to detach him from his current mental state.

He needed to be with him to show him what love, joy, and happiness look like, to help solve his lack of connection to a healthy reality. Connecting to God, cooperating with nature, and creating new healthy thoughts are all things Father Mike knew would help move him past his current condition. He knew he needed to be that person for Derek.

"The Bible says when two people join together in my name—" Father Mike projected his voice over the rattling. Even though he was directing his response to Alejandro, he wanted Derek to hear him so he could understand that when Jesus spoke these words, He referred to a collective state that can determine reality, which becomes most coherent in the heart and brain.

Father Mike continued. "Living in survival mode can cause an imbalance in the brain and body, leading to potential disease or breakdown. This emergency mode is not sustainable for extended periods. When our primitive fight-or-flight system takes over, it becomes all about ourselves. Emotions such as anger, aggression, fear, and depression are all results of stress hormones. In this state, we may feel separate from others and become materialistic and controlling to manipulate outcomes. Essentially, we revert to a more basic version of ourselves."

For a moment, there was silence between the men. Father Mike's kind eyes watched Alejandro closely.

Finally, Alejandro blurted out his conjecture again. "So, it's a lack of faith," he said, his conclusion clear.

Father Mike paused, his premature wrinkles deepening around his eyes as he frowned. "Perhaps," he said at last. "But sometimes, we must explore the darkness to get to know the infinite power of the light."

Alejandro remembered these familiar words spoken in the church that day; they had been the catalyst for lifting the weight from his chest. The burden of the loss of his family had fallen squarely at his feet. He had been the one who had decided to come out to this Godforsaken place to live.

It was as if Father Mike had opened a door for him, leading him toward a path he had long been searching for. As they continued talking, Alejandro felt a sense of clarity. The darkness of guilt still loomed, but now it did not seem quite as intimidating.

That day, Alejandro understood the true power of faith—not as a shield to protect him from the world but as a guiding light that would lead him through even the darkest times. As he left the church that day, he knew he would always carry that light.

Derek's thoughts drifted as he stared out the van window, back to the day he had sat on a worn leather chair, the kind that could swallow you whole. Across from him sat his therapist, Dr. Cole, her face noncommittal and her pen poised above a yellow notepad. He shifted uncomfortably, feeling the weight of her gaze.

"The solution lies within the problem," she'd said, her voice like silk. "And the answer is found within the question."

Derek had been struck by the simplicity and complexity of her words at the time. They held all the answers with all the possibilities, yet at the same time, he could not grasp their meaning.

"What do you mean?" he asked, his voice cracking slightly.

She smiled knowingly. "The problem you're facing is a part of you, and the answer you seek is also a part of you. You need to look within yourself to find it."

He had heard similar sentiments, but they had never seemed so profound. That day, he suddenly felt a weight being lifted, as if he had been carrying around a heavy burden for years and was just now realizing it.

He'd thanked the therapist and left her office, his head spinning with thoughts and questions. As he rode down the street on his motorcycle, he could not help but feel a newfound sense of hope and clarity. The solution was within him all along, and now it was up to him to find it.

Derek's gaze drifted back to the horizon. A storm was brewing in the distance, with dark clouds starting to mount. Above them, a small swatch of a beautiful shade of blue encircled them. His vision blurred as a single tear rolled down his cheek. It looked like something bad was coming their way.

It was a monotonous trip down the well-used but desolate dirt and gravel road. There were no satellite radios, streetlights, emergency call boxes, or telephone poles. They became accustomed to the pebbles that made a sound resembling small fighter planes bombarding the vehicle's frame. The monotonous sound of tires rolling over the gravel was only broken by the thud of the van's wheels hitting a bump in the road.

At last, after hours of driving, Alejandro turned off the main road—and took the curve faster than he should have. The van hit a loose patch of gravel. Gripping the door handle, Derek sucked in a breath as the rear axle scooted out from underneath, fishtailing and skidding. He caught a glimpse of the tree-trimmed town that lay ahead. Alejandro wrestled the van back under control.

They had finally reached their destination when they pulled up to a white-washed, flat-roofed building. The vibrating metal of the van stopped. The silence was deafening.

Sweat erupted from every pore as Derek stepped out, and a distant rumble of thunder echoed in the sky.

Alejandro's weathered face scrunched in pain as he stood outside the van's open door and stretched his arms high into the air, trying to straighten out his stiff back. Derek and Father Mike followed suit. It had been an uncomfortable ride.

As they exited the van, the locals cast curious glances. Tourists were a common sight, but Derek's appearance, covered in tattoos, piqued their interest.

After stretching momentarily, they entered the building through a creaky wooden door. Their guides, two sunbaked men dressed in long-sleeved shirts and trousers, sat patiently waiting on a bench inside. Alejandro spoke to the guides in Spanish. One, a younger man with broad shoulders who wore a wide-brimmed hat slung on his back and polarized sunglasses on a string on his chest, jumped up. While the older, burly man with a thick mustache stood back and listened intently, Alejandro gave them instructions for their journey ahead. The broad-shouldered young man reached around to grab his hat, placed it on his head, and put his sunglasses in place. They followed Alejandro back out to the van to unload the supplies.

The guide led the way down to the river at a determined and purposeful pace, carrying their supplies with ease and skill.

The sun beat down on Alejandro's weary shoulders. He periodically dabbed his face with the cloth he kept in his back pocket. He gave instructions from the riverbank in Spanish with a sense of urgency. The dark rain clouds hung ominously around them.

Alejandro continued to belt out instructions as he stepped onto the makeshift dock. His weight made the wooden structure creak and bend, reminding him how dangerous the river trip could be.

"The river runs northwest and is one of the largest tributaries of the Guaviare." Alejandro pointed downriver. "These men are your porters—your guides and security guards. Listen to their instructions. This river is the Inirida River, it will take you to the Orinoco River, where there is a small eco-village where you will stay." He pointed out into the horizon. "You'll have to watch for intermittent rapids."

Derek's eyes widened. He looked over at Father Mike, who stood on the berm ledge looking out into the river, seemingly unfazed by Alejandro's warning.

Here, at least, the water flowed gently, the last rays of pale sunlight bouncing off its surface in a mesmerizing dance. Derek tried to instill a sense of calm into his overstimulated mind. Taking a deep breath, he let the sound of the rushing water wash over him as he watched the men prepare the boat, an open skiff with an outboard motor.

The older man with the broad mustache was the driver, who now wore a light plastic poncho and sat on the rear portion of the wood wall attached to the back of the boat. Bench seats sat under the top cover. The boat looked like it had seen better days.

Alejandro spoke louder as he held on to the side of the boat.

"You'll stay in the eco-village for one night," he shouted over the rattle of the engine. "There will be a guide who will meet you there. He will take you on a trail to the jungle's interior, where the old shaman's village is located."

"How long?" Derek called out from the top of the berm.

"If you can get over the border without any problems, you should get there by this time tomorrow." Alejandro threw the last duffle bag to the young porter in the boat. "You will stay in the eco-village for the night, then enter the jungle on foot. It will take another two days or so to find the shaman village, depending on the weather and the conditions you run into on your way."

"That sounds pretty exhausting," Derek told Father Mike as they watched the older porter work on the engine from the embankment above.

Another clap of thunder sounded, this time much closer.

"You have enough supplies to make it to the eco-village. I sent what you will need for your hike ahead on the last trip to the village a couple of days ago." Alejandro took the cloth from his back pocket and wiped the sweat dripping down his face. "You must remember that the most important thing you can do is stay hydrated. Also, wear bug repellent. If something bites you, it can make you extremely sick." He felt a familiar painful pang in his chest—he knew this from experience.

"When we're in the jungle, we must be very careful not to touch the plants if we don't recognize them," Father Mike warned over his shoulder as he started down the embankment to the boat.

Derek knew he could not delay any longer. With a determined sigh, he squared his shoulders.

"Let's go. They're ready," Alejandro called out with one foot on the boat and one braced on the dock.

Father Mike stood at the edge of the makeshift dock, the damp wood creaking under his weight and the damp, earthy smell of rotting wood and fish heavy in the air. The Holy Spirit had summoned him here to answer a desperate call from his friend that he could not ignore despite the dangers ahead.

Behind him, Derek stepped out onto the dock, his face set in a determined expression. Like Father Mike, he knew there were risks involved in this mission, but they both felt compelled to answer the call. Derek for personal reasons, and Father Mike whom the spirit had moved to help a friend in need.

"Here, I got this for you in case of an emergency." Alejandro handed Father Mike a satellite phone he had unclipped from his belt. "Be careful, old friend."

A deluge of rain hit. "May Peace be with you, and may God bless you and guide you on this journey," he called out as the boat started to float away, followed by a clap of thunder.

Father Mike made the sign of the cross. And waved goodbye to his friend.

They floated into the river's flowing current without speaking, and the small fishing boat picked up speed, its rusted cleats and peeling paint a stark reminder of the perilous journey ahead.

Chapter 4

Once on the river, Derek felt the lull created by the diminished activity. The unease in his stomach started to settle as they floated on the current. He had read tales about the dangers lurking in the Amazon but pushed those thoughts aside.

His body started to relax and absorb the cadence of the motor's vibrational hum muffled behind the curtain of rain. The anticipation and excitement of the trip, on top of the stress he had experienced in the past months, left his body depleted of energy. The mist of the warm tropical rain on his face eased his breathing.

He looked over at Father Mike's flushed face under his military-style hat, water dripping from the wide brim, and remembered the priest's words from the plane: "Savor the magical moments. Stay aware of your senses and appreciate the beauty you are about to behold."

Derek watched the scenery pass as the boat was swept down the vast, murky water of the river that served as an artery into the rainforest. Small waves tugged at the hull, pulling them downstream in a steady and relaxing rhythm.

The rain disappeared as quickly as it had started. The steamy mist created a tranquil atmosphere that held a dream-like state. A subtle reality infused with a fantasia of optimism came on the slight breeze of the clean, fresh air. The immersion into the raw connection with nature had started.

He was fascinated by the jungle world he had just entered and how it could be so different from the world in which he lived, of sterile operating rooms and high-rise apartment buildings, traffic jams and shopping malls. A mind-body dualism started to penetrate his physical and spiritual being.

In this emerging meditative state, his body and mind started to experience a deep relaxation. His awareness heightened, things seemed more transparent, and his thoughts more manageable, allowing a sense of inner calm to develop.

His introspection traveled back to that fateful meeting with the old shaman woman. It had been a chance encounter that seemed insignificant at the time. He had been experiencing a panic attack when she suddenly appeared.

When they momentarily locked eyes, he could never have imagined that the deepest, hidden part of himself had been exposed in the seemingly random encounter.

Yet . . . Something about her had felt familiar, a past acquaintanceship, a feeling that they were meant to cross paths at that moment. When he stood looking down at her lying on the sidewalk, the weight of their unspoken connection had bound them together in a way he could never have fully comprehended.

As the days turned into months, he realized their encounter might stay with him forever. It was a small but significant moment that had left an indelible mark on his soul and a tapestry of ink on his skin.

As he flashed back to their encounter, he could not help but wonder about her . . . her life deep in this jungle and the experiences that had shaped her. She had also been searching for something, too.

Startled by a tap on the shoulder, Father Mike pointed ahead to a couple of military-style boats parked on the bank. With grim, anxious expressions, the men drifted past in the faded blue and red wooden riverboat, breaths held while taking an occasional covert glance. When ten minutes had passed, it was clear that no one was coming after them.

They relaxed back into the scenery, framed by pile-dwelling houses. The stilts had been driven into the ground for stability to help ventilate and protect the occupants from floods. Water buffalo, cows, horses, and occasionally children playing at the water's edge dotted the landscape along the banks.

Intermittent wakes from the flat-bottomed vessels of passing fishermen jostled the small boat. Derek understood that the river was a way of life for these people, a constant force that shaped their days. The vegetation grew denser while human settlements along the banks began to diminish as they floated along the river.

At sunset, the guides strapped on headlamps, a signal that Derek and Father Mike should do the same. The flickering lights across the water would catch an occasional snake slithering past on the water's surface. Derek tapped Father Mike and pointed to the capybaras—the largest rodent in the world—lying in the mud on the riverbank.

Later, in the pitch-black night, bats brushed against their heads, hunting insects attracted to their body heat. Derek's emotions veered from fright to joy as fireflies flickered on the shore. The low hum of the engine moved them along the river, and the red eyes of the monstrous caiman bobbed past.

Before daybreak, Father Mike tapped a dozing Derek on the arm and pointed to some heavy brush along the river. A jaguar slipped out from under the heavy brush to drink the river's water. It appeared to meander along the riverbank, waiting for its prey.

"It has the strongest bite of any big cat." Father Mike explained.

By sunrise, they were fully immersed in the wild as they watched pink dolphins swim alongside the boat. Derek laughed and felt lulled by the pleasure of this vibrant fantasy world.

Then he saw the churning whitewater.

The rapids were a frothing mass of waves that looked ready to devour the boat whole. The two guides' faces contorted in concentration. They quickly changed positions and started yelling in Spanish. The older river guide, a seasoned veteran with a weathered face and calloused hands, calmly grabbed a long pole from the side of the boat. It was apparent these locals knew the treacherous waters.

But now, as they approached the rapids, all of Derek's careful planning seemed insignificant.

Father Mike yelled, "Hold on tight. This could get rough. This is where the two rivers meet."

Just as he said that, the boat violently lurched forward as the water splashed into the air. Derek's stomach leaped into his throat, and his white knuckles gripped the sides.

The roar of the water was deafening, drowning out their shouts and the sound of the jungle around them. The river guide expertly navigated the boat toward the safest route, his muscles straining as he pushed against the rocks and powerful current with his pole.

For a moment, they were suspended in time as the boat teetered on the edge of a massive wave. Then, with a sudden jolt, they were thrust forward and into the main artery of the rapids. The boat bucked and started to spin, the water crashing over them and soaking them to the bone. But they held on, clinging to the sides of the boat and trusting in the skill of their guides.

The two guides' shouts in Spanish were barely audible over the roar of the water, but Derek could sense the urgency. His heart raced with both excitement and fear as the boat bucked, water splashing up around them. He could feel his stomach drop as they plunged into the rapids, the force of the river threatening to throw them off course.

But the guide's steady hand on the rudder and the second guide's long pole, used to push away from the rocks, kept them on track.

They emerged from the rapids, hearts still racing as they gasped for breath. Derek could feel the adrenaline coursing through his veins, a sensation he hadn't experienced in months. Since encountering the old shaman woman at the hotel and waking up two days later with tattoos covering his entire body, Derek's life had been a whirlwind of unexpected encounters and circumstances. It had been a year filled with despair, self-discovery, new relationships, and, ultimately, marriage to Kendal.

This adventure was exactly what he unknowingly needed.

He was grateful to have experienced it with such knowledgeable and capable guides. As they continued their journey, navigating through calmer waters, Derek could not help but think about what other challenges and wonders lay ahead.

Little did he know that this was only the beginning of a series of grueling obstacles and brutal challenges. Along their incredible journey, there would be temporary moments of triumph through small victories, but they would be by far outnumbered by the struggles that lay ahead.

Derek had never fished for piranha before. Actually, he had never fished before *period*. Each experience made it clear that this was a once-in-a-lifetime trip, a journey into a world that seemed to exist only in books and dreams.

As they cast their lines into the murky waters of the Amazon, Derek could not help but feel a thrill of excitement. The thought of catching a deadly predator, one that was feared by so many, was both exhilarating and terrifying.

When they finally reeled in their catches, Derek could not believe how small they were. The piranhas were no bigger than his hand, and their sharp teeth seemed almost comical compared to their size.

But when they cooked and ate the piranhas for breakfast, Derek was pleasantly surprised. The crispy skin gave way to succulent white meat. He felt a pang of disappointment when he realized how bland the taste was, but still found himself eating more than he thought he would.

When breakfast was over, he looked around at the lush surroundings, the sounds of the jungle filling his ears. Derek inhaled and let out a slow breath. He was grateful for the experience. It may not have been a gourmet meal, but it was a meal he would never forget. The memories of this trip would be more valuable than he could ever have imagined.

A rainbow of brilliantly colored butterflies gathered on the riverbanks. Electric blues, fiery oranges, sunshine yellows, and delicate pinks congregated in a kaleidoscope of color.

Despite the unrelenting humidity, they found ways to keep their spirits up by pointing out the wildlife. As they drifted along, Derek watched the water idly, his eyes scanning for any signs of animals.

An occasional caiman basked in the sun. Its black, scaly skin glistened in the sunlight, reflecting the water droplets in shimmering patterns across its back. Its eyes, with their vertical slits, watched lazily as it lay completely still on the muddy bank.

Derek recalled reading about this fifteen-foot predator, the most feared in the Amazon River basin and known for its attacks on humans. The thought of encountering one sent a chill down his spine.

Father Mike chuckled and pointed as a giant otter swam past curiously, looking up at the men in the boat.

They could hear the occasional scream of a monkey from the tree line. It was a haunting sound that seemed to echo through the dense jungle, filling the air with primal fear.

Floating deeper and deeper into the Amazon's heart, Derek momentarily forgot about his quest and simply marveled at the beauty and mystery of the world around them.

An endless diversity of trees, plants, and flowers grew along the fertile banks of the Amazonian basin. Birds covered the mud cliffs like a rainbow. Derek wished Kendal could have been there to experience watching the largest birds in the parrot family, the blue and red Macaws perched on the banks feeding on the clay deposits in the hundreds, their brilliant plumage flashing in the sunlight. Smiling to himself, he knew she would want to bring one home to live with Brutus, her Cockatoo.

Well into their second day in the Amazon, the small boat chugged along the murky waters of the living, breathing river. Occasionally, a deer could be seen drinking from the water's edge, its gentle movements a stark contrast to the wildness of the surrounding jungle. The air grew thicker and more oppressive, the humidity clinging to their skin like a second layer. The sun beat down, and they could feel the sweat trickling down their faces.

The atmosphere, an acoustic of the living, breathing jungle, became a concert made up of the distinct surrounding sounds, each with its own characteristics, like sections of an orchestra—bird songs, fluttering insect wings, and monkey hoots. The rush of water from nearby streams and waterfalls and the sound of raindrops cascading onto leaves. The steady hum of the boat engine and an occasional splash of a fish leaping out of the water like a cymbal's crescendo became a symphony of movements, each with distinct characteristics.

A sizeable green anaconda curled around its prey while devouring it as it lay next to the water on the bank. Derek could not help but empathize. Lately, he had felt like prey strangled by a giant snake that had been squeezing the life out of *him*.

They pressed on to what awaited them in the jungle's hidden depths. Derek knew that danger lurked around every bend, but he also knew that this was where the answer to his future hid—in this untamed, unpredictable place, where life and death swirled in a never-ending dance.

He thought about the tattooed chains that had recently returned around his ankles, symbols of a shackled life. A life spent trapped in cycles of violence and despair, a life where opportunities were allotted and desperation was abundant. Each link represented a struggle, a wound, a memory.

He thought about the bad choices he had made and how those decisions had ultimately brought him into the heart of the jungle, choices that had led him down a path of self-destruction, pain, and regret.

He told himself that his strength and resilience had allowed him to survive, his defiance had kept him going, and even when the odds seemed to be stacked against him, hope now burned in his heart.

He closed his eyes and took a deep breath. A pang of homesickness flinted across his chest. But this was his reality now, the cacophony of the surrounding jungle.

As he opened his eyes again, he made a promise to himself. He would break the chains, not just the inked ones that bound his legs but also the psychological ones that held him back. He would find a way out of this subconscious prison, both physical and mental. He *would* be free.

A family of capybaras lay sweltering in their fur coats, using the mud on the beach to help cool them down. "They are the world's largest rodents," Father Mike called out as he pointed to the pack of huge rat-like animals with partially webbed feet. They watched as the large rodents took an explosive jump into the water. Their eyes, ears and nostrils could be seen on the tops of their heads as they floated past.

"Capybaras hold their breath underwater for a full five minutes. They can walk along the bottom like hippopotamuses," Father Mike explained over the steady hum of the engine. "I watched a nature show about them!"

Small monkeys peeked through the pink blossoms that clothed the tree limbs along the water's edge. They watched the thirsty monkeys come down from the safety of the branches to drink the water. When the wake of their passing boat hit the shore, the monkeys sensed danger and scrambled back up to their perches in the treetops.

As the afternoon progressed, it reached one hundred degrees in the shade. Birds swooped down to cool themselves in the water.

A peccary, a medium-sized pig-like ungulate of the javelin family, rooting for grubs underneath the hanging branches, seemed out of place with the surrounding beauty.

Derek's rumination began to encourage a hypervigilant response. He started becoming aware of his thinking and psychological state. He continued to meditate on the scenic remote region, an isolated secret world of abundant life—a violent paradise far away from the cities where millions live. Here, life must battle to survive, caimans rule the water, and jaguars dominate the land.

Chapter 5

Father Mike had always been a man of unwavering faith, dedicating his entire life to serving God for the sake of man. As a young priest, he was filled with a burning passion to spread the word of the Lord and traveled to the farthest corners of the earth to do so. But he was still human and vulnerable.

Today, during the long day of journeying by boat, Father Mike sat on the wooden bench, exhausted yet content in his devotion. His body temperature had risen as he had sweated profusely. Dehydration had already started with this loss of core fluids, and he felt drained.

As the sun began to set and the boat gently pushed forth, he closed his eyes and drifted into a deep, peaceful sleep. As he slept, he dreamed of a vast, empty desert, the sand stretching endlessly before him. In the distance, he saw a figure walking toward him, their steps purposeful and determined. As they drew closer, Father Mike realized it was Jesus Christ, clad in a simple white robe and carrying a staff.

Jesus held out his hand without speaking and beckoned Father Mike to follow. Without hesitation, he rose and began to walk, the sand shifting beneath his feet. They walked for hours, but Father Mike felt no fatigue or discomfort, only a sense of calm and purpose as he followed the Son of God.

Finally, they reached the top of a small hill, and Father Mike saw a simple wooden cross standing tall against the setting sun. As he gazed upon it, Jesus turned to him and spoke, his voice filled with love and compassion.

"Your dedication and devotion to me have not gone unnoticed, my son," he said. "Continue to spread my message of love and forgiveness, and you will find eternal peace."

With those words, Father Mike awoke, looking at the sky. He knew he had only dozed for a minute, but the dream seemed like he was in it for an eternity. His heart filled with joy and renewed purpose. A single tear rolled down his face in relief at this revelation. He was fulfilling His purpose. He looked at Derek sitting next to him, dozing in and out. He knew he was on the right path, and nothing could deter him from his call to serve God and his people.

Thinking about his dream, he could empathize with what Jesus had felt during his forty days in the desert fighting the devil.

He grabbed his canteen and took a long swig, feeling the cool water replenish his parched throat. He also had a hydration power pack in his bag, so he opened it and sucked the gel from the foil pouch. This trip was going to be tough and exhausting. The sun's scorching rays were already taking a toll on him, and he could feel the effects of dehydration creeping in.

He gazed at the setting sun, painting the sky with pink, purple, and gold streaks. In this tranquil moment, Father Mike let his heavy eyelids close. He dozed, slipping back into a vision state. He now stood on the edge of a cliff, looking out at the endless expanse of ocean before him. He felt the sea breeze tousle his hair and cleanse his soul.

Father Mike's dream flashed him back to his church in San Diego. He could feel the weight of Jesus's sacrifice. It hung heavy as the congregation gathered for the Easter service. The sun peeked through the stained-glass windows, casting rays of colored light across the pews onto the altar in front. Reverence and awe permeated the space, a tangible presence of the Divine.

Father Mike began his sermon by speaking of the transformative power of Christ's death. "Through our faith, we have died alongside Jesus," he declared, his voice booming and filled with conviction. "Just as he sacrificed himself for others, so must we let go of our selfish desires and live for something greater."

The congregation nodded in agreement, their faces solemn and contemplative. For many, this was not a new concept requiring constant reflection and effort.

"Our task," the priest continued, "is to live authentically, to align ourselves with our new identity in Christ, and to consistently demonstrate our unique actions in the world. It is not an easy path but one filled with purpose and fulfillment."

As the service ended, the congregation stood and sang a hymn, their voices rising in unison, a beautiful harmony of faith and devotion. Father Mike could hear the angels' voices join the chorus as the words of the hymns floated up like puffs of smoke to Heaven.

Father Mike's attention was directed to a man sitting in the farthest corner of the church's sanctuary. When he lifted his head, he could see it was Derek. Father Mike knew exactly what he was thinking as he watched him sitting in the pew with his head down in prayer. He was contemplating the intricacies of his sense of self. From a young age, he was ingrained with the belief that his profession defined who he was. Without faith, his body had become an empty vessel waiting to be filled with God's love.

Father Mike knew this was the most crucial part for Derek to find the missing piece of his soul. Life events and experiences played a role in molding us, but ultimately, our relationship with Jesus Christ genuinely defined us.

Father Mike watched Derek pray and thought about his own journey with faith and how it had guided him through the difficulties of life. It had been his constant, his rock, his guiding light in the darkest of times.

Father Mike opened his eyes. He felt a strong sense of peace and purpose for this mission to spiritually guide Derek through the jungle. He knew that no matter what challenges lay ahead, he would face them with the strength and love of his Savior. And that, to him, was the most important aspect of his servitude and identity.

This was the confirmation he had been looking for. He was on the right path. This trip is what the Holy Spirit had inspired him to do.

He could not help but smile at how his relationship with Christ shaped and molded his own identity with His never-ending divine instruction and guidance. He knew that the Holy Spirit would be with him through this redemption path through the treacherous jungle.

Father Mike also intuitively knew that Derek's faith would have to become part of his identity—it was at the very core of his redemption. As a believer, Derek would have to learn to find his identity in being known and loved by God.

And from this identity would come his purpose.

Chapter 6

Derek had just left and closed the front door of their lavish penthouse in Los Angeles behind him. Kendal stared at the door; she couldn't help but feel a profound sense of loneliness. She could not help but feel abandoned. She felt like she had been thrown back into her emotionally unstable childhood. An eruption of memories from long ago came rushing back, filled with abandonment, disapproval, and rejection.

The sudden announcement that he was leaving left her reeling. She stepped back, the weight of his absence pressing heavily on her chest. How had it all happened so fast? He had been there, his presence filling the room. And then, with a single decision, he was gone, leaving her feeling empty and exhausted in his wake.

She tried to steady herself, her mind a tumultuous mess of emotions. She desperately searched for some semblance of understanding for his sudden departure, but all she could find was the lingering scent of his cologne and the memories of his touch.

She wondered if he had considered what it could do to their relationship before deciding to leave. She wanted to hate him for leaving her in this state, but she could not. She understood his desperate need to find the answers to getting rid of the tattoos.

But his deliberate omission of her opinion hurt her feelings. She could not help but feel ostracized by his decision-making process, as if she were not even a consideration. It was a sharp, stinging sensation that she could not shake off, no matter how much she rationalized it. She did not expect him to make a decision that would affect them both without even consulting her.

She remembered the day she had walked in on Derek working on his computer. He was sitting in his office, scribbling notes and muttering to himself. She'd asked him what he was doing, and he had replied with a dismissive "nothing important," not even looking up from his work.

She had left him to his research not knowing he was planning a trip. It was a clear sign that he did not value her opinion or consider her an equal partner in their relationship. When she had stood in their bedroom, watching him pack for this sudden trip, she could not help but feel a sense of resentment and isolation.

She reached for the door handle with trembling hands to run after him. Then she took a deep breath, willing herself to be strong. She knew she had to let him go, to let him find his path. But that did not stop the pain from searing through her, filling her with an ache that she might never see him again. The jungle could be a merciless beast waiting to claim its next victim. It was no place for the untrained, inexperienced traveler.

She felt like she was already grieving. It was a familiar feeling she had experienced countless times before. She needed to listen to her internal monologue. It was the only thing that allowed her to communicate the various complex emotions she was experiencing. The pain was so intense that it threatened to consume her.

She let out a sudden, gasping breath and began to weep uncontrollably. Tears streamed down her face like a powerful waterfall. She knew the tears were necessary, releasing pent-up emotions that threatened to consume her if not let out.

When her sobs finally subsided, she got up from the floor where she had collapsed and stumbled into the bathroom. The emotional breakdown had wracked her body, leaving her exhausted and drained. She removed her makeup, revealing the dark circles under her eyes as the layers of foundation and concealer were washed away.

She knew to listen to her inner voice. It was the only way she could navigate life. She had learned this from an incredibly young age when she had no one else to depend on but herself. Her inner voice had become her constant companion, a guiding light in the darkness.

Combing back her auburn hair, she took a moment to study her reflection in the mirror. The reflection was not kind, revealing a face marked with worry lines. She could see the dark roots of her hair, a reminder that she was due for a touch-up at the salon.

Exhaustion seeped into her very bones. With a sigh, she turned off the light and crawled into bed. Her body was spent, her mind heavy with the weight of her emotions. She curled up into a ball under the covers, seeking comfort in the warmth and darkness of her bed. She closed her eyes and let herself feel the grief. She cried softly until there were no more tears left. Sleep eventually came, bringing with it a brief respite from the turmoil that plagued her.

She rose early before going to work, having tossed and turned all night. She tried to busy herself by applying some much-needed beauty treatments. Maybe the pampering would cheer her up. Before showering, she put an herbal mask on her face and applied henna to her hair.

It seemed amazing to her how a painful experience could instantly reconnect the dots separated by a veritable lifetime. Her reflection felt like she was watching a marionette perform as she painted the mixture onto her face. She applied the herbal mask in a thin layer across her forehead and on each side of her nose, careful to avoid her eyes and lips.

The psyche never forgets, she thought as she extended the layer down her slim neck. It stores the most affecting memories in every cell of the body.

When Derek left Kendal to find the shaman woman's granddaughter, she was unprepared for the emotional flood of loss it had created. The sudden separation brought on a rush of despair and a myriad of other feelings she had not expected. Her self-esteem, confidence, and dreams for the future had taken a beating.

She padded out to the patio in her slippers and robe, then sat in a chair, waiting for the facial herbal mix to perform its magic. She slid her head back to let her facemask bask in the warm sun.

The most egregious feeling that had come from his leaving was powerlessness. Derek's actions made her feel helpless to control this huge part of her life. She had been left standing alone with this new reality.

Old memories of turmoil started creeping back in as she remembered the most upsetting times in their relationship before they were married. His emotions had been volatile when he first came to stay with her after his tattoos had appeared. He had scared her when she said something he didn't like, slamming his fist down on the breakfast counter in her apartment. She had felt threatened.

Derek was full of anger. Kendal sensed that he was becoming someone she did not know, distant and unrecognizable. She had wondered if *she* had somehow pushed him away with her fears and worries.

It happened again the night he left her apartment for the last time. They were sitting on the deck having a conversation right before sunset. She'd suggested he return to his penthouse to let things cool down when he suddenly stood up and threw his glass against the wall. She'd jumped in surprise, the shards of glass glittering in the fading light across the wood planks. He didn't say a word—just stormed back inside and slammed the sliding door, almost breaking it.

Kendal sat there in shock for a minute, trying to calm herself, regain control of her emotions, and make sense of his outburst. She had seen him angry, but not like this; it had scared her.

Darkness had fallen like a heavy blanket as she picked up the shards of glass and tried to adjust the sliding door back onto its track. Back inside, she found him still pacing back and forth, his hands clenched into fists.

She stood in the small apartment, unsure of what to say or do. She could not understand this emotional roller-coaster they were on. He turned to face her; his lifeless eyes had lost their usual sparkle. She stared at him, a man she loved, who now seemed like a stranger.

"I can't do this anymore," he said, his voice barely above a whisper. "You've made it clear how you feel." Tears welled in his eyes. "I know I can't stay here. I know I'm ruining everything."

And with that, Derek had grabbed his bag and left Kendal alone in the empty apartment. She sat on the kitchen floor that night and cried.

Now married, she was feeling the same type of loss again. She understood that he had left this time for entirely different reasons . . . yet she wondered, were they truly? His turmoil was the same, and his internal struggles had not changed.

She could feel her physiological being starting to slip back into old destructive, insecure patterns. She had to figure out how to re-empower herself.

Before he left, she had not been too proud to beg. What was that all about? She had always taken immense pride in her ability to provide for herself. She had created an independence that seemed to have been jeopardized, and now she felt deeply humiliated that her insecurities had crept back in. Her abandonment issues felt like they were written on her sleeve, like the tattoos on Derek's arm.

His forethought of planning without discussing it with her had broken her trust in him and shaken the confidence in their marriage.

Kendal's upbringing had been filled with chaos and abuse. She endured multiple abusive stepfathers and a neglectful mother. Despite the constant turmoil, she never lost sight of her goals and remained determined to create a better future for herself. She knew that education was the key to achieving her dreams, so she focused on going to school and becoming a nurse. When she finally had the opportunity to leave Michigan and come to California, she seized it and dedicated herself to making things right in her life.

She knew her expectations of marriage had been set high. She expected to have a lifelong commitment even though the thought of marriage had scared her to death. She knew it would be hard to fully invest in a relationship if she focused on the messy ending. She understood there would be no guarantees.

But she felt let down by Derek. She had let herself trust him and grown to depend on him. The cold disconnection from his actions had now put her into a spiral. It triggered all the hurt of the abandonment and abuse she had experienced throughout her childhood.

Her hurt and disappointment were palpable. How could he be so inconsiderate? After all the love and support she had given. The emotional roller-coaster ride in their relationship never seemed to come to a stop. She had done everything in her power to help him find his way. For him to grow into the person he was supposed to be.

She tried to understand the anguish he experienced because of the extreme number of tattoos. They made him feel as if his body was not his own. She wanted to help him with the struggle, but it was obvious that her words and love were not enough.

He'd made an important decision without a single thought about how she felt. He had let her down, and it felt disrespectful and dismissive. How could the relationship be the same after this?

Days before he had left, she had intuitively felt like something was going on with how he treated her, but she couldn't put her finger on it until he started packing his bag. By then, it was too late. There would be no conversation; he had made up his mind. He was going out into the jungle to search for something that probably would not be there—something so elusive that he could chase it forever—like an addiction that gnawed at him.

With her face turned toward the sky, she could feel the warmth of the sun penetrating her mask, and at the same time, the weight of sorrow pressing down on her chest.

Marriage to Derek had been a huge leap of faith. He displayed no signs of abandonment, just overblown expectations that she would always be there to support him.

She did not want to feel crazy or self-destructive for falling in love with Derek. He could be a great partner at times—when he needed to be—and romantic and loving when he wanted.

At first, he'd seemed sensitive to her emotions and tuned into her needs. Or had that been her imagination?

She felt satisfied with the relationship most of the time, but *his* insecurity could make her feel bad about herself. She had started to feel insecure when they were together *and* apart.

As the gentle warmth spread across her face, Kendal felt the tension in her facial muscles, and puffy eyes started to ease. It brought some relief from the headache that had been bothering her.

She needed to listen to her inner voice and acknowledge what was happening. She knew these signs were not good. Her self-reflection helped her to strategize, organize, and make tough choices. She needed to figure out if the relationship was worth holding on to. It had become necessary for her to reassess her marriage. From a young age, she had relied on her own thoughts and feelings for guidance, as she had no one else to look out for her.

The realization that she was on her own again with no one to turn to left a sharp hurt, a piercing sensation in her chest. It radiated outwards, like a spiderweb of pain, reaching her throat and making it difficult to swallow.

She tried to focus on the good times when they laughed and loved with abandon. But those memories now seemed distant, like a dream that had evaporated. But despite all the hurt and disappointment, a small flame of hope flickered deep inside. She could not let go of her love for him. She wanted to hold on, to fight. But how could she when he was so detached and now thousands of miles away?

Her heart ached as she realized that she might lose him, and there was nothing she could do to stop it. The tears threatened to spill over again, but she refused to let them.

She took a deep breath and straightened her shoulders, determined to face whatever came next. She would not let this defeat her. She would survive, even if it meant walking away from the man she loved.

She returned to the bathroom to remove the mask from her face and rinse the henna from her hair. She turned on the shower and stepped in, letting the warm water splash over her body. She lifted her face into the spray, to let the mask rinse away, and wiped her face with a soft washcloth.

Rinsing the henna from her hair was like washing out mud. Rinsing out the external grime had been easy, but the internal grime seemed to cling to her like a stubborn stain. She tried to push it away, but it kept resurfacing, clouding her thoughts and leaving her feeling drained.

Muddy emotions were like quicksand, she thought. The more she struggled against them, the deeper she sank. She needed to find a way out of this emotional muck before it consumed her completely. She massaged her scalp as the lukewarm water rinsed her hair to a shiny clean.

She looked up into her renewed smooth-sheen complexion in Derek's shaving mirror, which hung on the shower wall. Her reflection looked back at her with a renewed determination.

At the beginning of their marriage, he seemed to feel better about himself. So handsome, like a movie star. He could make her feel special. She had to admit that deep inside, she had admired him and looked up to him even though, at times, he could be insensitive.

She understood his problem with insecurities even though he had accomplished so much in his young life. It was becoming increasingly important for her to acknowledge the significant amount of time and effort she dedicated to boosting his self-esteem, which always seemed to be in need of support.

At the start of their marriage, she had been able to practice mindfulness. She could easily recognize when he was starting to feel anxious or angry, and she could help him shift his behavior. A small behavior change would always make a big difference in helping the relationship flow smoothly. As his self-awareness began to dissipate, he began to react badly.

She turned off the water and stepped out of the shower, wrapping herself in a fluffy towel. She looked at herself in the mirror. Her renewed complexion now glowed.

She toweled off and then applied moisturizer to her face. She stretched her neck and firmly rubbed the tired muscles, trying to loosen the tension.

She had to be realistic. What could she expect from their love? Had it all been a fantasy? Should she just give up? She knew he had some disorder created by his childhood trauma. It was hard for him to feel empathy. He struggled to find the right words or actions to comfort and show affection when she felt sad or injured. It was a constant struggle for him if not an impossible task.

As she dried her hair, she could not shake off the residue of emotions that had weighed on her all morning. They were a mix of anger, confusion, and hurt, a familiar and unwelcome trifecta.

As she combed through her damp auburn tresses, she could not help but replay the conversation. The one person she thought she could always rely on. But their intense argument had left her feeling betrayed and unsure about the future.

How does one wash away hurt and bitterness?

As she blow-dried her hair, the answer came to her: *forgiveness*. She needed to let go of the anger and hurt she was holding onto and forgive him for his lapse of judgment. It would not be easy, but it was the only way to free herself from this emotional mess.

With renewed determination, she dried her hair and styled it, feeling a sense of lightness and clarity as she did. The henna had left her hair with a beautiful red sheen.

It was not unreasonable for her to expect him to improve his behavior. But her unrealistic hope for him to fundamentally change who he was only added to the downfall of their relationship. She needed to see her part in all of this.

She reached into the vanity drawer and pulled out her makeup case, following her daily routine by applying foundation. As she carefully applied the makeup, she wondered: What was it about him that she genuinely loved? Were these qualities enough to keep their relationship alive? Could they compensate for the things that were missing? And could she learn to embrace the parts of him that she didn't necessarily find appealing?

He had undergone a transformation before. Would he be able to continue evolving and making positive changes, or would his insecurities and worries about his tattoos always be a part of him?

She reached for her concealer, hoping to camouflage the dark circles under her eyes caused by the sleepless night. The constant fear of not being able to trust him and the unending agony of his self-deprecation had taken a toll on her. She was grateful they did not have any children to worry about in this tumultuous situation.

She applied another layer of liquid makeup to her face, careful to blend it smoothly down her neck. The trust she had placed in Derek had come at a high cost. Her sense of safety and willingness to rely on others had once again been shattered. The hurt was a sharp, piercing sensation in her chest.

When they got married, she had felt a sense of stability and solace that she now understood was never truly there. "We promised to protect each other from the world," she reflected as she penciled in her eyebrows.

Her inner voice continued to chide: "I know our marriage problems should not have been ignored for so long. I should have made a list of issues—and not fear talking to him. I have become too defensive. I know I have the skills to resolve any new problems that should arise, but it also needs to be a mutually agreeable endeavor.

"It seems we fight about everything. My attempts to get him to change helped to invite his defensiveness. *I know that.* I understand that no one likes to be told what they are doing wrong. We both need to use our energies and intelligence to figure out how we can communicate differently.

"I long for a loving and positive relationship with him, but the frustrating aspects of our dynamic never seem to improve. He's just too focused on himself."

She tossed the eyebrow pencil back into her makeup bag and retrieved her eyeliner. With precise strokes, she lined her hazel green eyes from corner to corner. "The negative words and actions we exchange only bring us down. The constant criticism, complaints, blame, accusations, anger, sarcasm, snide remarks need to stop.

"We need to learn how to stay calm, exit the conversation civilly when it becomes heated, and reengage cooperatively."

She studied the arrangement of lipstick hues resting in a tray on her bathroom counter. After some consideration, she settled on a subtle shade to enhance the deep ruby tint of her lips.

"I'm constantly anxious now. Have I forgotten what a healthy, happy life feels like? Maybe we could start our marriage again from the beginning. But would that even be feasible?"

She gazed at her radiant reflection in the mirror, pondering if she had become consumed with achieving an unattainable ideal for her relationship. Was she using her marriage as a measure of her self-worth, pushing aside other aspects of her life? Had this tunnel vision led to this inevitable disappointment?

The sound of Brutus, her pet Cockatoo, screaming for attention from his cage in the kitchen reached her ears. She had forgotten to uncover him when she had gone out on the deck. She closed her eyes, hoping for a moment of peace and clarity. After one last look, she was finally satisfied with what she saw. She turned off the light and left the mirror behind.

Kendal entered the kitchen, approached Brutus's cage, and gently removed its cover. As soon as he saw her, Brutus began to swing and dance on his perch, serenading her with his morning songs. Parrots are incredibly intelligent creatures and can live up to fifty years. Brutus had been her faithful companion long before Derek came into her life. They had been living together ever since she moved to California, and their bond was unbreakable.

The penthouse always seemed brighter when Brutus was around, even though Derek wasn't initially fond of him. But over time, he grew to love the friendly bird who would perform tricks for scratches on the head. Brutus could sing, whistle, and even knew his name. Often, she would talk to him like a friend and confide in him about her problems. Even though he may not have fully understood her words, Kendal believed that Brutus could sense her emotions and comfort her in his own way.

Their bond had grown strong when she was a single woman and they had spent so much time together, but lately, Kendal had been busy with work and left Brutus alone for more extended periods. Sensing something was wrong, Brutus said, "I love you" more often than usual. At first, Kendal didn't realize what was happening, but eventually, it became just what she needed—a little light and energy in her day.

Despite being a bird, Brutus had a strong emotional intelligence and could sense the atmosphere in the room. He kissed her hand as she reached in to take him out of his cage. She smiled and said to him "I love you, too." In response, Brutus became animated as if he understood her words and repeated back, "I love you. I love you." At that moment, Kendal felt a sense of normalcy and comfort in their special bond. She petted his head, kissed the top, and then set him back in his cage.

She checked his food and water, and then grabbed her jacket from the closet, the one she knew Derek liked on her. She slung her bag over her shoulder and headed toward the front door. Glancing back at the vast, empty living room one last time, she told herself they would need to spend more time appreciating each other and finding common ground. Their relationship had reached a pivotal place right before he left, the way one can sense the shifting of tectonic plates deep beneath the earth. Decisions had to be made, and they had to be made together.

She knew that actively listening to him was a sign of love and understanding. Giving praise and showing gratitude were important as well. And in their free time, they should do more fun activities together. After negotiating a share of the practice and marrying Derek, she was thrust into a sea of responsibility. The magnitude of her newfound duties as office manager and now owning the majority share weighed heavily on her shoulders, as did the other partners' morale. It had become obvious to her that something had to change.

With these thoughts in mind, she closed the door to her personal life and stepped out to face the challenging tasks of her business day ahead at Derek's office.

Chapter 7

Just before sunset on the second day, the boat cut its motor as it slid up onto the muddy riverbank. The men spoke to each other in Spanish. The young porter pointed to the top of the berm.

"We get out here." Father Mike put his bag on his back, adjusted the string below his chin on his khaki hat, and jumped out.

"Here?" Derek looked around. "There's nothing here."

In truth, he was mentally unprepared for the trek. He had let his guard down, mesmerized by the river, and his subconscious had shielded him from the trials that lay ahead.

"It can't be seen from the river," Father Mike called over his shoulder. "We'll need to hike a path up to the eco-village in the jungle."

Derek hurriedly grabbed his bag and jumped out of the boat. The water was shallow here, but he could feel the force of the current tugging at his legs. He waded carefully, using his grip on the side of the boat to steady himself on the slippery riverbed.

He rushed to catch up with Father Mike, who had already started ascending the steep wooden stairs perched on the embankment. Father Mike had pulled out a small machete and began to hack away at the thick undergrowth that blocked their path. Sweat poured down his face as he cut through the dense vegetation.

Derek could not help but feel a twinge of fear mixed with

excitement for this new adventure. He glanced back when he heard the boat's engine start and saw the small boat push off. Their silhouette disappeared into the hovering fog that had hung over the river with the impending evening twilight. Having been cast off so unceremoniously, he felt the desolation of the remote and isolated environment.

Despite a tepid wind blowing through the dense canopy that loomed above them, Derek shivered and wrapped his arms around himself. He wondered what awaited him. Was it an opportunity or another trap he had set for himself? He could not shake off the feeling of unease that was starting to settle in his stomach like a heavy stone.

As the boat disappeared into the fog, he felt a profound sense of loneliness and detachment. Abandoned in this remote, unforgiving environment without ceremony or warning, he took each step one at a time like a march up to the gallows.

He had worked hard all his adult life, but all the hopes and dreams he had nurtured were destroyed overnight. He had tried to start a new life with Kendal, his new wife. And now, he had left it all behind, uncertain of what was to come.

But there was no turning back now. Father Mike waited patiently at the top of the steps. Derek took a deep breath, scaling the last steps with both determination and a sense of trepidation. Whatever was waiting for him, he had to face it head-on.

When he reached the top step, he looked up to see the treetops dominating the skyline. The dark entrance to the dense rainforest trail revealed little light. The canopy layer from ground level blocked the wind, rain, and sun. The two men stopped for a minute to listen to the loud, deep, hollow sounds that belched out from the black hole that was the entrance to the rainforest. The barking cries of spider and howler monkeys reverberated high above as they glided along through the slender, uppermost branches. They tried to take in the over-powering wave of surrounding sounds. The faint shrill of the scarlet macaws and rainbow-billed toucans could be heard in the distance.

Their senses heightened and on high alert, they cautiously stepped onto the well-trodden path under the thick jungle canopy. It was a humid, still, and dark environment. Derek's hands felt clammy, and his heart raced as he followed Father Mike deeper into the rainforest. With each step, the shadows seemed to grow longer, and the forest grew louder, more intense. The insect and frog calls were almost deafening.

One of the first things Derek noticed was the smell. It was like a well-planted greenhouse with a combined scent of soil, vegetation, and wood. The rainforest floor was the darkest of all the immersion layers, which made it extremely difficult for the plants to grow. That helped the leaves to decay quickly. Decomposer termites, slugs, scorpions, worms, and fungi thrived.

With heightened senses, Derek could feel something crawling on his skin. He listened to the insects swarming as they walked past the foliage that grew sparse at the tree trunks and then spread wide to the upper layer, reaching for the sun's rays. He could feel a stirring in his soul as the dark, remote environment awakened the ancient memory stored in his DNA. It evoked primitive feelings of fear. As they traveled deeper the dense vegetation started to dull the roar.

Derek could not shake off the feeling of being watched. He looked over his shoulder, half expecting to see something lurking in the shadows. Father Mike walked purposefully, his long strides easily navigating the uneven forest floor. Derek struggled to keep up, his feet stumbling over roots and rocks.

A short time later, faint lights flickered in the distance. As they came closer, Derek could see a light shining through the window of a long wooden structure with a thatched roof that sat off the main path. As they neared the clearing, Derek could feel his anxiety heighten. Each animal call magnified his fear, as he stayed close behind Father Mike, trying to absorb his calm demeanor.

The men stepped onto the lantern-lit planked porch, where a couple of sawed-off tree trunks used as chairs lined the wall and an empty hammock hung from the porch roof. Father Mike pushed open a large wooden door, exposing a large room filled with long wooden tables and chairs.

A thickset man with brown, weathered skin appeared from a doorway. "Tudo Bem, welcome!" His thick mustache framed a white, toothy smile. He brushed his hands on his pants. "I'm Rodrigo."

Father Mike stepped forward, removing his hat. "My name is Michael Korban, but most people call me Father Mike. I am a priest."

Rodrigo wiped his hands again on his khakis. "I have been expecting you. It is very nice to meet you, Father Mike," he said, shaking his hand with a steady smile.

Derek removed his cap. "I'm Derek Hollinger." Derek did not feel it necessary to tell him that he was a doctor. He would not believe him anyway, and he needed to trust this man. "Call me Derek."

Rodrigo briefly glanced over his tattooed, bald head and face, then shook his tattooed hand before gesturing with his arm toward the room. "Welcome to our main lodge. This is where everyone gathers for meetings and meals. Make yourselves at home. Would you like something to eat?"

In unison, both men replied in the affirmative.

Rodrigo disappeared back through the doorway leading back to the kitchen. Derek and Father Mike sat down at the nearest table. Derek glanced around the room and said, "This doesn't look too bad."

Father Mike smiled at his naivete. When he first became a priest, he had done missionary work in the jungle, which is when he met Alejandro. It had been the best of times and the worst. He had a good idea of what lay ahead. Derek was in for a surprise that would rock his world.

Along their journey, they would encounter various creatures, such as the fungus beetle with its putrid scent reminiscent of decaying meat. Yet despite the danger posed by venomous spiders, bullet ants, assassin bugs, and Amazonian giant centipedes that could inflict painful and even fatal bites, the tiny mosquito presented the greatest threat. Found abundantly in the region, mosquitoes carried dangerous diseases like malaria, yellow fever, dengue, chikungunya, and Zika virus. Father Mike decided not to mention this to Derek; he would soon learn about it firsthand.

Rodrigo returned with a large platter filled with ham, cheese, bread, vegetables, and nuts. "This is the diet of our Indigenous people," he explained. "We are skilled hunters and have provided fresh meat for this meal. This white-lipped peccary meat has been provided to us by the rainforest. From the local farmers, we have goats' cheese and vegetables grown in their gardens."

Derek felt a little queasy. He flashed back to when Kendal had taken him to his first hot dog stand. She had made fun of him because he was so inexperienced and hesitant. Since then, a new world had opened, pushing him out of his comfort zone. The queasy feeling that first night was the feeling he had now.

Rodrigo set three plates on the table, went back inside the kitchen, and came out with a pitcher of water and glasses. He sat down with the two men.

Derek became extra sensitive to the smell, taste, and texture of the food. His fussy eating habits were going to have to be set aside if he was going to survive the grueling trek ahead. The three men ate in silence. Rodrigo and Father Mike attacked their plates like starving men. Derek took small bites, nibbling at the contents on his plate until Rodrigo started to explain the trek ahead.

Derek set down his fork to listen to Rodrigo explain that he would be their guide in navigating the rainforest. In the days ahead, they would be living a relatively primitive life, surviving on his hunting skills. He would share his detailed knowledge of the rainforest and methods of how they would thrive in it. He would show them how to set up camp and where they would stay each night.

Rodrigo suggested that they rest first, and then he would go over the plan. They were to return to the main hut before dawn.

Father Mike took the barely-touched food from Derek's plate while Rodrigo prepared the dessert. He returned with an exquisite platter of Amazonian fruits and three cups of tea.

Perhaps this journey into the forest wouldn't be so bad after all, Derek thought. He lost himself in conversation with Rodrigo, forgetting his fears and enjoying the tranquility of the forest. Sipping his hot tea, Derek felt himself begin to relax.

When Father Mike had finished both their meals and indulged in the abundance of fresh fruit, Rodrigo cleared the items from the table and motioned for the two men to follow him. "I'll take you to your hut." He handed them both a large flashlight before exiting. "You will both be staying in the hut next to mine. If you need anything, you can just let me know."

Chapter 8

Kendal arrived at work early, fresh from her cosmetic routine, wearing her stylish surgical scrubs. She was the first to arrive at the office, which gave her an opportunity to walk through the surgical rooms and inspect inventory. Her non-slip shoes quietly padded from room to room. The silence of the clinic before the doctors, nurses, and staff arrived gave her the time to focus on the overall structure and cadence of the important work being performed.

It was her responsibility to make sure everything was in its place. She never wanted to experience what her aunt had gone through with an ill-equipped, unprepared surgery room. The nurses they hired were experienced, tough women who helped to make the doctors more confident in their work. She was instrumental in providing a safer atmosphere for both staff and patients.

After restocking and checking the inventory in the supply closet, she turned her attention to the equipment. She turned on and checked the function of all the safety devices and the monitoring systems. She checked to make sure they were equipped with enough sanitized surgical instruments. After inspecting to make sure all the equipment was safe for use, and all the systems were working properly, she went back to her office to take care of some paperwork.

She heard the front door being unlocked and then opened as the first of the medical staff arrived. She could not help but think about where Derek was right now. Had he made it into the jungle?

She signed into her computer and called up Google Maps for the Amazon rainforest. It seemed to be an amazing place, but it was also scary. The terrain looked like an inlet surrounded by dense jungle. Instead of traveling there, she would have to settle for seeing what it looked like through photographs. The collection of images captured various angles of the riverbank, forest, and sustainable eco-village, providing a comprehensive view of the area.

She wondered if he was scared or enjoying being out in the wild. She noticed the plant on her desk had started to wilt because it had not been watered.

She walked past Nicole's desk while retrieving some water and heard someone in the break room. She rounded the corner of the door to see Sandra, a large-framed, tall, middle-aged woman with brown hair pulled back in a braid, standing in front of the Keurig fixing herself a cup of coffee.

"Good morning, Sandra. How are you today?" Kendal inquired as she stood on her tippy toes to reach into the overhead cabinet for a glass.

"Good morning, Kendal." She looked over her shoulder at Kendal's petite frame. "I'm a little tired, to be honest. We've been really busy since Dr. Hollinger left. We have two extra surgeries today. I'm starting to get a little rundown."

"I restocked the surgery rooms this morning and checked the inventory. You should have everything you need for the day." Kendal tried to sound upbeat and cheery. "Let me know if there's anything I can do to help."

She stirred her cup slowly as she spoke. "Just inform Dr. Hollinger that we need him to return," she said. "We require an additional surgeon and nurse." Sandra was one of the few who saw Dr. Hollinger for his skills, not his appearance.

"I can assist Dr. Lee with a surgery today if you like."

"No, I can manage it for now. I appreciate the offer. He is particular and does not like change." She tapped the stir stick on the side of the cup.

"I understand," Kendal said with a slight smile as she filled the glass with water. "Dr. Hollinger is the same way," Kendal continued, her tone light and friendly. "He likes to have his instruments laid out in a certain way. He says it helps him think."

Sandra's eyes crinkled in amusement. "I've heard that about him," she said. "Guess it's their doctor thing."

Kendal nodded, her smile growing wider. "I suppose it is," she agreed.

Derek would only enter the surgical room after everything was in place and the patient was out under anesthesia. He would then turn on his classical music. He told her he had learned to do this when he worked with Dr. Casey. It made him relax and feel inspired while performing surgery.

"Maybe we could just start scheduling a little further apart?" Sandra took a sip to taste her coffee.

"Yes, we can do that. I'll talk to Nicole. Let her know not to overload you," Kendal said.

"I'd like that. I'm sure Dr. Lee will appreciate it, too," she said, adding a little more sugar, trying to get the combination right.

"No worries. That is what I am here for. Thank you, I appreciate the feedback. Please let me know if there is anything else I can do." After all, she was the majority stockholder since she married Derek and became vice president while performing the duties of the chief operating officer of the business.

"I will. Thanks." When she finished stirring her coffee, she sucked the stir stick and threw it in the trash as she walked out of the break room.

Kendal took a deep breath and sighed. She felt the heavy weight of the responsibilities that came with ownership. She knew it was only a matter of time before burnout would take its toll on the surgical staff. Not to mention the increased risk of malpractice. She returned to her office with the weight of the world on her shoulders.

Her mind wandered back to Derek and the Amazon as she watered her plant. She would probably like being in the Amazon jungle. He should have asked her to go. An adventure would be nice about now. But she knew that now was not the time to leave the business. She needed to make sure everything ran smoothly, and after the conversation she had with Sandra she feared they may be coming close to a tipping point.

The doctors and nurses needed a work-life balance. Right now, that would be difficult to achieve with the long shifts and weekend work. It was a prescription for widespread burnout and dissatisfaction. The extra load was making them particularly susceptible to physical and emotional exhaustion.

After this was over, everyone would have to take a vacation. She was going to take a long vacation. If Derek really liked the Amazon, they could go back there.

Or maybe she would just go on a more relaxing trip to Fiji or someplace like that. Someplace where she could lay on the warm white sand and soak up the sun.

She felt a little uncomfortable flutter of nausea. "Oh, I don't need this right now," she muttered. "The last thing I need is to get sick." She was trying to keep her stress levels down so that her immune system would not be weakened.

Between work and her personal life, it had been almost impossible for her to maintain a semblance of normalcy. She had increased her vitamins and sat in the sun to get a little vitamin D; hopefully, that would be enough.

She took a sip from the last of the water in the glass and sat back in her chair. Maybe she hadn't drank enough water. Dehydration could cause tiredness and nausea. A couple of hours of sleep just were not enough to wake up feeling rested and mentally alert. The lack of REM sleep from the restless night before caused her to close her eyes and drift.

She saw herself in the jungle. Walking a trail, she could see the monkeys above. A large colorful parrot flew past her and landed in a nearby tree. She could see the large bird prune its feathers.

She watched as a colorful butterfly fluttered past her face. She put her hand out and the butterfly landed on her finger. A sign of good luck, a symbol of hope and new beginnings, she considered it a good omen. She could feel the magic of being in such a vibrantly colored place.

The butterfly did not always have its wings, Kendal thought as it fluttered on her finger. It had started as a small caterpillar and had gone through a metamorphosis, then transformed into this colorful winged creature. It was a sign of perseverance through struggle and had come out stronger and more beautiful than ever.

She thought of a butterfly metaphor she had heard once: "A small change can give rise to a big tidal wave." She could feel that she was at a crossroads in her life, weary of life's twists and turns. The butterfly on her finger reminded her that change was inevitable.

Kendal heard a voice come from the front of the office. She quickly opened her eyes and wearily stood to continue with her day.

Chapter 9

Their flashlights flickered across the darkened landscape. The eerie sound of the ground-dwelling tinamous bird, coupled with the quails singing in the distance and the toucans crying their inharmonious protest from the treetops, sounded like a concerto of birds trilling and caroling, creating a cacophony of song.

Derek became aware that his vision and hearing were being processed at different rates. His visual cortex was slower to receive, decode, and process the information, while his auditory cortex swiftly managed incoming sounds. This imbalance impacted his overall sensory perception and influenced his emotions with an instinctual response before his brain could fully comprehend the situation.

They walked along the raised manmade pebble pathway connecting the thatched huts. Derek moved closer to Father Mike when the light caught the tail of a snake that had just slithered across the trail and back into the brush. They could hear more than they could see.

Derek jumped when his headlamp beam landed on a huge tarantula resting on the trunk of a palm tree. The night air heightened all the senses. They walked slowly, taking in the soundscape. Myriad eyes reflected the lights from their headlamps, so they were not difficult to spot. The rainforest was very much alive and crawling with bugs.

Derek's head was on a swivel as the constant buzz and sounds of millions of creatures reverberated through the rainforest. Occasionally, a loud, piercing noise would startle the two men.

Rodrigo slowly climbed wooden steps to a thatched door and then swung it open. He entered and lit a lantern on the small table between two cots that sat inside the primitive one-room dwelling with a steeply pitched thatched roof. The yellowish flame emitted just enough light to see by. The hut was equivalent to a nice screened-in porch with two beds and mosquito netting.

"There's no cell phone connection, TV or radio." Rodrigo pointed to a door. "This is the bathroom. It has a shower. The water is warm, but you will want to make your shower short so you don't run out. A solar pouch on the roof heats the water during the day. Get some sleep. We need to go over the plan in a couple of hours."

After the long boat ride, the rudimentary accommodations were welcome. They took short showers and climbed into their beds. With mosquito netting tucked in around their cots, they lay down for a good night's sleep before starting their long morning hike.

Derek felt a little freaked out after carefully adjusting the wick until the flame flickered. It was dark! Pitch dark. He could not see his hand in front of his face. He hoped he would not feel any creepy crawlies run over his legs.

Father Mike said a prayer aloud: "Lord, let us be the torch that lights up the dark path. Please clear any darkness that may stand in our way."

Derek lay fear-frozen in bed until the compulsive jungle rhythm lulled his tired body to sleep.

The sound of deafening rain came a short time later. Thunder rumbled in the distance. Then, as suddenly as it began, it stopped. It left a momentary, disquieting silence as Derek lay in his cot, unable to go back to sleep. In the distant rainforest, the monkeys began to howl almost in unison. It sounded like the low roar of a faraway lion.

A 5:00 a.m. wake-up call came with a knock at the hut door. Rodrigo had prepared their breakfast and supplies while waiting for them at the main lodge. "You will carry everything in your pack for the duration of the trip. Minimize as much as you can." He reminded them to carry only two pairs of pants, underwear, basic toiletries, a jungle kit with a headlamp, a safety whistle, and a sturdy rain jacket. They had twenty minutes to eat, and then it was time to head out on the trail.

Within the first hour, the auditory landscape of the vibrant Amazon rainforest shifted. During the sunrise, the clouds parted, and the sun's rays hit the canopy of trees, creating a tapestry of color that no human could ever replicate.

When Derek's body began to feel the effects of the strenuous exercise, the magic started to happen. He could feel the endorphins kick in as he tuned into the birds' melodious songs, frogs' deep croaks, and the mammals that added their occasional calls to the symphony of nature.

Their trek had started on an extremely muddy trail, increasing the demand for physicality. After enduring a few hours of the grueling hike, Derek's brain released another wave of chemicals. This was when the real transformation began. The new chemical signals started to positively impact his mood and thinking. The extreme exercise was now giving him a boost that slowly diminished his depression. He felt the darkness within him start to melt away.

The macaws and howler monkeys flashed above, creating a scene reminiscent of a circus tent. Meanwhile, a thousand different bugs and insects buzzed and chirped on the ground. It was a symphony of life, where each creature seemed to have its song.

The trio progressed deeper into the rainforest at a gradual pace along a twisting path around trees and bushes. Rodrigo chopped brush as he scouted ahead, intermittently calling out to look up or out as he spotted the indigenous creatures that lived in the rainforest.

The jungle echoed with the sounds of nature, a symphony of life. It was a place of secrets and splendor, inspiring awe and humbling anyone who dared to enter its depths. It served as a reminder of the wonders of the natural world and the mysteries of creation.

Father Mike's six-foot frame accidentally walked through the web of a crazy-looking spider, causing him to break dance along the path. This made Derek chuckle. Every so often, they would have a close encounter with a poisonous snake crossing the trail.

The macaws, dressed in feathers of glittering greens, blues, and glowing reds, flew over the trees in gregarious groups, filling the air with their shrieks and caws. The monkeys howled with piercing ambiance, swinging from tree to tree across the green canopy.

Derek's legs began to shake at the height of the steamy mid-afternoon heat. Rodrigo had been good about giving them breaks, averaging a ten-minute stop every two hours to let their bodies cool. Huge leaves funneled vast amounts of water for the men to hydrate, have a snack, and then continue. Hot and humid, their bodies full of sweat, they slowly trudged through thick vines and foliage.

It was impossible to stay dry. There were so many bugs that they were stung and bitten continuously. Derek's bee allergy so far had not come into play. The mosquitoes were the worst. Derek understood now why everyone had been so insistent about him carrying bug spray. Luckily, his clothes were treated with bug repellent as well.

Derek trudged through the never-ending jungle, surrounded by the constant chatter of spider monkeys that echoed through the dense and seemingly endless foliage around him. The thick greenery seemed impenetrable and limitless, stretching on for what felt like an eternity.

They trekked for hours, pushing aside ferns and vines that blocked their way. Derek stumbled occasionally, his feet catching on tangled roots that snaked across the path. The increasing humidity made it difficult, but he refused to stop, determined to keep up with Rodrigo until they reached the center of the rainforest.

This journey through the depths of the Amazon represented Derek's internal struggle as he grappled with his conscious, sub-conscious, and unconscious thoughts.

Just as the tropical rainforest is divided into three distinct levels, the highest level is the canopy, which blankets most of the forest. Below that is the understory, and finally, at the very bottom, is the forest floor. Derek began to consider the three levels of the mind: conscious, subconscious, and unconscious. He knew that his thoughts, actions, and awareness fell under consciousness.

His awareness heightened with his physical body pushed to its limit. He knew that his subconscious mind encompassed his reactions.

Finally, his unconscious represented the deep recesses of his past experiences and memories. He needed to think these through. It was obvious to him now that there was a correlation between his unconscious mind and the manifestation of the tattoos.

After walking for hours, Derek's shoulders ached from the heavy weight of his pack.

He began to think each level through while trying to ignore the fact that his feet had started to throb from navigating the rugged terrain.

The subconscious mind is like a personal assistant, always running in the background. It acts as a computer, storing and retrieving information from our senses and experiences and conducting automated processes.

These could include maintaining balance and coordination while driving or riding a bike without needing conscious thought. Our subconscious mind plays a major role in how we think, respond, and behave, dictating 95 percent of our actions to fit our self-image and beliefs.

Derek knew that this part of his brain had contributed to the manifestation of his tattoos. He understood that the depths of this area of the mind were not easily accessible and required thorough exploration to reveal. It could be likened to a secret chest with valuable insights and undiscovered capabilities.

The "unconscious mind" had dictated his behaviors without awareness of the stimuli that triggered them.

As they navigated through thorny vines and razor-sharp palm fronds, they finally reached a cool stream of fresh water. Taking a drink and splashing his face, he concluded it was true. All three levels of his brain had been triggered to manifest his tattoos. The unsettling question came to him: could it be possible that he was responsible for his own trauma? He had never wanted to face this conclusion before. Each time it had crept into his mind he had pushed it out.

The sunset cast a hazy golden light through the tree line. The water was just a short distance from the evening's selected campsite. Rodrigo instructed them to collect some firewood, and he would go out to find dinner.

The tropical sunset filtered by immense trees made the canopy above glow with an unearthly light. The air was thick with the damp rainforest smells. Everywhere Derek looked, he spotted something new and breathtaking.

He was anxious to take off his damp clothes and get clean. He quickly collected firewood while Father Mike started the fire.

Derek sat on the side of the stream, took off his boots, and saw blood-soaked socks. Alarmed and confused, he scrambled to see where it was coming from and removed his pants. To his horror, he found leeches. He let out a sharp high-pitched gasp at the sight of the bloated, black creatures covering his legs. Creeped out, he started to panic, trying to slap the slimy things off, but they only seemed to cling on tighter. He could feel their suction cups digging into his skin. He shuddered in disgust.

Hearing the commotion, Father Mike rushed over to help. He told Derek to sit down on a log so he could locate the head of each one and remove it.

Covered with the slimy, ravenous creatures that had been silently affixing themselves to his legs, Derek's body stiffened as each blood-gorged leech was removed. Every inch of his skin crawled as he sat, shivering. Derek shuddered in disgust while Father Mike pulled the skin from under the leech taunt and slid his fingernail underneath the mouth. He would then flick the leech away.

"I believe we got them all," Father Mike told Derek. "Turn

around, let me see." The priest examined him closely, like a mother tending to her baby. "We need to clean the bite holes and put band-aids on to protect from infection," he said.

Still a bit shaken, Derek felt a sense of relief. He took a deep breath and surveyed the damage. He sat for a minute, exhausted; the excitement had drained the last bit of his energy. The hot air encased them with buzzing insects.

He could feel those long-buried memories clawing their way to the surface. He tried to push them back down, to hold onto the false sense of control he had carefully constructed for himself. But it was no use. They came rushing forward, a flood of emotions and images that threatened to overwhelm him.

Tears welled in his eyes. "Kendal was right. She said that I might be getting myself in deeper and that I was just making it harder on myself. I have an EpiPen in my bag, too. I am allergic to bees."

"Now you tell me." Father Mike shook his head, his hand resting gently on his shoulder as Derek finally gave in to the tears building up inside him for years.

Derek started to sob as he momentarily set down the weight of his buried trauma. The veil began to lift, allowing him to see the world with new eyes.

He grew silent, looking at the ground and then at Father Mike. "*Who am I?*" he whispered, his voice thick with emotion.

Father Mike understood this to be a fundamental spiritual question. "It takes years to process traumatic events. You learn to live with them on *your* terms and *your* timeline."

Derek shook his head. "It's hard for me to determine what I truly want or what my next steps should be." The words kept flowing, each one more uncertain than the next. He struggled to make sense of it. He could feel himself unraveling as he spoke, the words spilling out as if he had no control over them.

"I'm not sure what it is I want or if I'm on the right path," he admitted, feeling his composure slipping away.

He knew how he could be when he acted on impulse. The flood of negative thoughts was creating a downward spiral. He could not make the right decisions in this frame of mind. He feared he had chosen incorrectly. The pressure was paralyzing.

Father Mike could sense Derek was on the verge of a panic attack. "This is a journey," he said softly, pulling out the medical kit from his pack. "It's not going to be easy, but neither of us thought it would be." He got down on his knees in front of Derek and poured alcohol on the open wounds.

Derek clenched his teeth and bit his lip, willing himself not to make a noise. "I'm a doctor, for crying out loud. I can handle a little bit of pain," he chided. He forced himself to stay silent though every instinct told him to express his discomfort.

Father Mike applied a small band-aid on one of the bleeding holes in Derek's leg. "We both know it was not working for you at home, the way things were going. You need answers.

"God tells us, 'Let not your hearts be troubled, neither let them be afraid.' I believe the best way to learn to trust God is to have faith in difficult times. He tells us not to worry and to pray. He will give you peace like you cannot imagine."

Father Mike finished applying the last band-aid and stood up. "Right now, you need to focus on the things within your control. This is a life-changing experience, no matter what the outcome. You need to lean into the tough and uncomfortable moments. We have traveled into the darkness now. Remember, we carry the light." He tapped Derek on the chest over his heart. "In here, we take on our responsibilities with faith."

Derek appreciated the personal care and comfort Father Mike provided. He felt calmer as he washed his clothes and the blood from his socks in the freshwater of the small stream. He remembered the day Kendal put her hand on his chest over his heart. He remembered how upset he felt that day. She had shown him support and love. Her empathy made him wonder, "Why would I have left her to come here?"

A feeling of despondency burrowed into the depths of his gut again. He reminded himself that Father Mike was right; he needed to find answers.

When he returned to camp, he put his hand on Father Mike's shoulder and gently squeezed. He gave him an affectionate look and then continued to finish readying the camp for dinner.

Neither of the men was an experienced camper, so they worked together. The novice campers strung up their mesh hammocks with overhead tarps to ward off mosquito attacks and other jungle creatures that might come their way.

Next, they hung their boots on makeshift wooden poles to prevent spiders and snakes from crawling in at night. Their bags had been stripped down to the essentials. They reapplied bug spray so as not to get eaten alive, put on a change of dry clothes, and hung up their wet ones. Father Mike rolled down his long sleeves and tended the fire, anticipating Rodrigo's return.

Derek sat resting on a log, looking out toward the small stream, when he felt a tinge of excitement. He had spotted butterflies with translucent wings fluttering along the bank. Immersed in this completely different world, he watched the optical illusion as they flew through the forest with clear wings. Bright pink and orange dots flickered through the air as they flew away.

He began to marvel at it all, feeling a sense of awe and wonder that had been missing from his life. He was being rewarded for this journey; what had taken him days to realize had only taken moments to appreciate. He lingered for a while, cherishing every moment, taking in the beauty, and feeling a deep sense of peace and contentment.

The quiet voice in the back of his mind reminded him he had taken a gamble coming to this place. For weeks, he had read stories and convinced himself that he could find the answers to his questions if he made his way to the shaman's village.

His intuition had urged him on. He knew he needed to be more thoughtful of Kendal in the future, but right now, he felt this was necessary. The path to the village proved to be treacherous, and every mud-filled step made him more aware of the risks he was taking.

The glow of the fire threw a faint light up several meters to just below the canopy, where Derek could see a darker and stiller layer. He looked around the perimeter height to see large flowers growing in the dimly lit environment. He watched the silhouettes of the jewel-toned squeaking parrots glide through the trees. A mantel of tranquility settled over his shoulders. A recalibration for a new perspective was starting to grow. The rainforest had felt intimidating and scary. Now, it felt full of life.

He took a moment to look at the flora from a doctor's perspective. He considered the compounds derived from the native plants to treat malaria, heart disease, diabetes, and many other health problems.

The hypnotic effects of the fire transcended Derek as he sat looking at Father Mike, the firelight flickering across his face.

Thoughts cascaded through his mind. *Why is he doing this for me? I understand he has a calling, and he helps people, but why me? I am not homeless. In fact, I probably have much more than I deserve. Why has he come on such an arduous journey like this for someone like me?*

As the sun sank below the horizon, the sounds around grew louder, more persistent and monotonous. The symphony of insect chirps was joined by a chorus of nocturnal frogs and the occasional rustling of mammals. Bats could also be heard, though their high-pitched calls were barely audible to human ears. Among all the natural sounds, there were unexpected noises, like a tree branch snapping and crashing to the ground or a ripe fruit dropping from a nearby tree. These sudden outbursts would catch them off guard and make them jump in surprise.

The sun set early in the rainforest, the dense foliage giving way to falling darkness. Father Mike sat by the fire, his hands resting gently on his knees. He looked back at Derek resting in his hammock, then turned back to the fire. He closed his eyes and took a deep breath, letting the warm air fill his lungs before slowly exhaling.

Ever since childhood, he had been drawn to the metaphysical and felt a connection to something larger than himself. As he grew older, he delved deeper into meditation and prayer. He had even started to explore a realm beyond the physical, where he felt closest to God and most at home.

His morning routine at home consisted of meditation and prayer with the Holy Spirit, where he sought guidance and inspiration for the day ahead. But today felt different.

He couldn't shake the feeling that this day had been significant in their journey. He opened his eyes and gazed back into the flames, feeling a sense of peace.

Father Mike knew he was on the verge of a breakthrough and felt ready to embrace whatever God had in store for him. He'd come into the jungle believing the Lord would show him His intentions.

That first night in the hut, as he slept, he received a vision in his dreams, a message that something significant was coming his way.

In the dream, Father Mike saw himself sitting in a dimly lit church, the gentle glow of the altar candles casting a peaceful aura around him. This was his home with the nuns. He would come here every night seeking solace and guidance for his struggles. Here, he found his faith, nurtured it, and watched it bloom into a steadfast companion.

As a very young child, he was fascinated by the Bible stories his mother read him every night before bed. The tales of miracles and redemption, love and forgiveness, captivated his young mind and and had planted the seed for him to follow in the footsteps of the saints.

But faith was not enough to shield him from the harsh realities of life. He had seen his share of pain, suffering, loss, and despair. His faith had been tested repeatedly, but it had never faltered. It had been his constant, his rock, the guiding light in the darkest of times.

As he watched himself sitting in the quiet sanctuary, a fog rolled across the floor and a sense of peace washed over him, consumed by God's presence. It was a feeling he could never fully describe, but it filled him with joy and comfort.

The flickering candles on the altar reminded him that there was always hope, even amid the deepest darkness. And as he thought of all the people he had helped through his faith, he knew he was exactly where he was meant to be.

He remembered his teenage years, when he first knew something was wrong. In his darkest moment, he could not look at himself in the mirror. He did not deserve happiness. A dark, suffocating feeling had consumed him, leaving no room for self-love or growth.

Father Mike had been raised in foster homes after his mother passed, until he was twelve, when he became too high of a risk. He started to rebel. He had been molested by one of the older children when he was young. It started around five or six and lasted until he was eight, when he started to run away. This caught the attention of the authorities, and he exposed his abuser. But the foster family got rid of Mike. The abuser was their biological son.

After that, he was in and out of different foster homes and ended up in juvenile hall until the nuns offered to take him in. He had become too old to adopt or foster out. People did not want that kind of trouble. He tried to hide his insecurities and put on a facade of confidence, but deep down, he was constantly belittling himself. His thoughts were a constant stream of self-deprecation and doubt. It was hard to find and connect with his authentic self. It had been lost in abuse and abandonment.

He navigated his youth, trying to find purpose. He had experienced intermittent bouts of depression, not knowing what was happening at the time. The heavy burden of guilt and shame weighed him down. It followed him everywhere, like vultures circling above, ready to swoop down and devour his soul.

But through the Grace of God and the devotion and nurturing of the nuns, he found the strength to keep going—to keep searching for that elusive sense of fulfillment and meaning. And even though the journey was long and treacherous, he knew it was worth it. Finding his purpose in life was the only way to break free from the chains of self-doubt and embrace his true self.

Derek roamed over from taking a quick nap in his hammock and poked a stick in the fire.

"How was your nap?" Father Mike asked.

Derek had something important on his mind. He ignored the question and asked one of his own. "You spend your time caring for people who don't deserve it, like me. Why?"

Father Mike drew in a deep breath. "When a person is facing judgment, they deserve justice. Just as your attacker did, the man called Spider. He wasted his life by hurting and killing people. Spending his life in jail is an incredibly sad commentary on how to waste a life, but it was necessary.

"However, it is also essential for the judge to consider mercy when it is warranted. In Spider's case, there is no humanity in making the man die in prison. In the face of judgment, every person deserves justice, including your attacker. He made many grave mistakes and ultimately paid for them with his life. While it is a tragedy that he spent his life in prison, it is also important for the judge to consider mercy when making his decision to release him to go home and die."

Father Mike shifted on the log, studying the flames. "But then again, in his case, it might have been more humane to keep him inside prison since when they let him out, he had nowhere to go and no one to help him. His was a sad existence indeed."

Derek gave a reluctant nod. "I guess so."

"As you know," Father Mike continued, "after he was released, I spent a little time with Spider. He told me he understood what he had done was wrong, but he was unable or unwilling to repent.

"You see, what was not shared in that courtroom is that Spider had been the victim of an alcoholic mother. His father had died of a drug overdose. He grew up on the streets. Not that any of these were reasons to do the horrific things he did, but it contributed to his mindset."

Derek had never taken the time to think about Spider's childhood. He never knew that at Spider's last courtroom visit, after being given a terminal diagnosis and living in the shadow of death, he sat with his head down, hands folded in his lap, his frail body weighing just over a hundred pounds. He was a flicker of his former self, with a thin line of gray hair, his brown eyes dulled by years spent in a cold, dark prison cell.

Spider's heart had pounded uncontrollably when he heard the judge's verdict. He knew he deserved the punishment for his actions, but he could not help but hope for leniency.

The judge's words were a distant echo, muffled by the weight of Spider's fear. He could not bring himself to look up, to meet the judge's eyes.

And then, the verdict was read. The words hung in the air, heavy and final.

Spider's head hung even lower, his breaths coming in short, shallow gasps. He had been given a chance to go home and die in dignity. But that would be impossible, for there was no home to return to. His mother had died long ago. He would never have a chance to make amends for his mistakes.

He could not change the past. The sting of hopelessness saturated his soul. At that moment, he vowed to spend every moment living the rest of his limited time making the best of a dead man walking, even when it meant facing his mortality.

The weight of his burden lifted slightly, and for the first time in years, Spider felt a glimmer of hope that his time on this earth would end soon and he could move on to the next life, whatever that would bring. But as soon as he hit the street, he fell back into the web that held all his old fears and propelled him back to his rebellious and predatory nature.

Father Mike tried to help him understand the error of his ways—to acknowledge that he had acted egregiously and make a conscious effort to change his behavior. He also explained the spiritual significance of how he had conducted himself in this physical world.

Father Mike continued to focus on the naked flame as he tried to explain it to Derek. "I have helped many people who have been incarcerated, so I understand this firsthand. People may label them as 'no good,' but they are still human beings with their own struggles and issues to face. We need to take the time to understand who these individuals are before locking them away. Of course, this does not apply to serial killers or other dangerous criminals like Spider, who was a predator.

"But for the average person who comes from poverty and has limited resources and options, perhaps they need more than punishment. Catholic charities often provide exceptional assistance in these situations, even though they may not receive much attention." He sighed. "In the end, mercy is crucial. The offender should take responsibility for their actions and make amends to society, but mercy should always be considered."

The fire's soft glow flickered around the landscape, instilling a subtle illusion of being enveloped in a warm, comforting embrace.

Derek stopped poking at the fire with the stick. "Is this how you see me? A person who needs an act of mercy?"

Father Mike looked up to meet Derek's eyes. "No, in your case, I see a person who has been knocked off the path of his original calling. I know that God has put it upon my heart to help you. It sounds weird, but the Holy Spirit continually prompts me to stay involved with you. I do not know what God has in mind, but I know I am here to help facilitate whatever you need to experience or learn."

He leaned forward, holding Derek's tortured gaze. "I am compelled to help you find whatever has brought you to this point. Maybe because God has plans for you, he needs to ensure you will have a better chance if I am here to help."

Derek's jaw muscles relaxed. "I can't express what that means to me."

The sight and sound of the fire had a calming effect on Derek as he gazed back into the flame. "My mentor, Dr. Christopher Casey, was a brilliant man. But I was treated as his protégé, his student. I never felt a paternal connection with him."

He absently twisted the gold wedding band around his finger. "Kendal was the first person to show me what love is since I was separated from my mother and grandmother when I was fifteen. Love still feels foreign to me, but sometimes I feel that flicker of hope when my heart seems to connect with hers."

Father Mike grabbed more wood for the fire. "You are blessed to experience that kind of love."

Derek paused. "Why did you decide the priesthood would be best instead of a relationship and family?" He watched the priest throw dry sticks into the fire. Sparks flew up into the damp air.

"In part because I was too broken," Father Mike admitted. "God placed me on a journey to find myself by helping other people. It worked." He brushed his hands off and sat back down. "My love for Him and the ministry has only grown through time. I believe this is where I am supposed to be—in this jungle, at this time, helping you find what you're looking for."

Derek chuckled. "Now I know there has to be a God because I could not imagine why anyone would volunteer to go through a struggle like this one if they didn't have to."

Father Mike let out a sardonic laugh. "Tell you the truth, I did not think it would be this difficult. I find myself having long and complex conversations with myself through this trek. I see how this is therapeutic and necessary for the breakdown of a person. This brings us to our core. Examine what we are doing and what we should do about it. It is a type of cleansing of the body and the soul." His brow furrowed. "It's hard to describe. I have never physically suffered like this before. I cannot even imagine the pain and suffering that Jesus went through on the cross. This experience brings me closer to Him."

"Wow, that is very profound." Derek stood stiffly and stretched. "I think it's going to take some time for me to digest this whole experience. It's been painful. But I'm realizing a lot of things. It brings clarity to my life that I have never experienced before."

Father Mike slowly stood. "Maybe that's why we've been put on this trek together. We can help each other grow through our own and each other's revelations."

"It seems to me . . ." Derek paused, startled by a rustling from the bushes.

They could hear the nuts tumbling from the trees. Father Mike moved closer to the fire when a loud crash erupted from the nearby bushes. They both froze, not daring to breathe.

Their eyes were fixed on a set of large elephant ear leaves. Out popped Rodrigo with a bamboo bow slung around his thick torso.

In his left hand he carried the carcass of a plucked bird. A skilled hunter, he'd caught fresh meat for the evening meal. As Rodrigo set the bird down, he explained that he'd cleaned it further downstream so as not to leave remnants that would attract a jaguar or other hunters of the jungle.

The bird looked oddly prehistoric; it had a long neck, and the head was disproportionately thin and small. The bill was baby blue at the base and cobalt-blue at the tip. Its legs were red. Derek realized this was the bird that made the slow high-pitched whistles.

Rodrigo looked around the camp as he took a drink from his canteen. "Looks good." He smiled. "I'll put dinner on." He cut a large leaf from a nearby plant and sat down on the log, placing his pack on the ground in front of him. He pulled out large pieces of Yuca (the roots resemble sweet potatoes), carefully laying each on top of the leaf, along with mushrooms, acai berries, three bananas, and a couple of mangos.

From the big, heavy supply bag he took out a small pot with a bag of rice. He threw in the rice and the mushrooms then poured some water from his canteen into the pot. He reached back into his pack and pulled out the bird's liver and kidneys and placed them in the pan. Then he threw in some homegrown herbs. Because the heart is rich in vitamins and minerals, he cleaned it and ate it.

As part of their cultural traditions, many Indigenous hunters consume the raw heart of a slain animal as a symbolic act. This practice is believed to grant them strength, courage, and vitality by ingesting the essence of the animal. It is seen as a way to honor and appreciate the life of the animal while also gaining its spirit.

Rodrigo then pulled out a second small pot and filled it with the Yuca root, seasoning, and water.

Derek and Father Mike watched as he transformed the campfire into a kitchen. Rodrigo placed both pots at the edge of the burning coals. He took his knife out and cut two small branches off a nearby tree. He pulled the foliage off the sticks and sharpened one end of each with the blade. Pushed the straight sharp edge in the ground and the forked curved end of the stick in the air. Then he placed them on each side of the fire. He cut another branch to make a stick to run through the length of the bird and put it over the fire then sat back down.

"It won't be long," he said, watching the fire.

They relaxed to the soothing sound of the crackling campfire. The hypnotic glow intensified their senses, enabling them to savor the smell emanating from the bird juices dropping into the fire.

When it was ready, Rodrigo slid the pans back from the fire. He pulled out three tin plates. One by one he dished out the dirty rice with vegetables. He took the bird off the fire, cut it apart, and put pieces on each plate. He handed a plate to Father Mike then to Derek, who eagerly sat waiting.

The nerves in Derek's tongue activated his taste buds. He had never eaten anything so delicious, and his aversion to strange food had miraculously disappeared. He asked, "What kind of bird is this?"

"We call it a piping guan," Rodrigo answered as he finished a leg, tossed the bone into the fire, and ran his finger around the inside of his plate.

Rodrigo wiped his mouth with the back of his hand and reached out to take the dirty plates from the two men. He collected the pots and utensils and then disappeared into the dark, heading toward the stream.

Finished with the rainforest delicacy, the two fatigued men sat mesmerized by the fire.

"Do you know the story of Joseph from the Bible?" Father Mike sat on the ground, leaning against a small tree with his cup in hand. "Joseph was the dreamer who was thrown into a well but still found the courage to keep going against all odds. This story helped me to realize that there are no logical answers to our struggles."

Derek sat quietly, watching Father Mike's silhouette against the flickering fire.

"I cannot predict your future, Derek, but you must make choices despite the uncertainty. Wisdom is being able to hold hope and despair in our minds simultaneously, but it can be hard to hold onto hope when despair starts to take over. Life becomes impossible without both."

"Then where is God in all of this?" Derek threw a stick into the fire in frustration.

Father Mike gazed into the flames for a few moments before speaking again. "The mind of God is beyond our understanding, but we can choose to live righteously. Despair is often rooted in pride that refuses to acknowledge that God's ways are greater than ours."

Rodrigo returned with the clean equipment and broke their trance when he began to talk slowly, his voice grim. "There is a jungle spirit that captures human souls in the rainforest." He looked up with the glow of the fire flickering in his eyes. "You are never *ever* to get out of your hammock in the middle of the night." He looked from one man to the other. "Even if you think it is I. It is the jaguar in disguise trying to lure you into the jungle. He will be attracted to the heat from the camp."

Rodrigo crouched down to poke at the fire, his voice lowered to just above a whisper, "The jaguar is an astounding hunter, a marvelous predator. He is filled with mysterious supernatural powers. He can appear and disappear at will. It stalks its prey with stealth.

"He's very muscular with a tan coat and spots." He swept his arm down his side. "Beautiful rosettes cover its body. The jaguar's hunting behavior is not confined to a specific time of day. He relies on encountering his prey while canvassing his territory." His eyes widened. "That is us."

Derek swallowed hard.

"He feeds on deer, capybara, and giant anteaters," Rodrigo continued. "He also hunts monkeys, birds, caimans, and turtles. His powerful jaws bite down on the base of their skulls, and his teeth pierce the brain for a quick and easy kill."

Rodrigo briefly stopped talking, his head swiveling to look out into the blackness. "It sneaks up silently until it is in range. A ravenous jaguar with night vision will launch an attack under the cover of darkness. The mysterious jaguar is not always nocturnal, so we must watch for him in the predawn hours. Listen for the warning sounds like snarls, growls, and deep hoarse grunts. Life and death are at stake—losers pay with their hide."

Rodrigo stood to put another log on the fire, then stirred the coals. "As we go deeper into the rainforest, we enter his territory. We must be vigilant and stay aware. The jaguar will stalk us. He is an ambush predator. That is how he got his name. It means the one who kills with one leap. His superpower has no physical origin. He appears from nowhere and is a savage fighter. The Indigenous people attribute his power to the spirits in the forest."

Derek, covered in goosebumps, rubbed the skin of the crouching jaguar tattoo on his inner right forearm. "Could it be related?" he murmured to himself. "Is it an omen?"

Or was it a reminder of his inner strength and courage? He tried to remember what Terry, the owner of a tattoo parlor back in L.A. who'd become a good friend, had told him the meaning of the jaguar on his arm could be. He tried to better understand this powerful animal and its place in human culture.

Rodrigo became animated. He stood with his arms stretched out. "They can easily carry large carcasses the size of a cow long distances through difficult terrain."

Derek felt a fearful anxiety ooze into his throat. "The jaguar tattoo means I have an inner strength with reserved power," he reassured himself.

Rodrigo continued. "He's an ambush predator with an uncanny ability to become almost invisible at will."

With fear, dread, and uneasiness, Derek imagined the jaguar stealthily approaching the campsite, completely unphased by a human with a headlamp—or the fire. His senses heightened. His inner voice reasoned back, trying to maintain a sense of calm despite the danger he was in. He had taken a risk by making his way here. What other choice did he now have?

Whether it was intuition or warning signs that Rodrigo was sharing, unbeknownst to the men, they *were* being watched. They had not realized they were under surveillance. Rodrigo knew the jaguar was close but would only show himself when he was ready to be seen.

He also knew it was rare for a jaguar to hunt people. "The jaguar has a disciplined energy. A shrewd awareness that makes it capable of unleashing its power in calculated ways."

Derek and Father Mike watched Rodrigo poke the fire one last time, then climb into his hammock and flip the tarp.

"Get some sleep," he yelled from his makeshift den.

The two men huddled around the fire. "Fat chance of that," Derek muttered wryly.

Father Mike sat with his hands folded in prayer. His words were reassuring as he spoke out into the night. "Our ultimate fate is not to reside 'up in Heaven' after death, but here on earth as it is in Heaven," he said, his voice calm yet assertive. "Our ultimate fate lies here, on a rejuvenated, tangible earth, in our transformed, physical forms. This will become a reality when Jesus completes all things, eradicating death and the old ways for eternity."

A sense of hope and peace washed over Derek as he listened to the priest's words.

"This is our fundamental belief of Christianity and our great hope for the future." Father Mike's sermon ended with an "Amen."

Derek was starting to feel a renewed sense of purpose.

Father Mike stood on the other side of the fire. "What you need to understand about the shamans' ways is that they represent the lower gods. As the Bible tells us, these gods are the fallen angels. The shaman is the intermediary between the separated worlds and dimensions. This practice Rodrigo talks of is discouraged in the Bible.

"Shamans believe in serving both the physical and spiritual realms.

In their worldview of connecting earth and Heaven, the proper functioning of the world relies on more than just social structures. It also requires a connection to the spiritual realm. The shamans function as intermediaries.

"When you think about it, why would you want to depend on another entity to get between you and God? You don't know if their intentions are good or evil. And if they belong to a group of individuals who have fallen out of favor with God, why would we want to deal with them at all?

"God clarified that He did not intend for his children to stumble around in the dark, grasping for His will like a blind man looking for a bone. No, He wanted His people to walk confidently, trusting in His plans and purposes. He wanted them to have peace amid uncertainty, knowing He held the future in His hands. This is why He gave us the Bible as a blueprint—our instructions for life here on earth."

Father Mike stood to go to his hammock and looked expectantly at Derek.

"I'm right behind you," Derek said.

Derek sat on the ground. Flickers of fire danced around him as he examined his tattoos in wonder. He traced his fingers over the intricate designs, each one seemingly representing a different aspect of his identity and purpose.

Unable to hide, the sight of them filled him with shame and fear. He feared the judgment and rejection he faced from anyone who saw them.

But now, in this moment of clarity, Derek understood that the tattoos were more than ink on his skin. They were a gift, a divine tool meant to be used for good. Each symbol and line held a powerful message and the potential he had yet to fully explore, a mystery waiting to unravel.

He knew he could not deny his tattoos any longer. It was time to embrace them and, in doing so, fully embrace himself.

Derek reached into his bag and pulled out the small hand-carved wooden angel; he could not help but feel a pang of sadness. The intricately carved figure had been crafted by his hands when he was just a young man, eager to impress his grandmother with his newfound talent. She had been his biggest supporter, always encouraging him to follow his passion for woodworking just like his father before him.

But now, as Derek ran his fingers over the smooth curves and intricate divots of the angel's wings, he could not help but think of his father. His father had been the one to teach him the art of carving, passing down the skill from generation to generation. And it was his father who had gifted him this piece of wood, telling him to craft something special for his grandmother.

Derek had planned to present the angel to his grandmother; the joy and pride in her eyes as she exclaimed over its beauty would have been his reward. She would have placed it on her mantel next to a photo of his father, where it probably would have remained until this day.

With his grandmother and father gone, the angel held even more weight and significance to Derek. It was a physical representation of his love for his grandmother and the memories he carried for his father. It was a miracle how it had found its way back to him after Spider had stolen it from him as a youth so many years ago. He could not bear the thought of ever parting with it again as he shoved it deep into the pocket of his bag.

Derek mulled over the events of his day, Father Mike's words, and how he had been so tolerant when Derek had panicked over the leeches. He was determined not to find himself in a similar situation again. He had embarrassed himself before the priest, and he knew he must make a change.

He turned his head to the side, watching the shadows of the trees sway in the moonlight. He thought about the other people in his life, the ones he had let down, especially Kendal. A wave of sadness washed over him like a heavy, damp fog.

Physically exhausted, the repetitive act of trudging through the mud, step by tiring step, had drained him. This ceaseless routine led him to a crucial insight: he had been trapped in a cycle of the same issues. It was time to alter his approach. His old habits and familiar feelings, rooted in predictable weariness, had led him nowhere. He realized with painful clarity that a complete shift in his mindset was not just helpful but necessary.

Before leaving home, he had been gripped by mental fatigue, leaving him emotionally numb and unmotivated, which in turn made him anxious, irritable, and hopeless. This exhaustion muddled his emotional processes, affecting his mental state.

He knew he had to make changes if he was going to make any real progress. This realization gnawed at him. He began to reflect on what was truly important and what was not. Father Mike's words echoed in his head: "As per Christian belief, our souls transition to a new dimension when we pass away from this earthly life. Those who have accepted the faith and been reborn are said to enter the Sixth Dimension, Paradise. In this realm, the departed are rejuvenated in a celestial body and await the return of Christ during the rapture.

During this event, they will leave their mortal bodies behind and take on immortal and incorruptible ones. These glorified bodies will then rule with Christ in the Millennium and the new Heaven and earth."

Father Mike explained it this way: "In the *Seventh Dimension* resides God, who reigns supreme over the universe with His boundless power and splendor. Thus says the LORD: 'Heaven *is* My throne, And earth *is* My footstool. Where *is* the house that you will build Me? And where *is* the place of My rest?'"

This message resonated within Derek. His body was exhausted, but his mind continued to churn. The statement "Heaven is my throne, and the earth is my footstool" highlighted God's immeasurable enormity. Derek thought this must signify that God cannot be contained in a physical building or structure made by humans. He transcends time and space constraints, encompassing all of existence within His being.

For the last couple of days, Derek had felt like he was in between realms, where he had to depend on sound to supplement his limited vision. In this chaotic and overwhelming soundscape, it was hard to discern what was dangerous and what was not. This uncertainty made him feel more connected to his spirit.

The fire cast a warm orange glow. Amid the hoots, chirps and howls of wildlife, he stood there alone and let the sounds of the jungle wash over him. It all blended into a symphony of chaos that left him unsure of what to anticipate next.

He closed his eyes and took a deep breath, trying to quiet the noise in his mind. But even with his eyes closed, the chaos persisted. It was as if the jungle was speaking to him, demanding his attention.

Finally, when Derek opened his eyes, he decided to embrace the chaos and the unknown and see where it led him.

He found himself restless. His hammock swung gently, the rope creaking, almost lulling him to sleep. But his mind was too full and consumed. He had been out in the jungle for days, searching for a way to solve the mystery as he approached the shaman's village.

He tossed and turned again in his hammock and finally gave up, sitting up and swinging his legs over the edge. He sat still, feeling the soft earth beneath his bare feet. Gazing upward to an opening in the canopy, he took in the vast sky with its countless shimmering stars.

He turned his gaze back to the trees and watched as the shadows danced and shifted by the waxing light of the moon.

He was determined to find a solution and hoped that discovering what had happened to the shaman woman would bring him peace. With a deep sigh, he drifted off. He felt uneasy and wondered what other challenges he would face in the wild. The jungle melodies lulled him into a deep slumber, blending seamlessly into his dreams in the untamed terrain.

God's presence, in the form of the Spirit of the Lord, infiltrated the physical space surrounding Derek with warmth and love.

"You were chosen, Derek," God spoke, His voice soft but powerful. "Chosen for your kind heart, strong spirit, and potential for greatness."

Derek could not believe what he was hearing. He had always felt ordinary but worked hard to become significant. Now, in this quiet, ethereal realm, he could feel the weight of his tattoos resting on his skin; he could feel each one with its own purpose and strength.

"These tattoos represent your true self, Derek," God continued as if reading his thoughts. "They are a reminder of your sins, inner strength, and connection to Me. Embrace them, and you will find the courage to fulfill your destiny."

Derek opened his eyes and released a shaky breath, overwhelmed by his newfound understanding. He no longer saw his tattoos as a burden but as a hidden treasure map, a gift, and a source of strength. With tears streaming down his face, Derek looked out into the expanse of the sky, feeling a sense of peace and acceptance wash over him.

"Thank you, God," he whispered, grateful and humbled by the revelation he had just experienced. He knew their journey ahead would not be easy, but with God by his side and his tattoos as a guide, he was ready to face whatever challenges came his way.

He got up and started to gather his belongings. He had a long journey ahead of him, but he was ready for it. He would not give up until he found the truth.

Chapter 10

It had been five days since Derek left her to find the shaman woman's granddaughter. Kendal stood in the penthouse's lavish marble and tile bathroom, looking at her gaunt reflection in the mirror as she prepared for work. She didn't know who exactly was staring back at her. Gazing into the woman's sad eyes, she wondered why she did not feel a connection.

Later that day, in a chance encounter, Kendal was approached by a woman who had been a patient. Derek had performed reconstructive surgery on her face and neck after she had been riding a three-wheeler and rode into a barbed-wire fence. On her post-op visit, she had tearfully thanked Derek for bringing hope into her life during such a dark time.

Now, as Kendal stood looking at this woman, she saw no evidence of her traumatic injuries. Only a slight scar on her neck remained. In that moment, Kendal was reminded of the true impact they had on people's lives—using their gifts for good. It was not about fame or recognition but about making a positive difference in the lives of others. She prayed that Derek could see it the same way.

Their wedding day had been a blur, a haze of colors and faces that Kendal could hardly remember. As the bride, she had been flooded with a cascade of emotions. Her head had been spinning with excitement, yet underneath it all, she'd been aware of a palpable sense of trepidation.

The night before, she had a dream that she was walking up to the church and collapsed, crying on the sidewalk in her wedding dress. She could not bring herself to go inside. She had awakened sobbing and was relieved when she realized it was Derek to whom she would be wed. She took this dream as a sign that everything would be okay.

Despite her hopes and desires, she could not deny the possibility that her expectations were too high. She could not rely on a prophetic dream to ensure a happy marriage. She had been building her hopes on a shaky foundation, one that she could no longer ignore.

On the day of her wedding, Kendal had been surrounded by familiar faces—her Aunt Sarah and all her new California friends. But they immediately became distant when she moved on to her new life. The carefree existence where she lived with her bird in a small apartment surrounded by community friends vanished into a boatload of responsibility for a new troubled husband, a large successful surgical practice, and a luxurious penthouse that had become her gilded cage.

She had decided to leave behind her old life and start a new one, leaping toward an uncertain future with no guarantee of happiness. One where she told herself love could prevail, one with endless possibilities. She had felt a sense of finality as the wedding had concluded. She now realized it should have been the promise of a new beginning, not the mourning of the freedom of a life that had passed. Kendal understood in that moment that everything would change.

Her wedding day had become a faint memory, but she would never forget the sense of unease that had come with it. She now realized that true love and marriage were much more complex than she had expected. A lasting relationship required hard work, dedication, and patience.

But now she felt as though her options were fading away. She felt desperate, ready to do whatever it took to get her life back on track. She could only take so much pain. If she were going to stay with him, he would have to come back with a genuine intention of reconciling and altering what needed to be fixed within himself and in their relationship.

The unbearably thin line of love had been stretched taunt like a rubber band well before Derek had left. Every morning, she'd awoken with the hope that maybe today would be different, that maybe today he would be ready to do the work needed to mend himself and their broken marriage. But each night it was the same story; they went to bed strangers.

Kendal knew that she could not bear it much longer. The thought of her husband, the person she had promised to spend the rest of her life with, constantly disappearing into the darkness of his mind was slowly killing their relationship. She was desperate to help find a way to make things right again—but that meant that he had to come back to her with a sincere desire to change or they would have to dissolve the marriage.

She felt like she was seeing herself from outside her body. She could see she was the person in the mirror each morning but could not feel anything. Getting ready for work made her feel like a robot going through the motions.

The last few days had left her drowning in thoughts, asking herself why she did not recognize who they had become. As she tried to make sense of her conflicting emotions, her inner thoughts struggled to define them. And the more she dwelled on it, the more intense they became.

The night before, in a hopeless bid to figure out how to get her husband back, she knelt by the side of her bed and said a prayer. She begged for a miracle, for a sign from God that things could still be saved between them. She waited, and when no immediate answer came, she closed her eyes again and silently vowed to do her best to make it happen, whatever the outcome.

The sun had set hours before, as she lay under the covers. The night seemed to stretch into eternity. Kendal tried to clear the cobwebs from her mind, but instead of achieving mental clarity, the darkness only amplified her sense of loneliness and anxiety.

She had been placed in an impossible situation, and it felt like the walls were closing in on her. She was desperate for a respite, a break, a reason to hope and believe—something to lighten her burdened spirit and ease her weary mind.

But no answer seemed to be forthcoming, so she simply laid there, waiting in the quiet. The emotional stress she was feeling was beginning to jumble her brain, and it felt like the only way to relieve the pressure was to talk to someone. She needed to release some of these turbulent thoughts to someone in the outside world.

In the morning, when she had finished applying her makeup, Kendal closed her puffy eyes and tried to bring awareness with her breath for peace of mind and to increase her focus and calm. Determined to find the place that would free her from the grip of her own thoughts.

When she got into her car, she turned on the music. It was not a conscious decision but an automatic one. As soon as the first song came on, she felt her heart sink. The songs she and Derek had chosen for their playlist were a nice blend of upbeat tunes that generally made her feel happy, but on this particular day, they were just another dagger to the heart.

It had been more than a week since Derek had left. She had to perform her laborious daily duties to ensure that the gears of the system stayed in motion. Since his departure, she had done her best to go about her daily life as usual, but the pain was constantly with her. She could hardly remember what it felt like to be truly happy anymore.

She tried to focus on the road ahead, but the lyrics of the songs kept tugging at her heart. Each one was a reminder of what she was missing, of what had gone wrong. She felt a wave of sadness wash over her, and a tear escaped her eye and trickled down her cheek. She wiped it away, determined not to give in to her sorrow.

As she drove to work, she impulsively decided to stop at her old apartment building. The wheels of her little red Fiat squealed as she made a hard U-turn. Kendal hadn't seen her landlord since her wedding. Mrs. Harris had been a close friend, a motherly type who always knew the right thing to say. They had an emotional connection. Their friendship increased Kendal's feelings of worthiness and belonging when she first arrived in California—a time when she had been alone and intent on starting a new life.

Mrs. Harris had quasi-adopted her into their little apartment family. Kendal reciprocated by watching out for Mrs. Harris and helping her navigate her health issues by using her experience as a nurse. Maybe stopping for a quick visit could help pull her out of those self-deprecating thoughts weighing her down.

Kendal parked in front of the apartment complex. A familiar feeling of happiness hummed through her chest.

She entered the big wrought-iron gate with a sense of coming home.

Kendal missed her landlord, the mature, full-figured woman with a somewhat old-fashioned sense of style whose presence commanded the respect due an esteemed older lady. Kendal reached up to knock on the old woman's apartment door. She could feel her body going through the motions, but that awful disconnection remained. When Mrs. Harris opened the door and Kendal saw her kind face, she was overcome with emotion and fell into her oversized bosom.

Chapter 11

Breakfast consisted of acai berries, banana, and mango—the colors of the sunrise spread out on a plate. The sweet, tangy taste of the fruits danced on Derek's tongue, a welcome respite from the harshness of the jungle.

Dark clouds intermittently marched in from the horizon, casting shadows over the serene landscape. The blue sky above was a fleeting sight, as if the Heavens were playing hide-and-seek with the earth.

A quick cup of coffee, bitter and invigorating, then they were off to trek through the mud. Derek unconsciously slapped mosquitos off his face. They were chased by howler monkeys in the lower part of the trees for the first part of the morning. The monkeys would intermittently swing over the trail and throw things at them to make sure they were aware they were there.

Derek found himself continually mesmerized by the vibrant colors and lively wildlife. The air was thick with the pungent smells of jungle flora, and the trees were so tall they seemed to reach to the Heavens.

They trudged through the thick, wet earth, their boots sinking with each step. This morning came with a new, unshakable determination. He was a seeker of truth, and nothing would stop him from reaching his destination.

As he continued the trek toward the village, Derek noticed the sky darkening again through the break in the trees. An incoming rainstorm was brewing, and the downpour descended upon them like a heavy blanket. They, too, hid for a minute under a canopy tree and watched as the forest's inhabitants adapted to the deluge. Monkeys huddled in the branches of tall trees, birds flew from branch to branch seeking shelter, and large catfish splashed in the nearby river, searching for morsels of food washed in by the rain.

As the downpour enveloped them, Derek could not help but feel a sense of wonder in the rainforest. It was as if he was in a sacred connection with nature as they trekked on. The only thing he could focus on was the sound of rain battering his protective gear. In this cocoon of water, the storm roared in his ears, but instead of feeling overwhelmed, he felt a profound serenity that he would never forget.

As the day unfolded, the gnawing ache in his legs and feet had become a numbing affliction. Each step forward came with a slight slide back in the mud. Even in the rain, sweat ran down his forehead and dripped off his nose. He could feel the punishing movement giving him the workout high he so much enjoyed each morning in the gym back at home, but that feeling soon faded, replaced by an ever-increasing sense of fatigue.

Yet he continued even as his body threatened to give out. He could not stop, not even when his vision blurred from exhaustion, and he could hardly take another step. He reminded himself that it was all worth it to get the answers about what had happened to the shaman woman and what her role in his tattoos might be. Even with the dream he had, where God had explained what the tattoos represented, he still needed to know where the shaman woman fit into the manifestation.

Only a few more miles, and then he would be able to rest.

Derek glanced up from under the hood of his rain jacket at his comrades ahead, marching one in front of the other. The path was barely visible in the dense jungle, their silhouettes mere shadows in the dismal light of the pouring rain.

Despite his fatigue, Derek quickened his pace. His feet blistered, and his throat parched, he pressed on, his determination unflagging. He was a man on a mission, driven by a burning desire to uncover the truth about his tattoos.

He longed for a hot meal and a soft bed. He was determined to keep up, so they could reach their camp destination before nightfall.

With the rain coming down harder, it did not matter. He kept his gaze forward and concentrated on putting one foot in front of the other, refusing to stop despite the discomfort. He could feel the fatigue taking over, the pain growing stronger, but he kept going, the strength of his determination carrying him through.

These marks had been etched into his skin against his will by some unknown force. He had awoken one morning to find them there, covering his arms, chest, back, everywhere. They were symbols of a language he did not recognize yet somehow felt familiar. The dream with God had planted an ethereal feeling. He began to realize that his tattoos carried a deeper meaning, a message that he *was* meant to uncover.

The journey was not easy. He had faced rainstorms, leeches, and exhaustion, but he never wavered. He was determined to reach the shaman's village and find out why these tattoos had been put on him.

He thought about his life before the tattoos had appeared. It was true, just as Kendal had said, that he was sheltered and naïve, but he had been content with his life. Maybe not happy but not unhappy, either.

He had made a world for himself, a shelter built from the ruins of his past. It was a world that was like walking through the rainforest during a downpour—all the familiar creatures were out there but mostly hidden from view. He had learned to protect himself from the elements in the city, just as he now had limited protection in the rainforest. But the danger still lurked at the edge of the trail, a reminder of the fragility of his sanctuary.

As he trudged through the endless mud, his thoughts continued to turn to the markings on his skin. They seemed to pulse with energy, a constant reminder of their mysterious origin. He did not know what awaited him at the end of this journey, but he knew he could not turn back. He had to uncover the truth, no matter how hard it became.

He had come to this place seeking solutions and to confront the memories that haunted him. The dense foliage and constant rainfall provided the perfect setting for his inner turmoil, allowing him to lose himself in the chaos of nature. And yet, even here, he could not escape the memories that had driven him here in the first place.

The words of the Bible were etched onto his back, like a permanent prayer. He had always been a solitary figure, even as a child, finding comfort and solace in his grandmother's endless recitations of scripture. After his father passed away, he, too, found solace within its pages. And now he felt drawn to wearing his faith on his skin, a tangible reminder of his newfound belief in God.

As he walked toward the village, Derek could feel the weight of his tattoo—both physically and spiritually—pressing against his back and heart. It was as if the words were propelling him forward, toward an unknown destination. He thought of his grandmother, who had taught him the significance of the written word, hoping she would be proud of the testament etched on his skin, a symbol of his newfound faith.

As he trudged through the rain, the drops pattering against his skin, he could not help but think of the past. Of the people he had lost, the mistakes he had made, and the pain he had caused. But as he looked around at the lush greenery, he felt a sense of peace wash over him. This was a place where he could let go of his regrets and find a new way forward.

When the tattoos originally appeared, it was like all his emotional survival skills had been stripped away. He had gone to Kendal for shelter. She provided him with a home and a sense of security that he never could have found anywhere else.

Yet, these detailed designs, with connecting spirals, winding up his arms and down his legs and back, binding tattoos all over his body, gave him hints of a secret life hidden within. The tattoos on his body told a different story from the one he lived out daily. The vibrant ink covered every inch of his arms, chest, and back, snaking around his muscles in intricate designs. Some people might have thought they were just ornamental, with each tattoo representing a moment, a memory, a milestone in his life. Happy memories to immortalize instead of painful reminders of what he had overcome. They would think they were his way of capturing his past and holding onto it forever.

The tattoos had started as catastrophic emotional distress; how they had gotten there, what they meant, and how to get rid of them overwhelmed his thought process. As time went on and Derek went out into public, he felt like a walking canvas, a work of art for the whole world to see. He longed for the simplicity and anonymity of his bare skin.

As a boy, he had spent many hours admiring and studying intricate design patterns. He had hand-crafted a wooden angel for his grandmother with fine, detailed feathered wings. But this sudden appearance of the tapestry of tattoos all over his body had been like a secret nobody could understand. In some ways, the tattoos had become a part of him. This week, he started to awaken to their meaning, as if they had been a part of his soul all along. He could not have understood until all the doors to the outside world had been shut.

He had never understood what the tattoos meant before. But now their meanings were clear—they were symbols of his destiny, of the power and strength that was embedded within him. He could feel the energy surging through him, and with it, a newfound courage to take on whatever lay ahead of him. He knew that no matter what happened, he would not be afraid. He had everything he needed to face his future. He was ready. No matter what he discovered when he got to the shaman's village.

He could not help but wonder how Kendal was able to accept him, and how he had changed so much since their first encounter. He could sense that these tattoos contained some kind of message with a power that had been unleashed when the ink had appeared on his skin. Whatever it was, it made him more captivating in her eyes.

Little had he known at the time what an exceptional woman she was. He was blessed to have a person of such integrity and loyalty at his side. She had become an integral part of his new life quickly. He had grown to depend on her in ways he could never have imagined depending on anyone.

Why then had he been unable to move on with life? What did it truly matter what people thought? On a personal level, it should not, but on a business level he had built his career on perception. It was all about the image. How could he be expected to ignore the way he looked—or to embrace it? His profession and his current body image were at odds with each other.

Derek stumbled as the tip of his boot caught a root sticking up in the trail. He glanced ahead to see Father Mike give him the thumbs up for catching his balance before ending up face-first in the mud.

His thoughts drifted back; his brain was distracted from the monotonous trek. Should this have been enough to have driven him to leave his new wife and home to venture out into the wilderness to find the shaman's granddaughter who may or may not be able to help? But he knew it was more. There was a lost little boy trapped inside this man's body. He needed to set him free.

He still carried the fears, insecurities, and anxiety of a fifteen-year-old boy. He had to battle those fears as one would if they matured in a normal environment where lessons could be learned, and growth acquired. These personal-growth lessons had not been experienced in his development. His emotional and spiritual growth had been stunted. And no matter how he tried he was unable to get past the barriers it presented.

The sun peeked through the tree branches between rain showers, intermittently casting golden streaks. It was a beautiful sight, but it did not distract him from his thoughts. He felt an overwhelming sense of determination as he took each step forward.

This was his official coming into manhood. Making the decision to take a life-altering risk to find out the truth about himself. It was something he had been driven to do. He was now beginning to understand the dynamics at play. It had all started on that fateful day of his violent childhood attack that had stunted his emotional growth. He had to do this.

The sun had moved slowly across the sky while Rodrigo, Father Mike, and Derek made slow but steady progress through the rainforest. The humid jungle air was thick and heavy, and the three men were damp with sweat.

Once again, they took shelter under the cover of low-hanging branches during an exceptionally hard downpour, which had been a welcome break from the relentless mud. Once the torrential shower had passed, they continued on their journey.

Father Mike did not get the chance to share his thoughts as the solitude still surrounded Derek. The sound of rain was too deafening, and when it finally eased up, Rodrigo hastily made his way down the trail.

A couple of sweaty hours later they stopped for a break. Drenched again from the latest afternoon rain shower, wet and hungry, they sat to eat a lunch of oranges, pineapple and nuts that Rodrigo had collected along the way.

The trio indulged in a quiet meal, relishing the delectable combination of sweet fruit and crunchy nuts. In between bites, they basked in the natural beauty surrounding them—the vibrant green flora, the babbling stream nearby, and the distant but soothing melody of birdsong in the treetops.

Derek lay back on the damp log and stretched his arms over his head. The sun had emerged from behind the clouds again, attempting to dry the sodden earth between a fissure in the trees. He closed his eyes and let the sun's warmth lull him into deep relaxation and contentment. He knew that he could not stay here forever. Eventually, he would have to leave the sanctuary of the rainforest and face the world outside once again. But for now, he would embrace this moment of calm amid the storm. Funny, how a place that had seemed so dangerous only days before now felt *safe*.

Father Mike watched Derek with a newfound respect for his resilience and determination.

The showers continued to start and stop throughout the rest of the day. It was an intense day of trekking through mud and over makeshift bridges.

Derek's mind continued to focus on his lack of emotional development. His brain seemed to go into a default mode that had him queued into thinking about his past. His divergent thinking was a reprieve from the unpleasant task of trudging through the mud, distracting him from the pain that came with it. He was having a breakthrough of sorts. He had concluded that changes needed to be made. He felt a block had been removed and he was beginning to refocus.

The worry, overthinking, and rumination that things might turn out for the worse were beginning to dissipate. His unresolved issues were starting to lean toward a guarded hope. He could feel himself drifting into mindfulness, which helped to change how he related to the present moment. He was starting to feel a little more empathy toward his situation, an emotion that did not come often or easily.

He did not have to force his brain to focus. His thoughts now seemed to have free rein coupled with a laser focus. With the long, arduous trek in the mud, focusing on his footing for long stretches seemed to help him concentrate and feel refreshed.

Rodrigo periodically gave them lessons on how to survive in the rainforest. He stopped to share a taste of milky sap dripping from an ancient tree and demonstrated how to tap water from a tree branch or collect it from a large, leafy plant. Hiking along the trail, he told them about the insects they could eat.

Derek hesitantly tried a grub. He popped it into his mouth; it tasted like almonds. Rodrigo told him it tasted more like chicken when roasted. The locusts were everywhere, full of protein and very nutritious. Crickets, he explained, were packed with calcium and phosphorus. But the most nutritious of all the insects were the termites. He gathered the insects by putting them into a sealed tin to supplement the evening meal.

They passed neon-blue butterflies and pineapples growing in the wild. When they came to a slow-flowing river channel that had created a calm body of water, Rodrigo decided it would be a good place to spend the night.

While Derek and Father Mike set up camp, Rodrigo went a little way up the river to collect long sticks and push them into the mud to make a funnel opening that he thought would match the size of the fish. He added some vegetation on top to create a shaded spot. The fish would find this area a good place to feed. Once they entered the funnel opening, they would be trapped.

Walking through the steamy jungle covered in mud had made it a hard day. Finding the water hole made it possible for them to have their first real bath in days. It felt like weeks to Derek; time seemed to stand still in the jungle. He sat in the deep water, listening to the beating heart of the jungle. The warm water soothed his aching muscles.

He looked at his legs and arms in the water. He could not help but feel a sense of disconnect. The tattoos were out of place on his muscular frame, like they belonged to someone else. But somehow, they were a part of him, a part of his story. He traced his fingers over the designs, feeling the rough texture of the ink against his skin. They might have just looked like tattoos to anyone else, but to him, they were a map of his life. He could not help but wonder that if he could not find the answer to ridding himself of them, what stories would his tattoos tell in the years to come?

He forced himself to get out of the water and change into a dry outfit to prepare for dinner so Father Mike could take his turn.

Not even Rodrigo noticed the deep scratch marks etched into the trunk of a nearby tree.

After a day of trekking, Derek was ready to eat anything. He had become more open-minded and prepared to try new things. His lips quirked in a rueful smile when he smelled the savory smoke and scents of food from the campfire. Of course, he had no other option. Eating in the rainforest had taught him valuable lessons in survival.

Rodrigo had used his knife to carve thin strips of wood, known as feather sticks, that would easily catch fire. He prepared the meal over the campfire. They happily ate pan-fried catfish caught from the river, ripe figs that grew throughout the rainforest, and insects they had collected along the way.

When it was time to retire to their hammocks, Derek lingered behind.

Like a nomadic Indigenous warrior with skin covered in eternal cycles of tattoos, Derek sat cross-legged on the ground in front of the fire. The flames danced and crackled, casting eerie shadows on his tattooed face. He traced his fingers over the spiral tattoo on his arm, feeling the intuitive connection with his touch. This symbol had become more than just a piece of art. It was a representation of the never-ending, winding cycle of his life. He had experienced the death of a past life twice. Once as a child and now again as an adult. He had also experienced the rebirth that came with it.

He gazed into the fire, lost in thought. Memories of his past flickered through his mind like dancing flames. He wondered if this would be a new chapter in the endless spiral of his existence. He closed his eyes and took a deep breath, feeling a sense of peace as he sat in the vibrant nocturnal place of life.

Life, death, and rebirth were all inevitable, but the journey in between was truly what mattered. And he was determined to make the most of it.

Chapter 12

Mrs. Harris had taken Kendal into her big soft arms and held her soothingly until her sobbing came under control. The plump elderly woman led her into her tiny little kitchen and sat her down. Then she put a kettle on the stove to make her a cup of chamomile tea.

When Kendal stepped into her apartment, she immediately felt a sense of comfort and warmth. The furniture was cozy with overstuffed chairs, fringed lamps, and crocheted doilies and blankets. A small hutch displayed a china tea set with delicate cups. Ruffled curtains adorned the kitchen window frame, while various knick-knacks were scattered throughout the small space, giving it a cluttered appearance. But to Kendal, it felt like being enveloped in a warm hug that brought about nostalgic feelings.

Mrs. Harris evoked a feeling of maternal warmth that Kendal had never experienced from her own mother during her childhood. Although this matronly woman was a stranger in many ways, Kendal was drawn to her as if by a powerful magnetic force as she sat with Mrs. Harris's pudgy, arthritic, wrinkled hand covering Kendal's, patiently waiting for her to come to terms with why she was there.

"I feel like my marriage is falling apart," she blurted out and began to cry again.

Mrs. Harris's eyes crinkled warmly in the corners. She handed her a tissue. Kendal closed her eyes, dabbing them for a moment, allowing the old woman's calming presence to soothe her.

Mrs. Harris spoke again, her voice a gentle whisper. "It's okay," she said, her voice soothing. "You do not have to be strong all the time. You can let go."

Kendal nodded, taking a deep breath. The woman's presence filled her with a new sense of courage and strength, and she felt a softness and warmth that she had been longing for since childhood.

Mrs. Harris patted her arm. "There, there, it's probably not that bad," she reassured her.

Kendal dabbed her eyes and blew her nose with the tissue. "He left. I asked him not to go but he just ignored me."

Mrs. Harris clutched her chest. "Oh my, why would he leave you?"

"Oh, no. I'm sorry." Kendal reached out to pat her hand. "I don't mean he left me for good. He left to go out into the jungle to find the shaman woman's granddaughter, who he thinks might have some answers as to why he has the tattoos. He's hoping that she might be able to shed some light on how to get rid of them."

Mrs. Harris wore an expression of concern, her gray hair framing her kindly face. "Oh my, that sounds quite perilous," she commented, wringing her hands. "He must be very brave," she added with a slight smile.

"It is very dangerous," Kendal agreed soberly. "That's why I'm so upset with him. I asked him not to go but he did anyway."

"That doesn't sound like Derek at all." She frowned and shook her head.

"He's not the Derek you know. He's changed a lot in the last couple of months, and these tattoos have been horrible for him to have to deal with."

"I can understand. The first time I saw him I thought you were out of your mind to be hanging around a person like that."

"And that is exactly his problem. When people see him, they automatically think the worst."

"You are right on that. He scared the wits out of me. I thought he was trying to kidnap you or something until you smiled at me and waved. Not until I had met him and spent time with him did I become comfortable with who he was. His tattoos are very frightening to an old woman like me."

"I know and I appreciate that you took the time to get to know him. He's a good man."

"Yes, a good man with a lot of troubles." Gnarled fingers smoothed the lace tablecloth in front of her.

"I thought I could handle it. It seemed when we decided to get married that he had resolved most of his deep-seated issues. But they keep cropping back up because of traumatic events that are constantly happening. I think the last one was the straw that broke the camel's back." Kendal snorted. "He was pulled over and taken to jail for driving with tattoos."

Mrs. Harris's brow crinkled, her eyes puzzled. "What does that mean?"

"The officer did not believe he was a doctor and dragged him down to the jail. I had to go vouch for him. It was very humiliating."

"That would be very humiliating, especially for a man of his caliber." Mrs. Harris clucked her tongue and shook her head.

"I'm trying to be understanding, but this is consuming his life—and mine too." Kendal's voice took on an edge of desperation. "I don't know how much more I can take of his emotional instability."

"I understand. But this issue could be approached like any other device that interrupts a marriage. Some people must deal with alcoholism or unfaithfulness. Decisions need to be made whether the person can be saved from themselves and are willing to do what it takes to make it happen for the good of the relationship."

"That is where I'm at right now." She started to cry again.

"Only you can answer that, honey." Mrs. Harris patted her hand. "But I will tell you this: You are married now, and you must make sure you do everything in your power to help this man become the husband he can be. When you have come to the point that you have done everything you can do in your power, and if it should not work, you can walk away with a clear conscience." She stood to take the whistling kettle off the burner. "You don't want to have any what-ifs or guilt for leaving the marriage."

Kendal slumped. "I know you're right. It's just so exhausting. I can't seem to have a normal day. He's sucking the life right out of me."

"Then when you have had enough, you will know in your heart. Right now, you are still going through the roller coaster of having an unstable relationship." She took two teacups out of the hutch. "This might be temporary." Mrs. Harris gave her an encouraging smile. "Who knows? Maybe he'll find the answers he's looking for on this trip." She placed the teabags in the cups.

"I guess I didn't really mind the trip so much as how he made the decision to go without me," Kendal admitted. "He sprang it on me at the last minute after he'd been planning it for a while. It felt disrespectful and like he just invalidated my feelings."

"It does sound disrespectful." She poured the boiling water over the teabags in each cup. "But has he explained to you his decision-making process?" she asked as she set a teacup down in front of Kendal.

"No, he didn't want to get into it. He was too focused on getting his stuff together to leave." The old resentment flared up. "To make it worse, he didn't just leave me, but he left the business too!"

"That's a lot for your young shoulders to hold. I know you've carried the major weight of the business for a long time. He has kept his involvement to arm's length." Her eyes twinkled as she set the sugar bowl down. "But I do have to admire the man. He stepped up to help those two young girls. One he performed a surgical procedure to remove a birthmark pro bono and the other to escape from those hoodlums who took her from her village, not to mention giving that young man Tyler a place to stay while he finishes school. That is a big-hearted man in my eyes."

"I know you're right. But where do I fit into all of this?"

Mrs. Harris sat back down and sighed, her gnarled fingers cupped her mug of tea. "Honey, I'm not sure. In my day we stayed home and supported our husbands, no matter what came our way. It was not about us, it was about the good of everyone else." She took a sip.

"Maybe I might feel that way if I didn't have the same or more responsibility than him," Kendal replied, as she mindlessly stirred some sugar into her tea. "But I'm the head of our household. His tattoos have taken away his self-esteem, and it affects his identity. He has a hard time figuring out where he fits in the world. That leaves him unable to settle into our marriage."

"I can see how that would happen." She stood and reached into a cupboard pulling out a package of cookies. "That is a lot for a strong, successful man to have to endure. His world has been taken away from him. All he's had in this past year is you."

"But obviously, I'm not enough!" Kendal choked back tears. "All

I want is to have a stable relationship with my husband. Right now, that's not possible. And . . ." Her eyes continued to well, "I'm not sure we'll ever be able to have the kind of relationship I need to be happy."

"Oh, honey, I'm so sorry." Mrs. Harris put her hands on Kendal's shoulders to guide her to stand so she could take her into her arms to help soothe the hurt. "Remember," she said kindly. "You are never alone."

Kendal felt a warmth and affection wash over her, and she was suddenly relieved of the isolated feelings weighing on her. The grandmotherly hug was precisely what she needed at that moment. It was an embrace filled with love and acceptance, reminiscent of a warm blanket enveloping her. The subtle scent of Mrs. Harris's perfume brought back cherished memories of her own beloved grandmother, who had passed away long ago when she was very young, and provided a sense of comfort and security. In that instant, she felt unconditionally loved.

Chapter 13

Third day in the jungle

Derek woke with a start. The keel-billed toucans led the natural symphony of different species of birds celebrating the new morning. He rubbed his eyes and stretched his arms, feeling fully recharged after a much-needed ten hours of sleep.

Each morning before emerging from their mosquito net, they would spray Deet on their bodies. They could not escape the insects in the rainforest. It became normal to sit down for a break and find their feet covered in ants.

He was getting used to living without any form of communication. He thought of Kendal often and knew she would be worried. Without the distraction of the outside world, it gave him time to think. It had become a type of meditation, with nothing to distract him from his inner thoughts.

With a newfound energy, Derek set out to collect firewood for breakfast. He walked through the forest surrounding their camp, taking in the beauty of the morning. The dew was still fresh on the tropical leaves and the air smelled of earth.

He had come to realize that his sudden displacement from his childhood home had created developmental challenges. It was becoming all too clear to him the deficiencies that he was experiencing were created by his never having been challenged by life itself. Sure, he had been tested in college, but tested by life was a completely different matter. He could never have understood what he was missing if he had not been forced out of the superficial world that had been created for him by his adopted father and mentor Dr. Christopher Casey.

While he collected the wood, he could not help but appreciate the beauty of this uncomplicated lifestyle. Away from the chaos and stress of the city, he found solace in the quiet of nature.

The solace gave him the capability to understand that his young body had healed from the brutal beating but the significant change in his self-identity had not. He was first laid bare after the abrupt outbreak of his tattoos, by the expulsion from his home and isolation from his business; he was like a man without a country. The fact was that he had only one choice and that was to go to Kendal for help.

Looking back helped him to understand how vulnerable he really was. He thought of himself as being protected, but he had been living life without a safety net. He had been like the emperor with no clothes. Posing as a world-class plastic surgeon when he knew he was not worthy. Walking through life letting everyone tell him how great he was. He had fooled himself and the people around him for many years. But now all had been exposed for the charade it really was. He had to find out if he was truly worthy, and the only way for that to happen was for him to figure out who he truly was and why he had this unwelcome tapestry on his skin.

The emotional adjustment to his current lifestyle had gone through many stages, including anger, despair, resentment, and depression. Ultimately, he knew he might have to come to accept his new body, even with all the limitations that came with it. He had to find the key to a fully enriched life. Reaching acceptance through this personal journey, no matter how long it took, would ultimately help him to move past the grief of loss. He was beginning to take one step at a time closer to the future through a more meaningful participation in life.

With a bundle of firewood in his arms, Derek made his way back to the campfire, ready to start the day with a hot cup of coffee and a hearty breakfast. He smiled to himself, content in this moment of peace and tranquility.

He told himself that he had to let go. He had to change his viewpoint from resentment to something more positive. He had to stop focusing on the loss; Father Mike had told him repeatedly to have gratitude just for being alive.

After the breakfast of insects, berries, and nuts, he helped to pack up camp to be ready for the day of trekking. It felt daunting but had become easier by the third day.

Rodrigo estimated that this would be their last full day of hiking. They should be coming to the shaman village by midday the following day.

As Derek trekked along the final leg of the trail, his thoughts drifted back to his childhood. He searched back to all the moments that had contributed to his decision-making process. He needed to understand the circumstances that formed the setting for the violent and traumatic event that almost killed him. The moment the clock stopped in his life. Where his emotional development had ceased to exist.

He knew that children who experienced the loss of a parent were at a higher risk for many negative outcomes, including mental issues. He knew from his own experience of losing his father and the attack that this could include depression, anxiety, post-traumatic stress disorder, and low self-esteem.

As they trudged through the mud with Derek deep in thought, the sky became dark quickly and caught them off guard. They stopped to put their rain gear on. Feeling hot and sweaty, the nice cool downpour ended up being a lovely surprise.

The rain streamed off his hat as he thought about his grandmother and how she had been the one to talk to him about his father's death. She explained how he had been ill and suffered no longer. She would listen to and comfort Derek when he cried at night. She would help him put his feelings into words.

He picked up a hiking stick at the side of the trail, which improved his balance when his boots were sucked into the mud holes. He tried to stay in the center of the trail, walking on exposed roots whenever possible. He had to concentrate on each step, careful not to expend too much energy by struggling in the mire. It occurred to Derek that this was a good analogy for how he had been living his life. He had been careful not to slip; his life had been choreographed so that he would not get caught in the mire. This, unfortunately, is what protected him from his growth and development as a man.

There were core issues that he was dealing with that fateful day of the violent attack. He had been torn between the love and loyalty of his grandmother and the allurement of newfound friends. But as a teenager, he had been consumed with focusing on himself and what he wanted. This is probably why he never attempted to explore friendship again. The punishment had been too much.

He trudged along weighed down by the Amazonian mud and the muck of his life. Hour after hour, he marched steadily, deep in thought. His daily struggle with depression before he left home had felt just like the jungle mud sucking at his boots, draining the energy from his soul. Each day had been getting harder and harder as he had started to lose hope.

He evaluated his childhood decision-making process, which resulted in being in the wrong place at the wrong time. When those thugs came driving around the corner, it was him that stood in the middle of the sidewalk. He could have run, yelled, fought back. Like a deer frozen in headlights he did nothing. An encounter like that had never entered his young mind. He had never been exposed to violence. His mother sheltered him to the point that he could not even watch television shows that had violence. She did not want her son to grow up being an aggressive man. Little did she know that she had handicapped him. He was unprepared for the events that happened that day. Not that anyone could prepare themselves to be beaten half to death, but he could have had something to relate it to. But nothing he had been exposed to in his young world could ever prepare him for what existed in his future.

As the years passed, by the grace of God, he had a mentor who focused on him. He blossomed like an orchid in a hot house. As long as he was not exposed to the outside elements he grew. The downside to the excessive attention was that he did not accept personal responsibility for his own actions. He was made to feel special by Dr. Casey.

The exhaustive hiking in nature had started to improve his mental health. He could feel the boost in mood as he remained deep in thought. The heavy feeling that weighed him down was starting to lift, and a renewed spirit was starting to form.

He had been a victim saved by a narcissistic father figure who had modeled Derek in his own image. He would always be grateful, but he realized that Dr. Casey had only one thing in mind: to have a successor. He had been groomed. He chose to live in the small cosmetic surgery world that had been created for him. It was better than having to deal with the reality of the outside.

Now he could understand that there were worlds out there that differed from his own. A world which he could never have known without this experience.

Rodrigo stopped periodically to point out shrubs or trees that would provide them with food for the evening meal. This now intrigued Derek and made him feel that they were invincible with the abundance nature provided.

When he had almost been beaten to death on his way home from school, it had shattered the illusion of his childhood. He no longer felt loved and protected. He felt vulnerable and scared. Living with Dr. Casey had given him a false sense of security. The man had built a gilded cage for himself and had brought Derek inside to live. When the tattoos appeared, they shattered the illusion of his life. Now he dealt with the fallout. He had not had the psychological assessment tools, nor a reliable emotional foundation to fall back on.

His childhood memories revolved around the grandmother who died for him. She had been his lifeline. Not being able to function as a normal adult had now led him to this new road of self-discovery. He now had to decide who he was going to become. He had to be prepared psychologically for whatever happened. He might or might not find out information that would lead him to understand and reverse what was causing him to manifest tattoos, and he had to accept that potential outcome.

Occasionally, a monkey would drop down from a tree to investigate the strange bipedal humans moving below. At midday, they stopped to eat and rest by the river that wound back and forth across their path. A caiman lounged on the riverbank and did not bother to swim away when Father Mike rinsed off.

After the break, he trudged through the mud again, thinking that a life unexamined was not worth living. The physical activity released endorphins, which energized Derek's spirit. He was starting to feel happy. It was time to look to the future. Before reaching the village, he knew he had to discuss protocol with Rodrigo. He did not want to come off as aggressive or disrespectful to these Indigenous people, but he needed an audience with the shaman who lived there.

Derek pondered whether the shaman in the village held any wisdom that could unravel the intricate markings inked on his skin. Would he gain any knowledge or insight?

Derek's first step had been for outside help from a therapist. Through therapy sessions, Derek had been able to confront internal struggles and identify past traumas that had been holding him back. He had started to understand the root of his fears and self-doubt, and slowly but surely, after being catapulted out of his comfort zone, felt more confident in his abilities. His tattoos had started to disappear, one at a time.

But then the unthinkable happened. They came back just as fast as they had disappeared. He felt like they had a stranglehold on him.

Every day became a challenge. There were moments when he doubted himself or questioned if he was on the right track. During one of these low points, when he was taken to jail for identity theft, Derek turned to God for guidance and clarity. He prayed for a sign that he was on the right path.

When he was released, he called Father Mike for a second opinion, the same man now who trudged along before him. "What a great friend," Derek murmured.

He did not have to come on this trip, but he'd sacrificed both time and comfort for Derek's spiritual well-being. He knew his guidance was needed and he had stepped up. There was no repayment for such a gift. When they returned home, Derek resolved to help the priest more with his charity work to aid the homeless. He could put in more time and money. He would talk to Kendal—she loved volunteering for good causes.

The common sight of monkeys jumping from tree to tree above their heads and whistling to one another only slightly diverted his attention. He watched as they moved in synchronization.

Now his choices were limited. He had committed to finding the old shaman woman's village. What would he say? Would someone have the answers he was looking for? He could be putting both their lives at risk. They were coming close to the end of their journey. He was starting to feel the trepidation that came with the unknown.

He now realized that his salvation could not be found in the external environment; it was a battle he had to wage within himself if he wanted to find peace. With each step, he forced himself to keep going, understanding that he would not be able to rest until he shed the chains of past hurt attached to him.

When they stopped for a well-earned break, he took in a deep cleansing breath. He stood still and enjoyed the beauty of nature, giving rise to a flicker of hope inside him. He understood that there was still an opportunity for redemption; all that was left was for him to take the risk.

Rodrigo identified fresh prints in the trail of mud. He stopped to measure the print as Derek and Father Mike looked on. It was the pawprint of the Amazon's apex predator, the jaguar. He put his hand inside the track of the pad—it was bigger than his fist.

"They are solitary and territorial cats," Rodrigo explained. "They do not roar like a lion, but instead make low-pitched growls and hisses. The average jaguar grows to be the size of an adult human. It has a strong body with muscular limbs designed to hold on to large prey. Its retractable claws can cut like razors."

Rodrigo stood and continued walking along the trail. He spoke quietly. "It will crush its prey's bone with an impressive bite. It can leap up to fifteen feet and can run at fifty miles an hour and is an ambush predator. So, stay vigilant."

Derek had been solely focused on survival since the first day he arrived in the jungle. The cacophony of sounds, the sweltering heat, and the constant threat of danger were enough to keep any man on edge. But for Derek, knowing that Rodrigo, a seasoned guide, was concerned gave him a sudden jolt of trepidation.

Rodrigo had seen the jagged teeth of a black caiman as it lunged out of murky water, narrowly missing his leg. He had felt the hot breath of the water buffalo on the back of his neck as he scrambled up a tree. These were nothing compared to the predator that now lurked in the shadows.

Rodrigo knew that the slightest lapse in concentration could mean death. So, he remained vigilant, constantly scanning his surroundings for any signs of danger. He had to be both predator and prey in this unforgiving environment. As they trekked through the dense underbrush, his senses on high alert, he gripped his trusty machete tighter and pushed forward.

Rodrigo hacked his way through a patch of dense rainforest where the trail had overgrown. When he came to a flat patch of jungle uphill from the river, he decided it was time to quit for the day and cook dinner under the observant gaze of several monkeys.

"When the jaguar roars, the Indigenous people call it thunder," he said. "The roar echoes across the Amazon."

As usual, it became quite dark after dinner. Derek told Rodrigo he needed to relieve himself. He walked out a short way from camp and unzipped his pants. He looked up to see twin orbs glowing in the beam of his headlamp. The two sparkling eyes were dangerously close. He quickly backpedaled his way into camp.

Rodrigo weighed their options. He decided to post rotating guards throughout the night. After a long day of hiking and swatting off swarms of bugs, they went to bed in hopes that they would not be dragged from their hammocks, killed, and eaten.

In the jungle at night, it became quite a scary prospect. Just like the first night, Derek struggled to sleep. All around he heard the buzz of insects, the shrill of birds, yelling monkeys and the splash of caimans and electric eels. The emotional high of the day had given way to the danger of the night.

Father Mike volunteered to take the first watch and keep the fire glowing. Derek had nightmares that the jaguar was chasing him. But to Rodrigo, the roar of the jungle was like a lullaby.

Chapter 14

Kendal woke a little more refreshed than the day before but still tired. Her visit with Mrs. Harris had been just what she needed. She'd felt more relaxed when she went to bed, but she had weird dreams all night.

She could faintly remember the first dream. The moon was high in the sky, its silvery light casting shadows on the forest floor. She stood in the center of a clearing, a sigil etched into the ground before her. The symbol glimmered in the moonlight, pulsing with an otherworldly energy.

With her wild auburn hair and piercing green eyes, she stood with her arms outstretched, palms facing upward. She began to chant in a language long forgotten, each word dripping with power and purpose. As she spoke, the sigil began to glow brighter, its lines throbbing and shifting as though alive.

Her chanting grew more urgent, her voice rising in volume and intensity. Suddenly, she stopped, her arms dropping to her sides. The sigil before her let out a blinding burst of light, and with a deafening crack, a figure emerged from within it.

The figure was tall and imposing, with wings of pure white feathers and eyes that seemed to pierce straight into the soul. It regarded her with curiosity and a hint of amusement.

"You have summoned me," it said in a voice like thunder. "What is it that you wish?"

"I seek wisdom and guidance," she said, her voice unwavering. "I have questions that only you can answer."

The winged figure nodded, a small smile playing on its lips. "Then ask away," it said.

Kendal began to ask it questions, her voice trembling with a mix of fear and excitement.

The figure answered each one, its words like drops of pure knowledge falling on her mind and seeping into her very being.

Kendal sucked in a deep breath. The haunting dream was unsettlingly vivid and lifelike, causing her to wake abruptly. Her heartbeat was rapid, filling her with a sense of foreboding. In those few moments before wakefulness, she could recall every bit of the dream. She could still feel the energy as the entity had spoken of secrets and mysteries, but now just minutes after opening her eyes, she could not remember the details.

She turned over on her side. The distress caused by her dream made it difficult for her to fall back asleep. When she finally closed her eyes and dozed, she dreamt that she was helping Brutus build a nest in his cage. She understood she was his mother, and she was feathering a nest for him.

When she woke up, she stretched her arms and legs to increase circulation and alleviate the stiffness. However, the irregular sleep still left her tired. She placed her hands on the bed in front of her and used them to push herself off the mattress, then swung her legs over the edge and tried her best to keep her back from aching.

Feeling groggy and weighed down, a heavy sensation lingered. She made sure to move her entire body at once, avoiding any twisting or bending at the waist, and relied on the weight of her legs to help her move. While standing up, she leaned forward from the hips, shifting onto the balls of her feet while tightening her stomach muscles for support.

"What is my problem?" she said aloud. A bit disoriented, she was not quite ready to start the day. It took a combination of arm and leg strength to fully stand up straight.

Probably after seeing Mrs. Harris, she had released some of her pent-up tension. The sacred role of their female relationship nurtured her soul. The emotional nourishment was probably helping her to bring a sort of balance to the areas where she had been neglected, exploited, and repressed of late.

She donned slippers and a robe and entered the kitchen. At the breakfast bar, a young man of Asian descent with the build of an athlete sat with his long legs stretched out beyond the barstool and his broad shoulders hunched over his laptop as he ate a bowl of cereal. Textbooks littered the counter. He was dressed casually in a plain white T-shirt and black jeans, and he kept his small backpack on the counter next to him with a sports drink hanging from the side pocket.

"Good morning," Kendal said as she uncovered Brutus's cage. He spread his wings and started to groom his feathers.

Tyler looked up from his book. "Good morning," he said, a friendly smile revealing perfect white teeth. "How are you doing today, Kendal?" He knew she'd been struggling since Derek had left her so abruptly.

"Much better, thank you. I went over to see an old friend yesterday."

"Cool." He took a bite of toast.

"How is everything with you?" she asked as she placed a coffee pod in the Keurig.

"Okay, I just have to get through these finals." He flipped the page of the textbook.

"Do you need help? You know I can help you with that medical stuff."

"Nah, I am okay. I just need to stay focused." He ran a hand through his short coal-black hair. "I'm getting tired," he admitted. "I can't wait for the break. To have a few weeks off will be great."

"Just let me know if you need anything." Kendal started to pad out of the kitchen with her cup of coffee. She stopped mid stride. "Can I ask you a question?"

Tyler's serious brown eyes looked up from his book, his eyebrows furrowed. "Sure, anything."

"I had a strange dream last night. It was pretty vivid, and I think it might mean something. It had magic symbols, and I wondered if you knew anything about them."

"I might." He eyed her with curiosity. "I studied sigils in Thailand when the priest asked me to participate in their ritual."

Tyler had come to live with Derek after he returned from a stint in Thailand, and his brother tricked him into becoming a target of a ransom scheme. The thugs wanted to use the magical tattoos that covered Tyler's torso.

"Sigils . . . What is that?" she asked.

Tyler put his pen into the crease of his textbook and closed the cover. "A sigil in the Bible is the Star of David. This symbol is associated with Jewish identity and is often interpreted as a form of divine protection, although its use as a magical sigil is not explicitly mentioned in the Bible itself, according to modern occult practices. A sigil is a pictorial symbol used to represent a spirit or deity or to manifest a desired outcome for the practitioner. In medieval ceremonial magic, sigils were believed to be the visual representation of a being's true name and were used to evoke demons, angels, and other entities."

Kendal stepped back into the kitchen and leaned against the counter, intrigued by what Tyler knew about the subject.

"As far as I understand, the theory on sigils is that once we create one and focus on the intentions of that sigil, we imprint it on our unconscious mind, which then influences our lives," Tyler continued. "Our conscious mind can act as a barrier, preventing us from achieving our desired outcome, and the true magic comes from harnessing the power of our unconscious mind. We can create our reality by changing our mental states through sigils."

Kendal watched as he took another bite of his toast, then seemed to remember something more and laid it back down.

"Now, some magic practitioners utilize sigils and other techniques to consciously reinforce their intentions. For instance, I have a bottle of water infused with lavender that reminds me to repel negative energy when sprayed in my room. I created this bottle by setting my intentions of warding off negativity, and every time I use it, those intentions are renewed in my conscious mind."

Tyler pulled the sports drink from his backpack, took a swig, and slowly put the cap back on as he stared down at the counter.

"I also have a sigil for self-love behind my mirror," he admitted. "So, whenever I glimpse myself in that mirror, my subconscious mind is subtly reminded of my intention without me being consciously aware of it. I have observed the Thai priests drawing sigils in visible places, like carving them into candles, keeping the symbol present in their conscious minds."

He turned to face her, his gaze distant. "I come from an artistic background and worked in advertising before I went to Thailand. Images have a profound impact on our psyche, shaping our thoughts, emotions, and behaviors. And when we craft them through design or illustration, that power becomes even stronger."

Kendal took a gulp of her coffee as she stood leaning against the counter.

"Consider ubiquitous logos," Tyler said, gesturing with his hands, "how the golden arches evoke the aroma of french fries, the Nike swoosh symbolizes speed and strength, and the Gucci logo represents luxury and extravagance. In my opinion, they hold more power when they become a constant presence, blending into the background of our day. I employ sigils to influence my thoughts."

He tucked the sports drink bottle back into the side pouch of his backpack and pulled out a notebook, holding it up for Kendal to see.

"One new practice I have incorporated is stenciling sigils into the front cover of my notebook. Each one represents a different purpose— whether it is boosting confidence in tests, sparking creativity, or alleviating my social anxiety. This practice resonates with me because the art of the design is meant to convey more than just words."

"Sounds like what I do with post-its," Kendal commented as she placed her empty cup in the sink.

"Pretty much." Tyler shoved the notebook into his backpack, opened a textbook, and went back to studying.

Walking into their home office always brought back a feeling of *him*. It was Derek's office. She had taken it over when she moved in, but it still had all his things. The Plastic Surgeon of the Year award hung on the wall. She ran her finger along the bottom of it. That was where it all started.

She remembered the day he had come into their surgical office, distraught, covered head to toe in tattoos. At first, she did not know what to think. She honestly thought he had done it to himself in some sort of drunken stupor. But it had become clear almost immediately that that was not the case.

Something traumatic had happened—supernatural, not to be explained in rational terms. She had tried to do everything she could to help him navigate the traumatic experience. She had ridden the roller-coaster with him, not letting him lose his footing. She had been his rock. She had little or no explanation for what was happening to him. Still, she had known him before the supernatural episode and watched as he had emotionally maneuvered his way through the devastating event.

She didn't know how she would have taken it if *she* had woken up covered in tattoos from head to toe. She did know that Derek would never have accepted her predicament like she had accepted his. She would have been alone except for her Aunt Sarah and Mrs. Harris.

But who knew how people would react to such an overall change in a person's appearance? Somehow, she had been able to empathize with him. Maybe it was because of all her work with the homeless. Going to the shelter had been an eye-opening experience for her. It helped her understand the personal plight of these faceless individuals on the street.

But Derek was more than a rescue to her. She had always held him in high respect, even though his treatment of her could be crude.

She hit the Harley Davidson biker bobblehead on the desk she had bought for him as she sat in the chair.

Illuminated by the soft glow of the computer screen, her fingers tapped lightly against the keyboard as she researched her dream. The words "Dream of making a nest" appeared on the blank white search bar, and she hit enter.

Page after page of results popped up, each promising to reveal the meaning behind her dream. Eager for answers, she clicked on the first link.

The website read, *"To dream of building a nest symbolizes protection and family. It may imply that you will soon create a safe and happy home."* A sense of trepidation washed over her at these words. Perhaps her dream was a sign of her apprehension of things to come.

She continued scrolling through the page, reading about various interpretations and symbolism associated with building a nest. As she delved deeper, she discovered that many women have a nesting psychology before their children are born. It is a psychological preparation for pregnancy, a way for the mind to prepare itself for the joys and challenges of motherhood.

She leaned back in her chair, reflecting on her own life. Could this dream indicate her desire for motherhood? Was she ready to take on the responsibility of creating a happy and secure home for her future family?

Not me, she thought, shaking her head. She quickly powered off the computer screen, not wanting to deal with any more problems. "That's the last thing I need," she muttered, standing up and heading back to her room to prepare for work.

Chapter 15

Fourth day in the jungle

Derek lay in his hammock in the darkness, drifting between sleep and wakefulness. He wondered what secrets and wisdom the shaman held for him. She had been the keeper of tradition, the guardian of her people's history and culture. She could communicate with spirits and ancestors and call upon their guidance and protection.

He let out a deep sigh, the sound of the crackling fire lulling him into a deeper, dream-filled sleep.

Derek sat up, rubbing the sleep from his eyes. He looked around, taking in his surroundings. The fire had died, but the embers still glowed, casting a warm light over the small campsite. The old shaman woman sat across from him, her face calm and serene.

"What was I dreaming about?" Derek asked, feeling disoriented.

The shaman chuckled. "That is for you to decipher," she said cryptically. "But I believe it was a dream of your true self."

Derek furrowed his brow in confusion. "My true self?"

"Yes," the shaman replied with a nod. "We all have layers and masks that we wear in our waking lives, but in our dreams, we often reveal our deepest desires and fears."

Looking at the old shaman's face with its bold and beautiful markings, he felt a strange kinship. The intricate tattoos depicted the stories and myths of her people. His gaze followed the lines and patterns etched into her skin, each telling a different tale. They seemed to dance and twist with a life of their own, moving and shifting with the flickering firelight embers.

Derek looked down at the intricate markings on his skin, which had started to pulse with otherworldly energy. With them came a revelation that unlocked a part of himself that had been hidden for years.

The campfire embers crackled the fire back to life, sending sparks spiraling into the dark sky above. He watched as a huge spider suddenly emerged from the flames, its long legs scurrying toward her. He watched as the spider crawled up her chest to her face, its movements mesmerizing. Without hesitation, the shaman woman opened her mouth and the spider crawled inside. She closed her mouth and smiled. The spider had become a part of her.

Just as it had become a part of him; the spider, with its eight legs and glowing red eyes, had been a recurring figure in his dreams and nightmares. Its thin legs skittered across his skin, leaving behind a web of intricate markings trying to trap him. Dreams of the spider always left him in a cold sweat, the spider's presence lingering in his mind long after he had opened his eyes.

But now, as he traced the markings on his skin with trembling fingers, he saw the spider in a different light. It was not a creature to fear but a messenger trying to communicate something to him. Derek felt a surge of excitement.

"In your dreams, you have seen glimpses," she said in a low voice filled with ancient wisdom. "You must be prepared for what is coming."

Derek's heart skipped a beat. "What does this mean?" he asked hesitantly. He was not sure if he wanted to know.

"It means that you have a connection to something greater than yourself," the shaman explained, her eyes sparkling. "It is a gift bestowed upon you by the gods, and it is up to you whether you choose to embrace it or not."

The shaman noticed his gaze and smiled gently. "Do not be afraid," she said softly. "You are one with the spirit world now."

"No, I don't want to be a part of the spirit world." Derek looked down at the tattoos on his hands, the symbols shimmered and shifted before his eyes. Then he watched her features become more jaguar-like, her yellow-green eyes glowing in the firelight with an intense fierceness.

Her face became a jaguar motif, its fierce and graceful form dominating her features. For a moment, he was transfixed, trying to make sense of the connection between her jaguar face, his tattoos, the spider, and the memories of his childhood attack.

"I don't understand," he said, his mind reeling.

"You will," the shaman smiled enigmatically. "But for now, just know you are not alone in this journey."

Derek's heart was racing, his body covered in a cold sweat. He glanced around the dim campsite. The old shaman woman had disappeared. He could not help but feel a sense of relief. But then he quickly checked his arms—the tattoos were still there.

Her tranquil presence had turned into a dark and foreboding energy. Dread settled in his stomach. It was like she was channeling something malevolent, something that wanted to consume him.

Still asleep in his hammock, Derek felt a hand gently touch his forehead. He opened his eyes to see his deceased grandmother smiling at him, her crinkled eyes filled with a knowing warmth. "You were dreaming," she said softly. "But now it is time for you to wake up and face reality."

Derek jolted awake. His eyes flew open as he was reminded of the life-altering assault he had endured as a child and the reason for his grandmother's demise. He sat up in his hammock, sweat beading on his forehead as he tried to make sense of his racing thoughts. He felt like he had just been pulled into something sinister and menacing.

And then it hit him like a bolt of lightning. The connection between the old shaman woman and the memories of his childhood attack by a gang member named Spider suddenly clicked into place.

Spiders can only detect differences between light and dark. Patient and persistent creatures, they wait for prey to get caught in their webs. Due to their venom and the slow death it causes, they are also associated with mischief and malice, often seen as a curse. The Bible told him to be careful of this type of witchcraft. Father Mike also warned him to be careful and not get in too deep when he researched the old shaman woman.

Father Mike had implored him to read his Bible. To give his life to Jesus. He was beginning to feel the spiritual warfare waging within.

An hour before daybreak, Rodrigo came over to shake their hammocks, calling out that they needed to abandon camp. The jaguar was nearby. At first, they were unsure as to what to do. He had warned them of this very thing. Should they follow, or should they stay safe in their hammocks? The hesitation lasted briefly before they grabbed their headlamps and backpacks. They packed their gear and left, hoping the jaguar was not in pursuit.

Rodrigo led the way down the trail, his senses attuned to any potential danger. Behind him, the two men walked briskly, trying to match his pace without breaking into a run. As they moved, Rodrigo shared his observations of when he had spotted the jaguar descending the river's berm.

"She didn't make a sound," Rodrigo said, his voice barely above a whisper. "Just slinked down and disappeared into the foliage outside our camp."

The men listened intently, their hearts racing at the thought of the predator lurking just beyond their campsite. Rodrigo continued, describing how he had watched the cat, estimating her weight to be at least two hundred pounds.

"We're lucky she didn't attack last night," Rodrigo said, his words filling the air with awe and fear. "She could have easily killed us with a single bite."

The men shuddered at the thought, their steps quickening as they followed Rodrigo deeper into the forest. They knew they had to stay on high alert to make it out alive.

Rodrigo suddenly stopped and held up his hand, motioning to the men. He crouched down, his eyes scanning the ground for tracks.

"Here," he whispered, pointing to large paw prints. "Fresh tracks, no more than an hour old."

The men looked at each other nervously, knowing the predator was close. They followed Rodrigo's lead. His senses were on high alert as he hit the branches along the trail, ensuring the safety of his companions.

He carried his bow in one hand, the string pulled taut and ready to release an arrow at a moment's notice. In his other hand, he gripped his trusty machete, its sharp blade glinting in the rays of dawn light that peeked in between the canopies. He swung and waved it in the air, trying to appear intimidating and fierce.

Derek and Father Mike followed closely behind, their eyes darting around for any signs of danger. They knew they were in good hands, relying on Rodrigo's expertise and quick reflexes to keep them safe on this journey through the treacherous terrain.

As the group continued, Rodrigo remained focused and determined, ready to face whatever challenges came their way. His years of experience as a hunter had taught him to always be prepared for the unexpected.

Suddenly, a loud primal grunt bellowed from the forest, causing everyone to freeze. Rodrigo quickly scanned their surroundings and spotted a large, dark figure lurking in the shadows.

Derek and Father Mike froze, unsure what to do. They came face to face with the stealthy cat as it slinked low to the ground into the middle of the trail. The stealthy jaguar had circled back. Rodrigo stepped forward and slowly sank to one knee while the other two men stood closely behind him, appearing to be a large target to the animal. The jaguar stood ready to pounce. An easy leap from where they had stopped.

Rodrigo slowly took out an arrow for his bow. As he pulled back, the jaguar sat back on its haunches unexpectedly. They stared at each other intently until Rodrigo released the tension on his bow, straightened up, and motioned for Derek and Father Mike to back away. The cat rose and slinked back into the jungle.

The rest of the day was an exercise in vigilance. Rodrigo knew that the cat was out there stalking them. He did not want to scare Derek and Father Mike, but he needed to let them know they were still in danger.

Rodrigo spoke loudly to the men to dissuade the cat from getting too close. "Stay behind me and make yourselves as big as possible. Derek, put your cap on backward. It may help to make the jaguar believe you are facing that direction. Make lots of noise with big movements. We need to avoid hiking between dusk and dawn. If we encounter her again, stand your ground and maintain eye contact. Do not run or give your back to the jaguar. Raise your arms and make yourself look bigger. Make loud noises and back away slowly. Remember, she will go in for the quick kill. She will aim for your head. Protect your head and neck as much as possible. Show that you are not easy prey."

They found a small clearing to make camp. Derek and Father Mike lay in their hammocks while Rodrigo stayed up again, watching for the stalking cat. The night passed without incident and they arose and ate breakfast quickly. Their headlamps constantly moved in great arced loops, scouring the surrounding brush as they ate. But all they saw were ghostly spiderwebs, glittering with tiny eyes that caught the light. The jaguar was just out of sight, quietly waiting and watching.

After breakfast, they packed their gear to return to the trail for the final leg at sunrise. The trio of men bound for the village kept vigilance. Rodrigo had estimated they were still a couple of hours away.

Derek felt another shiver go down his spine. The hackles on the back of his neck raised his heartbeat, a steady, hard pulse banging against his chest. He thought about the things he was supposed to do to avoid an actual attack.

He had to appear larger than he was. The instinct to flee was strong, but he would have to force himself to stay put. However, deep down, he was not sure if he was ready for a physical confrontation. Had they truly been hunted all night? The thought of finding out terrified him.

Remembering Rodrigo's advice about the jaguar attacking by biting its prey's head or neck, he focused on doing one thing: shoving his arm as deep down the animal's throat as possible. This would trigger its gag reflex, just like a human's.

This unexpected move could potentially throw the cat off balance and allow him to escape. He was well aware that the cat's sharp teeth could still cause damage to his arm and possibly even puncture a vein or artery. But it was better to have the cat bite his arm than his head or neck, as the jaws could deliver a fatal blow. Another thing he could do is push hard on the eyeball. His mind reeled with all manner of self-defense tactics.

If anything should happen to him, he knew he would lose the last shred of respect Kendal had for him. By leaving her behind to go on this trip of self-discovery, he'd crushed the dynamics of their relationship. He knew that it was important for him to communicate and be able to make these types of decisions together—he should have considered her feelings and been more forthcoming about the plans he was making. It might have helped to make her feel more comfortable with the arrangement he had made with Father Mike.

It dawned on him that his actions had made her feel excluded and ignored. She had warned him of the potential danger he was now facing. He should have taken the time to discuss the trip with her. Most importantly, he should have considered Kendal's needs and emotions more when deciding to travel into the depths of a dangerous jungle. But it was too late to change course now.

Midmorning, they stopped to take a break by a banana tree and sat down on a log, a spot where the sun peeked through the trees. As they rested, Derek felt something pounce on him. He instinctively yelped and jumped up, suddenly feeling a sharp pain in his back.

Rodrigo, always alert, reacted immediately and swatted the source of the pain from Derek's back. It was a huge spider, its legs stretching out in all directions and its venomous fangs glinting in the sunlight.

Derek let out a shaky breath, relieved that the danger was over. Rodrigo gave him a quizzical look. Derek shook his head. It felt like a swarm of bees had stung him all at once. He started to feel electric shocks throughout his body. His throat constricted and his chest tightened.

Rodrigo grabbed Derek's arms to steady him. "A Brazilian wandering spider just bit him," he said tensely over his shoulder to Father Mike. "It's one of the most toxic spiders in the world. It's also called the banana spider."

Father Mike looked at the spider that had climbed back on the tree. Its body was about two inches long, and the legs had to be at least six inches. The hairy brown spider stopped and raised up its two front legs to flash its scarlet-colored fangs, which served as a warning.

Rodrigo and Father Mike helped Derek to a tarp they had thrown on the ground. They turned him over to inspect the bite area. "They like to hide in dark places. It must have been living in this log beside that banana tree," Rodrigo said, examining Derek. "They are the most aggressive and venomous spiders known to humans. The venom is extremely poisonous."

Derek's lips and face began to swell and turn blue. It was apparent that he was having an allergic reaction to the venom. The skin around the bite mark had turned blister red. His body was clammy, and he started to sweat profusely. The muscle pain increased. He moaned as he cramped up, unable to breathe.

"Kendal," he whispered hoarsely.

Chapter 16

Father Mike quickly checked Derek's bag to find the EpiPen. Fumbling around in the pockets, he pulled out the little wooden angel figurine. He glanced over at Derek and threw it back into the bag. Then, he found the EpiPen. He injected it into Derek's leg, but nothing happened.

Rodrigo knew he had no time to waste. "I am going to the village. You stay here. I can make it much faster by myself. Keep him warm and hydrated, if possible. We still have a couple of hours to get to the village. They will have the antivenom. I will return as soon as possible. Wait here, and whatever you do, *do not move him.*"

With that Rodrigo disappeared, jogging down the trail.

Father Mike sat on the tarp next to Derek. He found a clean sock in his bag and soaked it with water. As he wiped Derek's face and stubbled head, he remembered their first meeting. The sermon he had given that day came back to him.

"There is a passage in the Bible that speaks of faith as a shield against the curse and the influence of the Devil," he had bellowed. "Faith means to trust in the LORD. The best way to eliminate a curse is to have a union with GOD."

He remembered marching across the front of the stage. "What I tell you is true! Curses are the work of the Devil, and the only way you can counter a curse is by spiritual means—by having a constant relationship with God."

A feeling of intuition had come over him. He had stopped and surveyed the crowd. "I know there is someone here today who has been sent specifically to hear this message. You are the best person to determine what this means to you."

Dabbing at Derek's colorless face, little had he known then that this was the man to whom he had been speaking. A feeling of trepidation came over him. "Was I able to give you the information you need? I pray the message of salvation was received."

He recited the sermon aloud to Derek. "There will come a time when that sinful spirit cannot curse you anymore. That wicked spirit will see *God* Himself in you." He made the sign of the cross on Derek's forehead, his blue lips, and then his heart.

"It will be afraid of *you!* This will happen because you are united with *God*. If you truly are a victim of a curse, you have suffered, and now you will be saved. You will take your power back with *God's* glory."

His voice softened. "I love You, Lord, and give You praise. I listen to Your voice come into our hearts." He clutched his chest. "Only You can set us free. We have repented and ask You for forgiveness for our actions."

He stopped to rinse the sock and placed it back on Derek's head. He leaned over close to his friend's ear. "I remind you now that your strength must come from your faith in the Lord's mighty power. Wear all of God's armor so that you will be able to stand safe against all the strategies and tricks that Satan will devise against you."

He raised both hands up toward Heaven. "For we are not fighting against people made of flesh and blood, but against demons without bodies, the evil rulers of the unseen world, those satanic beings and great evil princes. Against huge numbers of wicked spirits in the spirit world and all evildoers who rule here on earth."

Bending forward over Derek, he lowered his voice. "Know the Spirit of God. You have accepted Jesus Christ into your heart and now belong to God. I pray you use every piece of God's armor to resist this enemy! This attack will have no authority over you while you stand with Our Lord and Savior, Jesus Christ."

He stood up with his legs apart, jaw firm, and proclaimed, "To do this, you must wear the strong belt of Truth given to us in scripture."

He knelt back down on his knees. "In every battle, faith is our shield and love is our ammunition. To stop the fiery arrows aimed at our Helmet of Redemption, we must have confidence in God and do as He has asked. The Sword of the Spirit which is the Word of God I proclaim over you now. It will be your salvation."

Father Mike looked up to the sky. "We remain in You, and You in us. I ask You, Lord, for everything that aligns with the Holy Spirit's wishes." His praying hands clasped tightly to his chest. "I plead with You, Lord. I know that he belongs to You now. I know that the Son of God gave us the Holy Spirit to discern the One who is True."

He looked up. "I Pray for this man, that Your hand is upon his soul and that I offer the right words for Your Power and Glory be used to save this man. Lord. Amen."

His intense blue eyes closed. He bowed his head. His dark brown, dirty, disheveled hair hung limp with a strand stuck to his week-old growth of stubble on his face.

Derek moaned and choked as he started to vomit. Father Mike

turned him onto his side to avoid asphyxiation. He put two fingers in his mouth to clear his air passage. He then pressed his fingers against his throat, feeling the swollen lymph glands. He slowly lifted an eyelid to expose one bloodshot eye, then the other.

Father Mike became anxious when Derek's heavy sweating deteriorated into drooling. He knew death was imminent if the antivenom did not arrive soon or if God's intervention was not received.

As the light started to fade, Father Mike tried to comfort Derek the best he could and continued to pray aloud as he gathered wood and made a fire. He knew that intercessory prayer was one of his most powerful tools.

Chapter 17

Near death, Derek now faced his darkest fears. He lay there, helpless and immobilized, while the chaos of the jungle swirled around him. Another victim of this untamed land, he was forced to confront his mortality as he lay trapped in his own body. It felt like when the tattoos had initially appeared; he was now reliving that fear again.

He tried to repress the black memories that threatened his core, that still needed to be dealt with. He felt life slowly seep from his body as a flood of questions came to mind. What had he feared so much in life that it had brought him to this place in time? What did this say about him as a person?

When pieces of his life came into focus, a certain understanding started to settle over him. The memories flashed before him with a newfound understanding. His childhood trauma had altered his self-concept and views on reality. The brutal beating had caused such trauma to his brain that it struggled to comprehend the events fully. This confusion led to a series of reactions. Initially, he went into a state of denial, refusing to accept the new reality and holding onto memories from his childhood before his sense of safety was taken away.

He had shut down and disengaged from the outside world. The anger he had experienced was his brain's way of not having to experience the underlying emotions. Feeling on edge, lashing out. Placing blame was just another way to cope. The overwhelming sadness had come shortly after the attack. Depressed, with no energy and in extreme pain, he had cried continuously. He would lie in his hospital bed at night and bargain, making deals with God.

For the first time, he felt a sense of peace and understanding. He had gone through the different stages of grief multiple times in varying sequences. But this final stage of acceptance for the loss of his childhood gave him a newfound perspective on life and would help him move forward into a new reality—if he survived.

Derek lay motionless, beads of sweat on his sallow face. His shallow breath was not enough to raise and lower his chest. He could feel Father Mike's ear close to his nose with his hand on his chest to make sure he was still breathing.

Kendal flashed into his mind. His life had become her life. Why had he not made her life his? He had felt a total loss of power because he could not control things. Why had he been so quick to leave her behind?

Derek no longer felt pain. He could see a bright light as he detached from his body and floated above.

He hovered above, watching a concerned-looking Father Mike pat his forehead with a damp sock and pray over him. Derek knew his body was dying. The pain vanished. He felt blissful instead of panicked. The heaviness that he carried around every day had disappeared. His soul had separated from his body and expanded to an unimaginable magnitude. He had a feeling of great peacefulness, unconstrained by the confines of his physical body that had been controlled by space and time.

Suddenly, the tranquil atmosphere transformed into horror as he felt himself being pulled, like a puppet on a string, down to the edge of a pitch-black chasm, a black tar pit. As he edged closer to the immense pool of darkness, he started to panic, unable to struggle out of the invisible silk threads that held him. He could feel a malevolent force waiting for him in this desolate place. The black ethos was starting to saturate him with an unbearable burning sensation as it seeped into his soul.

The overwhelming pain and fear disintegrated into despair. He could feel all the intensified symptoms of the post-traumatic stress disorder that had been palpable when he lived in his body. He succumbed to the full force of the shame and social stigma brought on by the first beating and then the tattoos as he melted into the mire.

In that moment of total despair, the Holy Spirit prompted Father Mike to take the crucifix from around his neck, hold it up, say a prayer, and then put it around Derek's neck as an act of faith.

Derek could feel an immediate shift in his suffering. Father Mike spoke an intercessory prayer aloud: "Heal his soul and his body, Lord."

He heard Father Mike pray that he would take his place of suffering. He was making a solemn request that he carry the cross of burden. The symbol of death and hope through Jesus Christ.

Derek felt a hand clasp his wrist and yank him out of the mire's suffocation. He could feel his soul expand into perfect tranquility. The layers of psychological suppression that had permeated him melted away. There was no uncomfortable thought of existential needs—he just slipped into flawless oblivion.

He found himself surrounded by the echoing chants of Father Mike's prayers. Each chant penetrated his senses to create a sacred atmosphere. He became witness to Father Mike speaking directly to God, as his prayers twinkled like golden dust in the flickering light of the campfire.

Derek watched Father Mike make the sign of the cross on his forehead, lips, and chest. A white light streamed through a break in the trees, showing brighter than the sun. He recognized that his body lay lifeless, but he had no concern over it.

That is when he felt the bright light draw him into the sky's color. The warm, encompassing light lifted him closer and then enveloped him in a bright cloak. The compulsion came to start praising and worshiping God. "Thank you, Lord! I am here." He could see everything in his body—good and bad.

Then, a lucid intensity came over him with a great vividness. His soul was filled with detachment from the lower world and a proclivity toward the greater good.

His mind invigorated with thought after thought in rapid succession, indescribable and inconceivable to the natural mind. Traveling backward in time, every incident of his past life glanced across his recollection in a retrograde-type procession. The whole period of his earthly existence was placed before him in a panoramic view.

He began to reexperience his entire life. A shameful disappointment. He felt great sadness. Until he returned to where he lay on the ground, now void of hopes or fears. His mind and body seemed to be separate. He was still conscious of his body, but it was no longer him.

He could still hear Father Mike praying for God to give him peace and that he may be healed and repurposed.

Derek felt no judgment but was wrapped in love and affection. He recognized the metaphysical reality that life on earth had been a lucid experience of his spiritual being. He had lived in his body for only a short time. Eternity stretched out before him.

Father Mike understood that prayer matters to God, intercessory prayer specifically. Anything asked in His name would be done. Derek could feel him focused on his soul not on his body. He could hear his prayers to cleanse his soul for his suffering to lead to his redemption.

Derek saw a man in a white robe and gold sash so bright he could not see his face. He had His hand on Father Mike's head. He realized this man was his only way to Heaven. This was Jesus Christ.

Derek immediately felt himself prostrate on the ground. He was then lifted to his feet.

Jesus embraced him. "Remember your prayer to me."

An immediate flood of unending unconditional love infiltrated his being.

He understood that God needed his full cooperation as an eternal being. He had prayed to him standing in the penthouse living room with Father Mike. He had asked him to come into his heart. When Jesus touched him, Derek saw all people as people of worth, people that God created and for whom Jesus died.

He had now granted him a vision of Heaven and hell.

Derek seemed to float in a quiet void for a long time somewhere between the lower world, earth, and Heaven.

Then he remembered the prayer Father Mike had given him. He started to pray to Jesus. He asked Him to forgive his sins and come into his heart. A warm light encased him. He could feel himself being lifted. He could feel the overwhelming presence of the Divine. The fragility of his life was stripped away. His consciousness expanded. It felt as though there were no beginning or end. He could still see and hear Father Mike on bended knees in prayer. His prayers had risen with a sweet, flowery scent.

Then as suddenly as he had left, he was sucked back into his body. His soul had taken flight and now returned. His soul felt like sausage meat being stuffed into a casing as it reentered his body. Below the canopy of trees, he lay in excruciating pain. But as he lay paralyzed, Derek knew he had experienced a divine encounter with God, and this experience would give him newfound strength and determination to continue his journey.

Chapter 18

The Village

Rodrigo knew that he needed to reach the village quickly to get the antivenom that could save Derek's life. He pushed his body to the limit as he ran through the muddy, dense rainforest. He sprinted across a field of corn outside the small settlement right before dark.

The village was filled with communal structures made of wood, bamboo, and straw. It bustled with life. Each open-sided round hut held a family, with a fire and hammocks strung up inside. The village men were the hunter-gatherers, and the women ran the household, growing the crops, caring for the children, and cooking. The tribe's people shared a fundamental respect for the spirit of the rainforest. When fishing, they used plant-based poisons to stun the fish. And when they hunted game, they shot darts tipped with curare.

The Warao people believed that they were the first inhabitants of the earth. This belief was rooted in their origin story, passed down from generation to generation. According to the story, they were once inhabitants of the Heavens, living among the gods and spirits. They lived in harmony and had everything they needed.

But one day, while hunting for birds, they came across a magnificent creature with vibrant feathers and a long beak. The Warao people had never seen a bird like this before, and they were determined to capture it. They chased it through the skies, but the bird was too fast and elusive.

Finally, the bird made a sudden turn, and its beak caught onto the clouds, tearing a hole in the sky. The Warao people, in hot pursuit, fell through the hole and descended to the earth.

As they landed on the ground, they realized that this was a new world, unlike anything they had ever seen. The land was rich and fertile, bursting with life and resources. The Warao people saw this as a sign from the gods, that they were meant to live on this land and call it their home.

From that day on, the Warao flourished on the earth, building their villages and living in harmony with nature. They never forgot their origin story and believed that their ancestors watched over them from the Heavens above.

The men and women who took care of their business in the village were partly naked. They wore loincloths and coconut grass skirts, and some even wore a mix of Western clothes. Tribal symbols were painted on some of their faces. They stopped to look at Rodrigo as he scanned the buildings.

He identified the main hut and was quickly approaching when two villagers stopped him. He asked them in Warao Spanish if he could speak to the shaman. The banana spider had bitten his friend. The two men's eyes became large. One rushed into the hut while the other told Rodrigo to wait.

The first villager came back and waved for Rodrigo to enter. He motioned for him to follow deeper inside the hut where an old woman sat by a small ceremonial fire in the corner. The villager stood by the old woman.

Her culture believed that she had true spiritual knowledge. She practiced the art of healing by performing sacrifices. She preserved their traditions by telling stories and singing songs, fortune-telling and acting as a guide for souls.

The villager who had led Rodrigo into the hut motioned for him to sit down.

The shaman stared into the fire. "You bring despair."

This woman, by nature, had been born a shaman. She was a healer, herbalist, shapeshifter, and priestess of the ancestors. She would receive spirits into her body to help her heal and prophesize under their inspiration. After she had absorbed the negative energies into her own body, she would return to the sacred fire of her ancestors, who would release them. The villagers believed that she was able to restore life to the dead.

Rodrigo explained that he was with two foreigners, and the banana spider had bitten one. She waved to the villager, and he immediately left the room. She picked up a plate and cup that sat next to her and then handed them to Rodrigo for him to eat and drink as he explained what had happened.

The villager returned with a vial and syringe. All the villages had been given antivenom medicine, but it had never been used in this village. The old woman told him that she would send her men to help Rodrigo bring them back.

Chapter 19

Father Mike continued to pray as he sat on the tarp, wiping Derek's brow. He was leaning over close, trying to listen to Derek's faint breathing, when he heard the sound that he hoped he would never hear.

A growl, followed by a deep, hoarse grunt from behind them. He knew that sound. It was the sound of death coming for them both.

He quickly looked up, his heart pounding as he saw a large, prowling figure moving in the shadows. He slowly rose to his feet, his eyes widening as he watched the creature move closer.

Its eyes gleamed from the flickers of the fire. He could feel the vibrational low grunts, its hunger emanating from its body. Father Mike stood his ground, his hands held high in the air trying to make himself seem bigger. He slowly took a step forward off the tarp.

The jaguar snarled and then growled. Father Mike took another step forward, his heart racing as he held his hands up in prayer. He closed his eyes and prayed that it would pass them by. After an eternity, the jaguar slowly retreated into the darkness.

His knees shaking, he sat down on the tarp next to Derek. He thought, *This is how Jesus must have felt waiting in the Garden of Gethsemane.*

He listened to Derek's low, faint breath. He knew that if Rodrigo did not return soon, Derek might not make it. He could feel his heart hurt, thinking he would no longer have Derek in his world. They had become close. He considered him a friend.

Derek had first appeared to him as the illustrated man who had taken a seat to hear him speak in the homeless church tent. Father Mike had never seen someone with tattoos so vibrant and complete. The tapestry on his skin made him seem lost and isolated in a dark world. The illustrated man's intense blue-eyed gaze made Father Mike feel like Derek was some sort of messenger.

After his sermon, the illustrated man approached him, smiling a weak yet enigmatic smile and extending his hand. Inquiring about the man he knew as Spider.

Spider, Father Mike would soon find out, was the gang member who had almost beaten Derek to death as a child. Father Mike had been in the process of finding Spider a place to stay so the hospice could care for him in his last days.

Somehow, from the moment he met this illustrated man, Father Mike knew there was something special about him. He felt like God had sent him specifically to facilitate a new growth in his faith. There was more to the spirit than what happened in the physical world—Father Mike could feel it in his heart.

He knew their encounter would help Derek apply those revelations to his daily life. He would guide him to a relationship with God as the veil was being removed from his eyes.

He now felt no pulse in Derek's limp, cold wrist. Derek lay on the ground, his body still and lifeless. Father Mike's fingers searched for a heartbeat that he knew was no longer there. The air was thick with the stench of vomit and death as he gazed down at this man with whom he had become so close.

He had tried to steer him onto the right spiritual path, but Derek had been too stubborn to listen. And now, it seemed, he had paid the ultimate price.

Father Mike stood up, feeling the weight of grief heavy on his shoulders, wondering if there was anything he could have done to prevent this tragic end. But he knew that dwelling on these questions would only bring him more pain.

When they first met and shook hands, he felt a sense of something bigger. A spiritual connection that reached his heart. "I'm here to help," he had reassured Derek. "I believe in the power of the spirit, and I want to share it with you."

Derek had hesitated at first but had been drawn back to him repeatedly.

Father Mike peered into the darkness and saw what he had prayed he would not see—the silhouette of the jaguar had returned. He had to act fast and do something to protect Derek's body. He made the sign of the cross as he scrambled to his feet, his heart racing with fear.

Father Mike realized that he only had one option. He began to speak, his voice loud and clear as he recited verses from the Bible, hoping to send the jaguar away without incident. He prayed while searching for a weapon and spoke louder as his fear grew. All the while, the jaguar lurked in the darkness.

Finally, after what felt like an eternity, the jaguar slowly began to move away, fading into the night. Father Mike fell back onto the tarp, exhausted and relieved. The jaguar was gone, and Derek's body was safe. For now.

Father Mike had been tested and faced with his mortality. But he had held onto his faith, and it had seen him through this dangerous moment.

Father Mike had never had to face this type of danger. His heart pounded in his chest as he sat there, barely able to breathe. He knew what he had to do next, but he felt scared and inadequate for the task.

He had never even been in a physical altercation before. He had never had to fight for his life or anyone else's. He had never even had to raise his voice in protest. But now, he felt a force within him that made him feel confident that he had the power to protect Derek.

He stood waiting, unable to breathe. The predator sensed his helplessness and let out a low, growling hiss. He closed his eyes and braced for the attack.

Then he heard a grunt come from behind. He whirled around in confusion, unsure where the sound had come from. Father Mike could tell that his uncertainty gave the animal the upper hand; he continued to hold his ground. He could hear the rustling stop and then a pause.

Father Mike stepped away from the tarp, strengthening his resolve, ready to confront the beast. He knew there was no way out, but he was prepared to do whatever it took to keep Derek's body safe. With a steady gaze, he investigated the surrounding foliage with a resolute voice: "You will not desecrate him," he proclaimed aloud to the beast.

A low growl came from the wall of large green leaves. A distinctive guttural sound. Just as he had heard the first night sleeping in his hammock, he suddenly heard *the jaguar*. His heart began to beat faster. He could feel the sweat drip down his back. He continued to pray aloud.

From the surrounding foliage, the hoarse grunt would grow louder each time it came a little closer. Father Mike now gripped a knife in each hand. He held one up at the side of his head so that when the jaguar tried to bite his head, he would get the blade instead.

Rodrigo had told him that jaguars are known for their powerful jaws, making them formidable predators. They kill prey much larger than themselves by crushing their head or spine, demonstrating their superior strength and hunting abilities. Men had been paralyzed as they were forced to watch the predator eat their bodies.

Rodrigo's words repeated in his head. It would have extremely powerful jaws with very sharp teeth and razor-like claws. He heard the guttural sound come from behind. The hackles on his neck raised as he spun around.

Then he saw the feline face looking right at him. A full-grown jaguar. He suddenly was not sure if he could survive an attack. This massive cat seemed hungry as it walked slowly in a crouch around him.

"Stay calm," he stammered quietly. "Hold your ground."

He turned slowly, making sure his back was not to the animal. The urge to run and climb a tree came to him, but he knew that the only way to try to intimidate it was to wave his hands with a knife in each above his head. He yelled at the monster as it slowly retreated into the foliage.

He swallowed hard and walked around Derek's lifeless body on the tarp. He could feel a sinister force brewing as he clutched the knives. Remembering what Rodrigo had done, with his legs shaking he got down on one knee, preparing himself for the attack. He said a quick prayer for God to be with him just like he had been with David when he killed the lion. He held one knife out in front of him and one at his head. He heard the growl again. He continued to pray. It seemed to be toying with him, enjoying the fear it instilled in its prey.

The stealthy jaguar reappeared. Like a cat playing with a mouse before ultimately catching and killing it.

With a snarl, she showed her teeth with her hair bristling. Father Mike heard a deep, hoarse grunt right before the jaguar hit him.

He was punched with the force of a speeding car as the knife that had protected his head flew from his hand. He was now in its death grip. He could feel its teeth sink into his head and claws rip into his shoulders trying to grab him by the back of the neck. Fighting for his life, with the second knife, he continuously stabbed the jaguar in the side.

He started to choke; he could taste his own blood. At one point, he locked eyes with the jaguar, reflecting a haunting yellow-green glow that seemed to pierce right through him while holding him in her deadly grip.

Father Mike repeatedly stabbed the cat as it wrestled for a better grip. He could feel its breath on his face, hot and fetid. At one point in their struggle, it started to drag him, then let go to adjust its grip as it grew weaker. At that moment, Father Mike shoved the knife into the belly of the beast. And with all his might, he pulled forward.

He could feel the warm, sticky contents, soaked in blood, pour out from its body. The jaguar tried to find its grip again but started to weaken as life oozed from its body. Father Mike summoned the strength to punch the cat in its snout as it rolled over next to him.

Chapter 20

Kendal spent the morning at the clinic supervising the multiple scheduled surgeries. The clinic was as busy as ever, and she tried to keep her mind busy. The nausea she had when she had awakened that morning still plagued her.

She tried to shake the feeling that something bad was going to happen. The intensity of her psychic discomfort resulted in a feeling of extreme uneasiness. A sense of being powerless to deal with the anxiety left her feeling tired.

She tried to convince herself that it was only normal wifely worry that plagued her. After assisting with a long reconstructive surgery, she returned to Derek's office to take a minute to collect herself.

The nightly dreams she was having left her feeling anxious and exhausted. When she entered his office, she closed the door, ripped the mask from her face and took off her surgical gloves, then sat down at his desk. She began to sob. The loss she felt was profound. It felt like he had died. She could not explain the deep grief she felt with his absence. She gave herself permission to let the pressure of the emotion out.

She understood that he was under great mental strain and stress from his tattoos. But running after the shaman woman's granddaughter was not the answer. It was grasping at straws.

She had to stay busy to evade the burning chasm she felt bubbling inside. The consuming emotional pain would have been unbearable if she had not kept herself occupied.

The weight of grief hung heavy on her chest, pressing down with an unrelenting force. It was as if a boulder had settled on her sternum. She tried to go about her daily tasks, but each movement felt impossible. How could she continue with her life when her heart and soul felt so shattered? She had no choice but to carry on, to function as if nothing had happened. As if her husband had not abandoned her, possibly forever.

Even the simplest tasks felt like insurmountable obstacles. As she washed dishes the night before, her hands had shaken so badly she dropped a plate. The sound of it shattering on the kitchen floor echoed through the empty penthouse, which was silent except for a shrill cry from Brutus on occasion. She collapsed onto her knees, tears streaming down her face as she tried to pick up the broken pieces. It was a stark reminder of how fragile and shattered she felt inside.

But she had to deal with it. She had to find a way to move forward. She could not let the weight of grief consume her. Gathering her strength, she stood up and continued with her chores. Each step was a battle, but she refused to let herself give in to the darkness. She had to be strong, even when she felt so broken.

Her undulating emotional pain was controlled by negative thoughts that kept popping into her head. Intermittently she would feel the urge to cry. Consumed by an overwhelming sadness she grabbed another tissue and blew her nose.

She had barely been able to get up that morning. Her body ached all over. The emotional pain of abandonment had given her physical symptoms she had never experienced before. The nausea and muscle pain made her feel that she may be coming down with something. She had tried to be careful wearing gloves and a mask since coming into the office that morning in case she was sick with some virus.

Her emotions continued to run high. She was trying to keep them in check. She was determined not to make any rash decisions that she could not trust. She made a concerted effort to shut off her emotions and try to become numb to the pain so she could get through the day.

She would eventually have to find a way to release the feelings that had been bottled up. This is what had led to their initial breakup right before they were married. She had let her emotions build until there was an explosive release. She and Derek both had experienced the complicated problems of crippling emotional pain in their early childhood lives.

Derek would shut off his emotions, then manifest them into new tattoos. It had been devastating to their relationship.

Kendal now found herself in the same place. She had to manage the pain by distracting herself. Derek had developed self-sabotaging habits. Little did he realize that when he had shut off the pain, he had also shut off the possibility for happiness with her in his life.

As tired as she was, she knew she needed a healthy distraction and some physical activity. She would take a run after work to get some sorely needed endorphins. She knew that physical activity was the best way to get out of her head.

But when Kendal arrived the next day at work, it seemed no different. Her wariness was as palpable as ever. The anxiety had been building all morning. When she finally took a moment to get a little relief, she went into Derek's executive bathroom and splashed some cool water on her face. She patted her wet face with a hand towel and looked into the mirror. What was the matter with her? Why was she so emotional? As she checked the bloating of her face, it occurred to her what time of the month it was. She went back out to his desk to check the calendar. She was three weeks late. With all she had been going through with Derek leaving for the Amazon, she had been preoccupied and had not kept track of her cycle.

The missed period, unexpected changes in her body, soreness, headaches, fatigue, nausea—with the unexplained mood swings . . . Could she really be pregnant?

The thought gripped her like an iron fist. This had been the farthest thing from her mind. A baby? She was still dealing with a new marriage and running a business with the possible abandonment of her husband. How could she possibly manage a baby?

She sat down in his chair and a tinge of happiness started to bubble somewhere deep within. It was like a bubbling spring as she absorbed the full meaning of what she had just realized. She had a human being inside of her. Part her and part Derek. How wonderfully the spark of life shifted her whole body and mind. As the realization sank in it started to transform her mood. It was as if she had taken a happy pill. She could not help herself. She still worried for Derek, but she did not feel the grief of loss, only the joy of life.

She picked up the phone and made an appointment to see her doctor. She needed to know for sure right away. She did not want to experience any confusion or disappointment. The range of emotions she had felt since Derek left was enough to deal with.

The news brought her great joy and relief. She was pregnant with Derek's child. She wondered how he would react as she walked through the penthouse door. She could hear Brutus squawk from the kitchen when he heard her come in.

Tyler walked out of the hallway with his laptop under his arm. "Hi Kendal! Have you heard from Derek?"

"No, nothing. I'm trying not to be worried. He told me that they'd have no connection to the outside world once they entered the jungle. All I can do is hope and pray that everything is going as planned." She took a pitcher of orange juice out from the refrigerator.

"I understand," Tyler said. "I sure wish I could have gone with him. He didn't want me to miss any school, but I could have made it up when I got back."

"I'm sure he appreciates that." She took a glass out from the cabinet. "But you know your schooling is as important to him as it is to you." She poured the juice into the glass. "So don't have a second thought about it. You are right where you're supposed to be." She took a long swig from the juice. "Who knows how long this is going to take? He's on a hunt that could take months."

"Hopefully, it won't take months," Tyler said as he watched Kendal pour a second glass of juice. "He'll be going into the wet season. There's lots of flooding where he'll be. The villagers start to move around. He could chase them for a long time if his timing isn't right."

"Sounds like you've done your homework." She gave him a weak smile. "That would be a terrible blow to get to your intended destination and find they've all gotten up and moved." She reached into the cabinet and pulled out a box of crackers.

"I believe he and Father Mike picked this time specifically because this is when they would have their best chance to find the village." Tyler ran a hand through his thick black hair.

"You're probably right," Kendal agreed. "Derek is great at figuring things out and planning. I know that he thought this through before he left." She ate two crackers, finished the second glass of orange juice, and wiped her mouth with the back of her hand.

"The good news is that Father Mike has spent time in the Amazon. He has at least a little knowledge of how the ecosystem works," Tyler said.

Kendal nodded. "One of the only comforts I have about this whole thing is that he didn't go alone. I trust Father Mike to guide him and help to protect him." She closed the package of crackers and put the box back into the cabinet. "He was getting pretty anxious before he left. He's looking for answers and hasn't found them here."

She took her empty glass to the sink, rinsed it, and put it in the dishwasher. "Whether it ends up being that the old shaman's granddaughter is the person who can give him some answers or that he can just get the time to think all of this through without the everyday interruptions, I think the trip will be invaluable."

"I wish I could help him," Tyler said. "I owe him so much, and I want him to be happy like he has made me."

"I know," Kendal said with a smile as she reached to set the orange juice bottle back into the refrigerator. "Just focus on school, which will make him happier than you could ever know."

"Thanks," he hugged her quickly and left for school.

She sat down. She suddenly felt exhausted. *Here we go*, she thought.

Chapter 21

The sky was an oppressive blanket of dark gray, threatening to burst into thunderous rain. In the distance, lightning cast a faint flicker of light in the darkness. The air was charged with electricity, a reminder that a storm was coming.

Derek lay semiconscious but with a sense of clarity and purpose. He had faith that no matter how dark the night was, eventually, the sun would rise. "God, give me strength," he silently prayed. "Give me the courage and wisdom to persevere in my darkest hour. My faith will serve as a guiding light. Amen."

Derek's new growth of blond stubble gleamed damp with sweat while he lay fiercely determined not to die. Staring up at the sky, he lapsed back into unconsciousness.

A short time later, pain jolted him awake, yet his body still refused to budge. "Where is Father Mike?" he murmured. "Did he leave too?" He had heard Rodrigo tell Father Mike to stay put. Rodrigo had left to get help. Was that right? Or did they both leave? He didn't know.

He felt a tinge of fear as he lay incapacitated. The jaguar, would it come into camp? He faded back out. He dreamed he could feel the hot breath of the jaguar on his face. Paralyzed, he lay motionless, terrified, not able to move. He could feel the jaguar touching him, its fur brushing against his arm. It had come near his face; the barrier of safety had been broken.

Then Kendal's smiling face flashed into his mind. This reminded him that she adored him and was always with him in his heart.

He tried to take a breath and made a conscious decision to survive. He had to get back to Kendal. What had he been thinking? The only thing that mattered was seeing her again. He no longer cared whether he had tattoos or not.

Assigning blame was the last thing on his mind—it did not matter anymore. He had spent his life feeling wronged and victimized, always feeling inferior to others. But he was tired of that story. He didn't want to be just a survivor—he wanted to be a thriver, to take control of his narrative.

A wave of understanding broke over him like someone had downloaded a new program into his mind. The familiar thoughts and beliefs he had held onto for so long now felt like they had been erased from his system.

His thoughts were directed toward something more positive, and his emotions had changed, too. He would declare himself renewed and accept that sometimes things were not under his control and bad things could happen.

He had finally let go of his grief, loss, and negative experiences. The once insurmountable obstacles and challenges in life no longer weighed him down. The childhood trauma that had caused his PTSD and consumed him was a distant memory. Even the rage that had once consumed him had been released. It was as if he had been punching a heavy emotional bag filled with tension and suffering, but it was now empty. In its place, he felt the bright light of faith and hope shining through the darkness.

The quest to find the shaman's granddaughter in the jungle had been his last resort to ease his unbearable pain. But now, lying still for an unknown time, he felt a sense of inner peace. He longed to return home to Kendal and tell her how much he loved her. He was ready to turn the page and leave the past behind. But he would have to survive this to see her again.

Chapter 22

"Attachment to our mothers is important to secure a healthy foundation that lets the child explore the world and have a safe place to come back to. This is the first way that babies learn to organize their feelings and their actions by looking to the person who provides them with care and comfort."

Kendal put down the book, turned off the lamp on her night table, and fell comfortably asleep. She slept through the night until early morning when she remembered this quote as she woke from a dream about a baby jaguar—a newborn jaguar. She groggily rose from bed and went to the computer in the office. She felt it was some premonition but was unsure what it could mean.

She wiped her eyes with the back of her hands, then turned on the screen and typed into the computer, *"Dream about a baby jaguar."* Different links to different websites popped up. She clicked on one.

"The dream symbolizes your idealized self-image, perhaps because it feels difficult to communicate your emotions openly. You need to make a quick decision. This dream also symbolizes your aims and aspirations. Others have control over you, but the manifestation of a jaguar in your dream encourages you to recognize and embrace your own unique identity. A task may need to be completed concurrently".

She read on to the next link. *"Having a dream of a tiny jaguar symbolizes dedication and loyalty to family members. Both you and your partner are held together in each other's life by something that binds you. You have been too swayed by your bodily cravings. You need to remember to be more conscious and thoughtful in certain circumstances or relationships. The little jaguar is a symbol of collaboration, balance, and unity. You are having doubts about who you really are."*

She sat back in the chair looking at the screen. She smoothed her hand across her taut stomach. Gently massaging her micro-bump, she wished Derek were here to massage it for her. The soft gentle movements brought her back to memories of when she and Derek lay together soothing each other with long soft gentle strokes exploring each other's bodies.

A profound sadness came over her when she walked back into their bedroom to get ready for work. The big, expansive room was now empty of the happy life they had known for such a short period of time. Tears ran down her face as she pondered the unknown future that lay ahead. This was not how she had planned her life to be, she thought as she stepped into the shower. She had done her best to secure a solid, balanced life—and then Derek happened.

Chapter 23

Fifth Day in the Jungle

Just after dark, Rodrigo and the two village men quickly crossed over the harvest of beans and wild rice next to a field of corn that surrounded the village on their way back out to the jungle trail.

Farming was critical to their survival, but hunting was the most crucial skill taught to the villagers from an early age. They hunted game with blowguns, poison-tipped arrows, and spear traps. Rodrigo knew these men were expert trackers and would be hard to keep up with as they made their way through the jungle.

In just over an hour, they approached the area where Rodrigo had left Father Mike and Derek. They found jaguar scat. Rodrigo's heart sank.

"Stay alert and trust your senses. Something is not right. There is a big animal around here, you can smell him," one of the village trackers cautioned in his native tongue.

An exhausted Rodrigo followed the men closely as they came upon Derek lying peacefully on the tarp. Rodrigo called out for Father Mike. There was no answer.

One of the village men pointed to jaguar prints coming into camp and then the drag marks going out the other side. There was a blood trail leading back into the bush. One man loaded his arrow into his bow. The other loaded a dart into an extraordinarily long blow pipe. Rodrigo readied his bow and stayed back to guard Derek as the men disappeared into the brush.

He felt Derek's pulse; it was very faint. His breathing was shallow. Rodrigo took the syringe and vial out of his pack and gave him the antivenom shot. There was no reaction. He sat waiting, bow in hand, for the men to return with Father Mike.

One villager returned with a grim look on his face. They had found Father Mike critically wounded but not eaten. There had been a fight to the death, and he'd killed the jaguar in the struggle. The blood they had seen was mostly from the cat. But Father Mike had multiple deep lacerations that covered his body. The worst was on his scalp, shoulders and face. A few more laced his torso. But the puncture wound to his skull was the most egregious. He appeared to have obtained fractures above his right frontal bone. His scalp and face were completely swollen, with the lacerations gaping out of proportion. It was hard to determine at this point if he might have a bleed in the brain.

The village men quickly started to give aid. One collected ants to put on the wounds. The ants were used to clean out the bacteria and keep infection out. A jaguar's bite, just like any other big cat, could be lethal since the cat's mouth was full of bacteria. The right side of Father Mike's face had been ripped open from the chin through the nostril across the eye orbit. His ear hung from the side of his head. He also had an open fracture of the right mandible. It had been a severe, life-threatening attack.

The Indigenous men quickly scanned the area for the powerful rainforest plants they had used for thousands of years. First, they would use the Sanipanga plant as an antiseptic by rubbing it onto his wounds.

The men found the Una de Gato (Cat's Claw), which was a tall vine that curled upward on a tree trunk with tiny twisted green thorns located under its leaves. They used it to control the pain of Father Mike's deep wounds. This also helped to fight the bacteria.

They wrapped his head in dry gauze to keep his ear from detaching any further and protect the wounds from any further contamination. Then they stuck a Cordoncillo leaf in Father Mike's left cheek to stop the blood hemorrhages.

Rodrigo bowed his head, crossed himself and said a prayer. The two villagers returned from administering aid to Father Mike. They quickly built a fire to boil the Matico plant leaves to make a brew of tea.

Rodrigo lifted Derek's head and opened his mouth to pour a little of the liquid inside. It was given to help his muscle pain and sore throat, as well as inflammation and body aches.

The village men quickly built two bamboo sleds to carry Derek and Father Mike. They had covered the jaguar with palm fronds and would return for its body. It was believed to be sacred.

Father Mike, a priest whom God had filled with the Holy Spirit, would be honored. The jaguar (the earthly spirit companion) was believed to protect religious figures from evil spirits while they moved between the earth and the spirit realm. For some unknown reason, this possessed jaguar clashed in a battle to the death with a mediator of the Almighty God.

Chapter 24

Shaman Village

In the Western world, spirits are considered Heavenly, but in the shamanic world, spirits are everywhere—plants, animals, and even rocks. Spirits circulate between dimensions and impact one another.

As Rodrigo and the village men rushed back, carrying the unconscious Derek and Father Mike, the urgency of the situation was palpable. In a desperate attempt to save his comrades, Rodrigo rummaged through their bags and found Father Mike's satellite radio. He called for help, his voice trembling as he detailed the dire situation. The person on the other end assured him that an emergency team would be sent out, but they would have to land their helicopter several miles away and hike in. It was estimated that the team would take at least a day to reach the village after finding a suitable landing spot.

Mari, the shaman's granddaughter, emerged from the depths of the rainforest carrying a bundle of precious plants. With delicate care, she stripped the bark off one plant and separated it into fibers, revealing Ayahuasca, also known as "the vine of the soul." She added Chacruna, a small shrub, to the mix before boiling it into a potent tea. Her grandmother used this brew in sacred rituals to induce an altered consciousness and connect her patients to the spiritual realm.

Mari came into the hut with the brew ingredients. Despite facing the unimaginable childhood hardships of human trafficking, Mari was developing into a young woman with a steely resolve. Her petite frame and long dark hair only added to her fierce demeanor.

To her astonishment, she recognized Derek and Father Mike lying on the bamboo sleds. Their faces were etched into her memory after they had rescued her from the clutches of the ruthless human traffickers. Mari rushed to tell the woman who was busy preparing for the ceremony, hunched over with a deer pelt draped on her shoulders.

The elderly shaman's resolve strengthened. Learning this new information would only deepen the intensity of the ritual.

Mari, known to Derek as Maria, gently lifted Derek's head to pour a sip of the brew into his mouth. She rubbed his throat to help him swallow.

The ceremony commenced first with Derek. The aged shaman woman used her medicinal abilities to neutralize the venom and alleviate its effects. She wore a headdress made of antlers and blew smoke toward his motionless tattooed body. The smoky atmosphere in the hut was designed to awaken something within him, trigger an unconscious response, and unleash his spiritual side. This ritual aimed to aid in the therapeutic changes that would purify and heal his body.

The shaman woman's deep connection to the spiritual plane allowed her to enter a trance. Her spirit reached out, searching for Derek and Father Mike's spirits. She sensed that their souls had been separated due to their harrowing struggle for survival. She witnessed a fierce battle for Derek's well-being and Father Mike's physical recovery in this otherworldly realm.

Mari proceeded to the ravaged body of Father Mike, who lay unconscious on the other side of the fire pit from Derek. She slowly lifted Father Mike's head and poured a sip of the brew into his mouth but could not rub his throat because of the extensive wounds to his face and neck. She put her finger into his mouth, pressing down on his tongue, allowing the throat to open, consuming the small amount of liquid.

The shaman woman's bare feet underneath deer hooves pounded against the ground to the beat of the drum as she marched around Derek. She sang, danced, and shook her rattle as she called upon spirits to aid her in healing the two men. She could feel her spirit enter the supernatural realm, where she would have to interact with benevolent and malevolent entities.

Her melodic chant and steady shaking served as a gateway to heightened enlightenment. The psychotropic plants acted as guides, unlocking the doors to her consciousness.

She danced for the gods to seek their blessings. The shaman's drumming, accompanied by the mournful notes of her tibia-bone flute, filled the hut and echoed through the thick air. The dense atmosphere in the village seemed to stand still, only disrupted by the eerie music that drifted through it.

Mari tossed a mix of incense, herbs, and copal resin into the blazing fire, invoking the power of ancient wisdom. With rhythmic movements, the elderly shaman circled the flames and then circled Derek and Father Mike.

She stared into the flames. In her native tongue, she asked her ancestors to connect her with *The Wisdom*. She circled Derek and stomped her feet to invoke the earth. She moved her hips to invoke the water. She made dramatic movements to invoke the fire and she swayed her hands over his body to invoke the air. With a wave of her hand, she called upon the venom and fear lurking within Derek's body to be banished into the depths of the universe.

Next, she focused on Father Mike and performed the same ritual, walking around him in a circle. She called upon the spirits. She stamped her feet and called upon the elements to aid her in this task. She asked the spirits to heal Father Mike's battle injuries.

In the village's center stood a totem adorned with a carved jaguar spirit animal. This powerful creature was known as the gatekeeper. It held mystical energy and offered lessons on reclaiming inner strength. The arrival of this secretive and graceful creature signaled the need for spiritual rebirth in one's life.

The villagers were shaken by the sight of the jaguar being carried into the village and laid outside the hut. Its exposed teeth represented the weapon used upon the man of God. The villagers gathered around the scene. They whispered to each other in hushed tones, many believing this was an omen and a sign of something dark and sinister. Others concluded that it must have been the almighty power of God.

The jaguar, with its sleek golden coat and piercing green eyes, had been revered by the native people for centuries. It symbolized power and strength, a force to be admired and feared. But now, as it lay on the ground, its mighty roar silenced, it had shattered their perceptions.

The man of God, a priest, with a different kind of power and strength, now lay inside the shaman's hut, his body battered and bloodied from the fierce attack. The jaguar had lunged, clawed, and tore at his flesh until he was nearly unrecognizable, but he had prevailed.

The villagers had gathered around the jaguar's lifeless body, their eyes wide with shock and fear. They had never seen anyone, let alone a man of God, attacked in such a brutal and unexpected way—and survive. Once a majestic and revered creature, the jaguar now lay defeated and broken at their feet.

And the man of God, who spread a message of peace and love, even though his body lay shattered his beliefs and convictions still intact.

As they examined the scene, the villagers could not help but question their beliefs and perceptions. Had they been wrong all along in worshiping the jaguar? What did this mean for their future beliefs as a people? As they grappled with these unsettling thoughts, they could not help but feel the unease and uncertainty settling over the village.

The jaguar protected and guarded the rainforest's secrets and mysteries. The totem reminded all who entered the sacred rainforest that the creatures were not just animals, but guardians of a magical world hidden within the jungle's depths.

Though most feared for its ferocity, the jaguar was respected and revered equally. The locals had come to view the jaguar as a source of strength and resilience, a symbol of their own will and determination. This belief, now shaken, hung in the balance.

The jaguar had become more than just an animal to the Indigenous people—it had become an integral part of their culture and identity. Its spirit was said to pervade the surrounding area, inspiring all who encountered it with its strength and courage. But their image of this creature now came into question, destroyed with its attack on this man of God.

It had attacked Father Mike with an evil intent far beyond an animal looking for a meal. It had pounced on him with a force far beyond that of a normal beast. It must have been possessed.

Father Mike had a high level of spiritual regulation. The old shaman woman could sense his unwavering spirit and unshakable faith. His soul remained impenetrable.

She could see in her mind's eye the brutal battle between Father Mike and the jaguar. He had not gone down without a fight. The wild animal, a demon, was sent to challenge the priest. Father Mike faced certain death without the protection of the helmet of salvation.

Taking the life of the jaguar symbolized the victory over internal struggles when faced with mortality. He did not let fear consume him—instead, his strong belief in Christ allowed him to remain calm and composed as a faithful servant, even in the face of death. His dedication to serving God showed an unwavering desire to fulfill God's plan and protect those in need.

She felt the rapid decline of her request. She could feel her shamanic journey with the spirits disconnect and end abruptly.

Chapter 25

Father Mike interpreted the jaguar as a symbol of the malevolent force that had been following Derek since he was young. This journey through the jungle was not just a test of physical endurance but a spiritual battle against evil that would push Derek's faith and bravery to their limits. The constant threat of danger from this unseen entity made every step a struggle for survival, both physically and spiritually.

Father Mike had been taking care of Derek as the intense afternoon sun blazed over the thick jungle. When the jaguar suddenly appeared, it startled him. Its deep guttural growl echoed through the air. Even the most courageous of fighters would have cowered in its presence. The jungle was a realm of secrets and peril where anything could occur.

He had stood alone, his body tense as he waited for the inevitable attack. He knew he had been summoned by a higher power, given a task he could not refuse even if he wanted to. And now, as he stood alone in this shadowy place of death, he could feel the weight of true evil bearing down on him. And then, suddenly, the jaguar slunk out from the shadows.

Its coat was tan with black spots, glistening in the sunlight. Its intense eyes stared right through Father Mike, sending shivers down his spine. He could not help but be entranced by the grace and strength with which the jaguar moved around him, both mesmerizing and terrifying at the same time. Father Mike could only watch in awe as the majestic creature confidently prowled around him, every step deliberate and purposeful.

He was paralyzed with fear. His heart pounded in his chest, and he struggled to catch his breath. The jaguar sensed his fear and crept closer, its deep growls reverberating in the ether. The thick jungle closed around him, trapping him with the powerful predator just feet away.

He recited, "*Yea, Though I walk through the valley of the shadow of death, I fear no evil . . .*"

The jaguar gave a guttural snarl that made him pause, but he did not let fear overcome him. "*For thou art with me; thy rod and thy staff they comfort me.*" With a sudden burst of speed, the jaguar appeared in a blur. He lunged at Father Mike, his movements precise and deadly.

His attacker sent him sprawling to the ground. The creature tried to lock its jaws onto his head but he was quick to recover, and soon they were in a fierce battle of life and death. Father Mike had felt the predator look deep into his soul during the struggle when they had locked eyes, trying to communicate something he could not comprehend. As the fight raged on, and Father Mike had stabbed it repeatedly, he could feel the jaguar's strength starting to wane. He refused to give up. And with one final, powerful stab of the knife, he cut it down.

He had done it. He had fulfilled his task. He had protected Derek's body from mutilation. And as he lay there covered in blood, he knew that he had just faced true evil and emerged victorious. He felt a sense of satisfaction and power that he had never experienced before as he drifted into unconsciousness. Father Mike knew his end was near; his love and faith for God never wavered.

As they stood around the hut, the jaguar continued to captivate the imagination and evoke a sense of awe and reverence among the villagers.

The natives' view of the jaguar as a representation of sheer power, capable of striking fear into anyone it encounters, had been eclipsed by Father Mike's survival with the obvious protection of God.

The gifts and sacrifices offered in his name could not perforate his conscience, for he was a worshiper of the Almighty God.

Father Mike was suspended between life and death as the infection spread through his body. He began to hallucinate, then fell back into dark unrest. He began to dream. He stood on the edge of a riverbank, his body throbbing with the wounds of battle. He had come to the riverbank because he knew the Holy Spirit dwelled within its living waters.

He gazed upon what he intuitively knew to be the River of Life. The water shimmered with a brilliant light. An inner stillness allowed him to connect to the river's energy flow as it coursed through him. A sensation of warmth and peace exploded within him and then enveloped his entire being.

He silently asked God to transform the wounds of his battle into something new and abundant. He felt a gentle breeze kiss his face and knew the Holy Spirit was within him, listening to his plea and granting his wish. He opened his eyes to see the river had turned into a glowing, soft, golden light. He knew then that the transformational healing had begun.

He stepped into the river, feeling its healing power washing away his pain. He emerged from the river renewed, his wounds healed and his heart full of hope for the future. Jesus stood on the bank.

Father Mike fell to his knees, bowed his head, and clutched his praying hands to his chest, thanking his savior for this gift of transformation. Jesus turned to walk away, leaving him with a newfound sense of peace.

Little did he know this was only the beginning. There would be more battles to come.

God had anointed him His warrior.

Chapter 26

The Shaman Woman

She moved back to where Derek lay. His rage blazed in the distance, no longer a part of him. His diminished expectations and disappointments floated around and through his spirit.

His dead grandmother appeared in the scene, holding a baby in her arms. This was a sign to the shaman that he was bound by familial ties and would enter the prime of his life with the power and vigor to continue the lineage.

The shaman could feel the void created by his disconnected spirit from his grandmother and how he missed having her in his life. She had been a major contributor to his sense of safety, kindness, and protection. The shaman woman knew that his grandmother's presence meant that a new life was imminent. The next generation was on its way.

She watched as he spoke to his deceased grandmother. It was a strong sign that he now had the necessary information to make wise decisions. She could see his grandmother smiling at him. It seemed that fortune would now be in his favor.

The dead jaguar had been placed outside the hut's door. It waited to have the malevolent spirits expunged from its body. The breath of life, which invigorated and stirred the consciousness of village life, was believed to come from animal spirits that existed within every object.

They believed that some spirits were helpful, and some were malevolent. The death of the jaguar and the attack on the priest brought consternation to the village. If an evil spirit had possessed the cat and caused it to attack a priest, that was a sin against the Great Spirit.

The fierce jaguar was worshiped as a deity. But the one that had killed the priest was not the one they worshipped. Just like the ancient rulers, the warriors of the village adorned themselves with the animal skulls, skins, fangs, and claws. They circled the shaman's hut where Derek and Father Mike lay unconscious. Throughout the night they performed the ceremonial dance to expel the spirit from the village.

The breath of consciousness, the sacredness of spirit, and the community wisdom that embraced the notion of animal essence inhabiting all things were the foundation of village life.

The whole village understood that she needed to save his life. The ceremony would be critical to the belief system of the village.

Chapter 27

Derek was vaguely aware of the shaman stomping around him as he lay on the ground. He could feel the effect of the hallucinogenic. It released natural endorphins and increased the dopamine in his brain.

The smoky air in the hut stirred something deep within him, awakening his spiritual side. He felt his body relax as the air filled his lungs and his mind cleared of thoughts.

As he lay in the hut, he was aware of a subtle shift in his energy. His chest broadened as the air filled with a gentle warmth. He felt his lungs open, and the hut walls seemed to expand around him.

He closed his eyes and let himself be taken over by the experience. He felt the muscles in his body loosen as his heart rate slowed, and he was aware of a calm settling over him. The air seemed to hum around him, the vibrations creating a sense of weightlessness.

When he opened his eyes again, the hut seemed brighter. Sunlight now streamed in through the gaps in the wall, illuminating the room and its contents. He felt a sense of clarity.

The flickering of the fire was intertwined with the rhythm, creating a waking dream state. Derek had never believed in shamanism or anything mystical, for that matter. He was a man of science, rationality, and logic. But when the shaman woman held his hand and spoke her incantation, he felt a primal force surge through his body, a feeling that he had never experienced before. It was basic and potent, evoking feelings similar to those originating from the most ancient parts of human nature.

His heart rate increased, his palms became clammy, and his legs trembled uncontrollably. It was as if the shaman woman had unlocked a hidden door in his mind, unleashing a torrent of memories, fears, and insecurities that he had long buried to cope with the physical hardships he had endured.

He opened his eyes briefly. His weakened gaze fell upon the intricate tattoos covering the shaman woman's face and it triggered a PTSD flashback. He was back on the sidewalk, surrounded by the men who had beat him. He could hear his own screams, smell the blood inhaled through his broken nose, and saw his blood spilling onto the ground.

He was suddenly back in that moment, reliving the pain, the fear, the helplessness. And then, just as suddenly, he was back in the present, his breathing ragged, his body drenched in sweat.

The shaman woman's grip on his hand tightened. With a deep breath, he tried to steady his breathing, to push the memories back into the depths of his mind where they belonged.

But the first time he met the shaman woman, she had said, "I need someone to find my granddaughter." And in that moment, Derek understood. She had orchestrated this encounter based on her needs. She had seen the pain in his eyes and used it to her advantage.

Derek now recognized the shaman woman's cunning, realizing he had been manipulated. Her connection to the other world, with her special powers and paranormal abilities that influenced the good and evil spirits, had triggered his demise.

Derek floated in and out of semiconsciousness next to the fire, unaware that Father Mike lay on the other side of the fire ring, close to death.

Chapter 28

The phone call came early in the evening. One of the men had been attacked by a jaguar and the other lay unconscious from a spider bite.

Kendal's heart skipped a beat and she dropped the phone, feeling like she might pass out. *Don't faint, don't faint.* She managed to pick up her cellphone and half-fall into the nearest chair. Her heart pounded. She couldn't breathe. She tried to answer but nothing came out.

Derek's absence had weighed heavily on her psyche, and she'd had an ominous foreboding that something bad was about to happen. Had she manifested her feelings strong enough so that he could feel her missing him?

"Mrs. Hollinger?" prompted the person on the other end of the line. "Are you still there?"

She let out a breathless, "Yes."

"We will have more news once the emergency team arrives on the scene. It takes a day to fly to the location and trek back into the jungle. They will update us once they have contact. I will call you back at that time. Do you understand?"

"Yes." Her psychological response to the terrifying news surprised her. The surge of strong emotions and corresponding physical reaction had completely caught her off guard. She was finding it hard to function.

She had not been ready for the intense rush of emotions. She might have gone into a state of shock.

The phone went dead. For a minute she prayed it was just another bad dream, but she knew it was real. She felt numb. Physically unable to move. She felt like nothing around her was real—with a weird sense that she was watching this happen to someone else.

Had her mind been trying to warn her of impending danger through her dreams? She had felt it deep in her bones. Derek was her soulmate. She had dreamed that morning that he lay with her hugging her from behind. His arms wrapped around her felt so real. For a few seconds, she thought he was actually home, there with her.

In the weeks before he left, there had been shifts between her emotions and his, a blend of their connection. Even now, she could still sense the bond they shared.

Her worst nightmares were being realized. She had warned him of the risks, cautioned him not to go, but Derek wouldn't listen. She had the familiar feeling of abandonment accompanied by a new fear of whether he was hurt but still alive—or worse.

She missed him deeply and questioned if he had missed her in the same way. She struggled to find her composure, worried that any tension or anxiety could put her baby in jeopardy. She knew that it was important to immediately take steps to relax her body. She took a minute to breathe so that she could try to think clearly without feelings of panic and grief taking over. She would have to wait for communication from the rescue team once they arrived on the scene. It had not even crossed her mind to ask about the last spot where Derek and Father Mike had been seen or to determine what area they would most likely be located in. She would have to wait to get the detailed information. She just wanted to talk to him, to touch him. All she could do now was hope and pray for his survival.

She nestled into the couch as she gazed out at the serene penthouse view. The lights of Los Angeles twinkled in a vibrant display. But for all its beauty, her mind was elsewhere, lost in thought.

She tried to shake the impending sense of doom. It was as if the walls she had previously built and worked so hard to tear down immediately sprang back up. Clutched in her hand was her cellphone; the call had been delivered without emotion. She had no idea what to expect or what to do next.

After some careful thought, she concluded that she should have faith and get ready for whatever was to come. She lay on the couch in a sort of suspended animation, for how long she didn't know. Despite her best efforts, she couldn't help but feel overwhelmed. She was pregnant with an unexpected child, and the reality of it was beginning to sink in.

She knew she had to be strong, but it was a daunting task. How was she going to cope with a baby without Derek, when she had no idea what she was doing? But she had also felt a strange sense of excitement when she had found out; knowing that a new life was growing inside her had changed everything.

She took a deep breath and slowly exhaled. She had confidence that eventually, everything would work out—she just needed to have faith.

Her mind shifted to business. During this uncertain time, her normal office and clinical duties would have to fall to the wayside. She sat up on the couch. Her cellphone lay next to her. She picked it up and called to leave a message for Sandra, Dr. Lee's nurse, saying that she would be taking a couple of sick days. She then called Nicole at home to tell her not to schedule any new appointments for the next couple of days. This would propel the office into Defcon One, but there was nothing else she could do. Nicole had been curious but polite and did not ask any questions.

Not knowing what might happen next or what the future held, Kendal had to keep her personal and business life in a state of perpetual motion. While all she could do was wait in desperate uncertainty for news as to Derek's and Father Mike's condition, it was imperative that she continue life as usual.

For now, she could feel herself physically hitting a wall. Feeling a sharp pain in her lower abdomen she went into her bedroom to lie down. She crawled into bed and covered herself with the blanket. She started to shiver as a cold feeling came over her.

Chapter 29

Sixth day, Shaman Village

Derek tried to open his eyes, but his eyelids seemed to be sealed shut. Sensing movement, Mari rushed to his side. She grabbed a wet cloth from a bowl of water that had been used to keep his fever under control. She wiped his eyes as he lay wondering who could be gently administering to him. He finally managed to look up at her face. With great surprise and confusion, he saw the face of Maria. The girl he had rescued from the drug pushers and human traffickers.

He lay in a makeshift bed on the ground. He was able to move his neck so he could glance around, yet he was too feeble to lift himself up. He needed somebody to explain to him why he was in this small hut. The light that spilled in from the smoke hole in the roof of the hut could not lighten the weight of the darkness that still clung to him. He could feel it in his veins, a slow-moving poison that had been injected into his bloodstream.

He tried to recall what had happened from what felt like a dream, but he couldn't remember much. He had received a mysterious vision, in which he stood in front of towering gates. A man had stood guard in front and checked the Book of Life for his name.

The Bible frequently mentioned a celestial record where the names of those who are part of the Lord's flock are written. But what

Derek had found once he crossed through those gates was unclear. He remembered strange symbols and secret languages, conversations and revelations that had left him reeling.

Now, in the light of day, it was difficult to remember. It felt like an ever-shifting tapestry of half-remembered images that receded before he could get a good look. He felt like he had been shown something remarkable and important, and yet he could not even remember what it was. He knew that with his Book of Life, he had been the author.

He had glimpsed the narrative of his life—a Heavenly testament to what it takes to live one's unique story yet remain in alignment with the Book of Life and all that comes after. The chapters of his life on earth, including the stories he had written about himself, had been revealed. Through this, he would be able to gain a better insight into what steps should be taken for his future progression. He had only to remember the specifics of the insights he had been given.

He had been given the freedom to accept the truth and learn from it or reject the truth and run toward hell. It had been revealed to him that he had an outer cerebral memory and inner spiritual memory. The details of what he had said or done and what he had heard and seen were inscribed on his inner spiritual memory. He was shown that there is no way to erase anything there.

Everything he had experienced in his life had been written in his spirit and on parts of his spiritual body. This meant that his spirit was fully formed in accordance with what he had thought, how he had responded, and what he had done intentionally because of his expe-riences.

But he realized that his life story had also been written on his physical body. Angels had come to help him through this examination of his life.

When faced with his deeds, the angels were tasked with examining the whole body, beginning with the fingers first on one hand and then the other. The things that had been inscribed in his memory from his intention and consequent thought were also inscribed not only on his brain but also on his whole person, where it had taken the form of patterns and designs all over his body.

By looking closely at his body, the way a doctor examines the state of a person's health, the angels had shown him how to become more aware of the true state of his mind and heart. They examined and studied the inner patterns he had established. They let it be known that the state of spiritual health is not a matter of adding up how many positive deeds or negative deeds he had performed but a mixture of these things. The tattoos reflected the overall deeper goals and priorities during the span of his earthly time.

Had it always been about serving himself? Or did he also consider the welfare of others? He had to fully review the life he had led on Earth. Actions he regretted could easily fall away if he discontinued doing the things that would cause the problems. He had to be shown how to purge evil to detox his body. This clarity being given through his life's review was necessary—a map of sorts.

It had been transmitted to him that he needed to know where he wanted to go but he also needed to know from where he had started. This is how he could figure out how to get to his desired destination. Then ultimately, he had to be willing to take the steps to move forward. He needed to dump the negative burdens picked up in life. To relieve this tapestry of affliction, he must be stripped of his negative worldly qualities. Live in the present and build a foundation for a stable future.

But only if his consciousness was ready to accept this information.

Chapter 30

The morning twilight streamed through their master bedroom window. Kendal still lay in bed exhausted from not sleeping. The hardest part was the waiting. Her emotions vacillated between hope and despair—she was not ready to say goodbye. She prayed that he was safe, but a tiny voice inside her warned her to brace for the worst.

The spacious bedroom was filled with a tranquil silence, except for her gentle breath and Brutus's occasional chirps as he talked to himself from beneath the cover of his cage in the kitchen.

She flung off the covers, rolled her body toward the edge of the bed, and sat up. Her legs felt heavy, and her head was still foggy from the lack of sleep. She felt a chill that made her skin prickle. Instinctively, her gaze sought out the expansive view of the penthouse window, and she took in the pale pink light of the morning sun, wondering if Derek was looking at it too.

She got to her feet and shivered, her toes touching the hardwood floor. She pulled out her oldest and most comfortable jeans, ruefully noting that they were already getting tighter. As she buttoned up her shirt, the memory of the phone call the day before flashed in her mind.

Hearing the news about the men being wounded or possibly killed made her acutely aware there was still a strong bond between her and Derek, and their hearts were still connected. According to the Bible, a married couple should unite in purpose, serve God, and make their marriage a priority. Their souls were entwined, making their two hearts beat as one, which made her realize why the pain of a possible breakup had been immense. For her, it was not a matter of two hearts going their separate ways but the fracturing of the one.

His painful departure for the jungle made her realize her mourning had already begun. She perceived it as a sign of the relationship's failure, decreasing her self-esteem. She had tortured herself with worries about what might have gone awry and her trepidations about what was yet to come. Now all she could do was pray that he would return to her unharmed.

She left the bedroom and headed to the kitchen, stopping briefly at Brutus' cage. As soon as she removed the cover, he was up and running along his enclosure in excitement. She opened the door of his cage and carefully removed the water and food trays.

Her time alone had allowed her to think. If she were being honest with herself, she had selfishly approached the situation. She recognized her mistakes and was not going to repeat them. This now allowed her to dig deep into her pain. She asked God to protect him. She asked for forgiveness for her part in sabotaging the marriage.

She had known for some time that Derek was feeling trapped— not by her but by the tattoos that marked his skin with years of tortured pain, a constant reminder of his life before her. He rarely discussed it anymore. She had seen it in the way he avoided eye contact and the lack of effort he could make toward their relationship.

She emptied out the contents of the small water dish into the sink; a mixture of seed and water dribbled out. She rinsed it out and refilled it. She then took the birdseed out of the cabinet, refilling the empty food dish.

But right before he left, she noticed something different in Derek. His frustration had reached a new level, and he had become increasingly distant from her and their life together. Now, standing in the dimly lit kitchen, she finally understood why. After months of searching fruitlessly for a remedy to his tattoo dilemma, Derek had yet to find a satisfactory solution. This lack of progress had taken its toll on his emotional well-being.

She was filled with an aching sadness for him. She wanted to reach out and take his hand, telling him she understood that everything would be okay. But before she could do any of that, Derek had to return home.

"I'm sorry," she whispered.

She had misunderstood when he had said, "I can't stay here any longer." Tears had stung her eyes as she watched Derek turn and walk out the door. She now understood it was not her he had left.

She returned to Brutus's cage, slid the tray out from the bottom, and then returned to the kitchen. She disposed of the paper she had placed at the bottom and refilled the tray with fresh ones.

Even during the awful time of Derek's tattoo manifestation, there were moments when he tried to focus on her and their relationship. Yet she became resistant to his efforts.

She would have to trust him again, recommit to helping him, or let him go. At this point, she had come to the realization that she was not willing to let go.

Before he departed, they had reached a state where they stopped bothering to make each other content. This was a serious setback for her. An air of pessimism had become commonplace between them, ultimately leading to their marriage's breakdown. It had already begun when they spent less and less time together.

She returned the fresh tray to the cage and removed his mirror. Brutus's protest could be heard throughout the penthouse. She hoped it wouldn't disturb Tyler. She padded back to the kitchen and put the mirror under the faucet, wiping it clean. She took another paper towel and dried it off.

It slowly dawned on her that her unhappy mood had caused the marriage to deteriorate. Although it had started off promisingly when she had been happy, respect had steadily drained from the relationship as her perspective of his behavior changed.

Initially, she was able to easily look past Derek's mistakes. However, as time passed, she became increasingly aware of the lack of mutual respect in the relationship. Both seemed to enjoy pointing out and ridiculing each other's flaws.

Acknowledging her unhappiness, she questioned whether it was a long-term issue or a passing phase that would resolve itself.

Since he had left, loneliness had set in. She had started to feel like she had already lost him—and now it seemed that could be the case. He might not make it back alive.

She returned the mirror along with the food and water trays to the cage—to Brutus's obvious chattering delight.

Right now, all she wanted was to communicate with Derek and know that he was safe. The lack of communication was tearing her up inside. She needed to hear his voice, feel that intimacy of their emotional closeness, and have his physical touch to reestablish the bond they had once felt.

She wanted to give him an opportunity to make everything right. His flaws had been a sign of his uniqueness. She wanted to resume a cheerful outlook and the intent to support him in his quest to free himself of the burden of his tattoos.

She returned to the kitchen to make herself a cup of coffee. She opened the door to the patio, stood in the doorway, and felt the cool, damp breeze on her face.

She had plenty of time to consider how she would react if he returned home, but all the thoughts in her head made her cry. She wished with all her heart to be able to utter those three simple words one last time to his face: "I love you."

She wanted to forgive and apologize too. She wanted him to understand that their connection had been something exceptional and important. She still felt connected to him. She told herself that if he had died, she would have known it instinctively—wouldn't she?

They would have to set down rules of engagement, setting the right tone and positive influence to inspire changes in the way they communicated. They would have to make long-term changes.

She realized they both needed to forgive themselves for past mistakes, get back to practicing mindfulness and empathy by being conscious of each other's efforts.

She closed the patio door, deciding to remain inside. Aloud, she said, "None of this means a thing unless he returns home."

Chapter 31

Seventh day, Shaman Village

Derek's eyes shot open. He stared at the thatched ceiling of the hut, trying to understand what was happening. He heard a movement and turned his head to see Maria tending a fire with a pot hanging over it. How had she come to be here to help him? Then he remembered the old shaman woman had been her grandmother. He tried to sit up.

Mari saw him try to move and rushed over to his side to help him sit up. She smiled, patted her chest, and said softly, "Mari," then said something in Warao and left the hut. He sat up, looking around. Before he could collect his thoughts, the hut door opened and to his surprise in stepped the old shaman woman.

The woman who had vanished without a trace.

The shaman woman whom he thought was dead.

A powerful sensation of awe and amazement washed over him in response to seeing her for the first time since her body had lain on the gurney in the hospital morgue.

The old shaman's eyes flashed bright. She maintained eye contact. She seemed extremely happy seeing Derek awake.

Rodrigo entered right behind.

Derek noticed that she was wearing ordinary clothes instead of the robe and headdress he now faintly remembered seeing her in during a ceremony. The doctor of the community. She sat down beside Derek with Mari at her side. She spoke in a smooth, soft voice. Derek looked at Rodrigo with amazement and shock at seeing a presumed dead person alive and well.

"She is asking how you are feeling today," Rodrigo explained.

His swollen and inflamed vocal cords left his voice a mere whisper. "Like I've been hit by a bus."

Rodrigo translated the words, and she smiled.

"What happened?" Derek rasped. "How is she here?"

"You had a very bad reaction to a very venomous spider."

Derek felt as if he had undergone some transformation. As if he had completed an initiation rite. Something within him felt healed, different, and fundamentally altered in his core.

The old shaman woman spoke again.

Rodrigo repeated, "She says she works with your spirit energy."

Derek noticed that she had a keen intellect with a sharp mind. He devoted his undivided attention to her. As the conversation progressed, he grew more confused. He looked over to Maria-Mari and wondered how she had been able to bring her grandmother back here. Mari had a close relationship with her grandmother, her teacher. Being from her lineage she'd studied with her one-on-one for most of her life. She had developed some sort of power unknown to Western culture.

Derek was looking for more information about the shaman's granddaughter and her kidnapping. He wanted to understand the connection between his supernatural tattoos, the shaman's powers, and their connection to everlasting life through faith in Jesus.

The old shaman's words were gentle, punctuated by occasional moments of lightheartedness, prompting her granddaughter to laugh. She seemed almost impish as she spoke.

When Derek first met her, he thought she was wicked, but after observing her for a while, he could tell that she was caring, understanding, and incredibly grateful. She explained to him that she had performed a healing ritual and that he was now healed from the terrible spider bite.

He questioned her, wondering how she was standing before him. He remembered Father Mike and Cecilia saying that they had seen her in the hospital morgue, lifeless.

"I was not dead. I slowed my heart rate down to an undetectable level."

He looked at Mari. "But how did you two escape the room in the morgue without being seen?"

Rodrigo waited for her response, then translated for Derek. "I asked Father Mike to leave me alone with my grandmother. I knew she carried a special herb in the lining of her dress. I put the herb in her mouth, bringing her blood pressure back up. We shape-shifted into nurses and then walked out quietly as they stood in the hall with their backs to the door. We then left the rear of the building. As they stood talking, they were unaware of our exit. I am sorry, but I wanted to say thank you. But we knew that people could still be looking for us. My grandmother was afraid they would take me away. My grandmother had already purchased a round-trip ticket and the documents to get back home. We went straight to the airport."

He asked her, "Why do I have all these tattoos on me? Did you put them there?"

Rodrigo again waited for the shaman's response.

Her parchment-paper hand lifted up in front of her weatherworn face. "I hold up a mirror to lead you toward your real story. I will help you get to a place where you can heal yourself. You must be realistic." Her crooked finger swiped up and down. "I do not have the power to manifest tattoos on you nor change your Book of Life."

Rodrigo sat in silence, staring at Derek, waiting for him to answer.

"Then why did this happen when you grabbed my arm?" Derek pointed to his face.

Rodrigo began to translate again. "I had to do something when my granddaughter was kidnapped, so I opened myself up to the spirits for guidance. That is how I ended up finding you. I think there must have been something in your soul that I needed to help rescue. My consciousness grew, and I became aware of your being. I reached out with my mind, and I was able to link with yours. You had a void I could manipulate, so I used it to guide you toward finding my granddaughter.

"I cannot control you, for we are all granted free will—unless you give me that power. We all have been given the power to choose. However, I can influence and guide your spirit to help affect your decisions, and that is what I did. What happened afterward was your doing. You accomplished the rest on your own. I will always be eternally thankful for that."

"After our encounter, I became sick and woke up with tattoos head to toe. How do you explain that?" Derek kept his eyes trained on her.

"This is your journey. I do not know exactly why. I do know that it was meant for me to be there at that place and time. My goal was to find my granddaughter and you appeared. That is all that I know.

"Rodrigo has explained to me that you carry judgment and doubt.

You believe that I have attached this stigma to you. I can only guide you through your shadows. I can only help you expand your consciousness and explore the dark as well as the light. I am here to help you connect with Spirit. You need to release what no longer serves you."

Her voice was gentle. "I can only help you interpret your experience. You must release the dark and reach for the light within you. I am here to assist in your personal empowerment and spiritual growth to work in harmony to remove blocks and life obstacles. You are here to restore balance to your mind, body and spirit. You have been provided the tools to release what no longer serves you and integrate the learning from which this journey has provided."

Derek wasn't sure how to process this. He was not getting the answers he'd been looking for. He had found a connection to the Great Divine but not through her. He had become aware of his path's purpose. He had reached deep into the shadow and released the pain and past trauma created by his early childhood issues. So then where did this shaman woman fit?

As Derek uncovered more information about the shaman's powers, he started to question the wisdom of coming to the village. He wondered if not finding these answers would cause more turmoil in his life.

The shaman began to speak in a soft tone, as translated by Rodrigo.

"I do not believe that I have affected you, but you have affected me. I went out to search for my granddaughter who had been taken from me. I had invoked the spirits to help. I was led to you. At the time I did not know how you were going to help, but I knew I had been led to you for a reason. I became deathly ill. The evil and darkness almost took me. But then just when I needed you most you provided me with the medicine I needed, my granddaughter."

She gazed at him calmly. "I am sorry that we left the way we did. I needed to come back home with my granddaughter to protect her and so that she could help me to heal. I was going to contact you but then thought it best to leave it alone. I had no idea that this thing had happened to you. My granddaughter told me of your appearance once we returned to the village. It seemed to me to be a strange thing for a Western doctor to do. To submit his body to such an extreme transformation like a body full of tattoos."

"Then you are telling me that you have no connection whatsoever to my transformation?" Derek felt like all the air was being let out of him, as his hopes were crushed. He was deflating like a balloon quickly losing its shape.

"No, I do not. I am forever grateful to you for returning my granddaughter to me. You and Father Mike."

He stiffened. "Where is Father Mike"?

She dropped her head. "We do not know if he will survive," she said feebly.

Rodrigo hesitantly repeated the words.

"Survive? What do you mean?" His eyes scanned the hut.

Rodrigo looked at the shaman woman then back to Derek. "The jaguar attacked him. He has sustained critical injuries. We're waiting for the emergency crew to come and get us. They should be here at any time."

Derek started to get up, but his weak legs betrayed him, and he sat down again.

"Where is he?"

"He is lying right over there." Rodrigo pointed.

Derek turned his head to see a motionless body under a blanket. "I want to see him."

Rodrigo jumped up to help Mari lift Derek to stand. They assisted him to the other side of the hut where Derek kneeled next to Father Mike. He gasped when he saw his mentor's ravaged face. He began to weep.

Mari placed her hand on Derek's back. "I am so sorry. We honor this great man of God. He fought the jaguar spirit. No one has done that and lived. I believe he is under God's protection."

Derek could feel the sense of loss and responsibility brought on by Father Mike's condition. For Derek, every moment had been a battle, a test of his will and his strength. And he wouldn't let the jungle defeat him. He did not want the jungle to defeat Father Mike either.

"He killed the jaguar," Rodrigo said.

Derek looked at him in disbelief. "How did he do that?"

"It appears that he had a knife when the jaguar attacked."

"Where was he when this happened?"

"From the tracks we found, the jaguar came into the camp. We believe that Father Mike was protecting you. The jaguar pounced and there was a struggle. Then it dragged Father Mike out of camp. Father Mike continued to stab the cat as he was carried by the head. He had a knife in each hand. The cat succumbed to its wounds. We found them both lying in a pool of blood just yards from the camp. You, however, seemed to be untouched."

"I need a minute with Father Mike alone," Derek said firmly.

Mari and Rodrigo stepped away, back to where the shaman woman sat waiting.

"I can't believe you did this for me," Derek said quietly. "I can never repay you. But I want you to know I understand now what you have been telling me about God. Father Mike, I have felt the love. I have seen Him. I pray that you will live. I know that God is protecting you. He loves you and will heal you. Faith, Father Mike, I give you my faith and my forever gratitude. You represent to me what God wants us to be on earth."

Father Mike, a priest of God filled with the Holy Spirit, had fought with the jaguar spirit (an earthly spirit). The Holy Spirit had led him here with Derek to protect him from these evil spirits that moved between the earth and the spirit realm.

Derek now knew that the shaman woman presided over the spirits of the underworld and the material world but had no power in the Heavenly realm. Her position in the spirit world was that of a communicator. He had deceived himself into thinking that she had the power to inflict the tattoos on him.

He now understood that she had been looking for someone who could help return her granddaughter. That she had the capability to manipulate benevolent and malevolent spirits on earth but not to manifest physical changes that could change the direction of the Divine.

He was not sure if the shamanic medicine had anything to do with it at all.

The door of the hut opened, and a villager came rushing in. Rodrigo approached Derek to announce that the emergency team had arrived to evacuate them both.

Still too weak to stand and walk by himself, he said his goodbyes to the shaman woman and Mari, who knelt beside him. As Mari wrapped him in a warm embrace, her grandmother watched. He felt a mixture of emotions as he accepted their final blessing—sadness, grief, and a sense of loss—but also a flicker of hope reignited within him. He was going home. It was bittersweet; this hunt for her was coming to an end and it left him feeling slightly empty inside. He couldn't help but question himself, wondering why he had given the idea of her so much power in the first place.

On the flight back to civilization, Derek lay in the helicopter next to Father Mike.

He never could have anticipated what this journey would bring. During the time he had left his body he had experienced the ability to sense other people's emotions. It had been coupled with the ability to imagine what Kendal might be thinking or feeling.

From the start, she had been a source of encouragement. A kind and supportive companion. She was an enthusiastic person who had always wanted the best for him. Her intentions were good.

Derek's body lay on a cot in the helicopter next to Father Mike. Relaxed now, he faded back into the black. This time he dreamed about Kendal. He could see her auburn hair and warm green eyes. She was wearing her favorite sundress and smiling. She whispered something to him, then gave a little wave for him to follow. She turned to walk away then her head turned to look back over her shoulder to make sure he was coming. He could see she had a tear in the corner of her eye.

His new awareness revealed the broken life contents that had been stuck in his mind. He had failed to face the darkness, and it had almost destroyed the only thing he absolutely loved in the world.

The helicopter landed on the roof of the hospital. Father Mike was rushed into emergency surgery. Derek was taken to the ER for examination.

The surgery on Father Mike was extensive. He would need more operations eventually, but for now, he was disfigured but stable.

The wounds were deep and severe. The slashes ran diagonally down his face, neck, and scalp, his ear almost completely severed, barely hanging by a thread. The doctors had managed to close the gaping wounds and stabilize him. They were hopeful that they could contain the infection coming from the bacteria-riddled bites. The lacerations on his arms and hands, where claws and teeth had dug in deep, still needed time to heal.

Derek was confined to his hospital bed, connected to several machines and intravenous bags of medications. Vivid dreams of Kendal played out in his mind, teeming with powerful emotions that threatened to overwhelm him.

The realization that he had died and then returned diminished the fear he had once felt inside. He had gone to the brink and come back. What else could there be? All his worries and earthly concerns had dissipated in the knowledge that there was more, much more. He had seen the Book of Life.

So, he had no choice but to ponder and examine the paths that led him to the brink of destruction. He was now required to take a journey deep into his thoughts. This allowed him to look back at previous decisions and understand how he had arrived in this situation. His recollection of the days and years that passed was all he had to make sense of it.

He had been hard on himself since arriving at the hospital. The negative self-talk threatened to entrap him once again. He felt over-whelming guilt for Father Mike's attack. It was impossible at this point to reframe his negative thoughts into positive ones. It felt silly to even try to pretend that all was well.

Derek had brought Father Mike with him, but now his best friend was lying in a bed down the hall unconscious. His body had been ripped apart trying to shield Derek from danger.

Since Derek had returned to the physical world, he found himself questioning his true purpose in life and pondering what the future held. This shift of perspective was an undeniable fact that he would need to treat the people he loved with a greater awareness of their contributions.

At this point, he understood that the powerful, mystical experience of dying would lead to the permanent transformation of his life. The body is just the vessel that contains our soul. The lessons he learned changed him. He now had self-sufficiency, knowing that faith was the only thing that could be linked to his immortal soul, transcending even death.

Derek heard his voice come from within: "My spirit belongs to God and my body belongs to me."

When Derek first rolled into Father Mike's room in a wheelchair, the bandages covering the priest's face and torso were a stab to his heart.

Derek sat by his bed after his most recent surgery. When Father Mike finally woke, he looked over at Derek with his one good eye. The left side of his face was covered in bandages. He had lost his eye. Derek could not see the damage hidden behind the bandages. He gave him a weak smile.

Derek reached over and squeezed his one good hand. "There's my friend. I've been worried about you."

"About me?" His weak half-smile turned to a grimace.

"Yeah, you had me worried."

"Hmm," he closed his eye.

When it was clear that Father Mike had drifted off again, Derek pushed his IV pole down the hall to his room and climbed back into bed. Still weak, he rested. He dreamed he had been in what seemed like an art gallery. Each framed piece of art reflected a place in a specific time in his life.

He had stepped into an alternate world where he relived the scenes that played out before him. As he studied the framed artwork, it brought back memories of his past. Important moments that had shaped him. He had stepped into another realm surrounded by the echoes of his past.

He realized that he was reliving the experience he had in the jungle. The time he spent in Heaven was revealing bits and pieces to him.

Derek no longer required a wheelchair. It had taken more than a week for his body to regain some of its strength. He feebly walked into Father Mike's room and found him awake. He had just finished eating a cup of soup that sat empty on the tray in front of him.

"You look like you're feeling better," Derek said.

"I am." He dabbed the corner of his mouth with a napkin and laid it on the tray. "You look like you've had some sort of revelation." Father Mike could see immediately that his tattoos were gone from his face. "How are you feeling?"

"Fine." Derek smiled. "I'm ready to blow this popsicle stand and go home."

"Have you spoken to Kendal?" Father Mike took a swig from the straw that sat in a glass of water.

"Yes, we've been spending a lot of time on the phone." Derek ran his fingers through the new crop of light brown hair on the top of his head.

"You should go home." Father Mike sat the glass and straw back on the tray.

Derek's bearded face contorted into a frown. "I'm not going home without you."

"I'll be ready to go home soon. You don't have to wait."

"Of course I do. We came here together, and we'll leave here together." Derek reached for the water pitcher to refill his glass. "So, you're quite the legend around these parts."

"What do you mean?" Father Mike's gaze lasered in on Derek.

"The story of you killing the jaguar has grown to great proportions." Derek grinned.

"Really?" Father Mike said flatly.

"Yes, good conquered evil."

"Doesn't the Lord work in mysterious ways?" He slumped back onto the pillow.

"Yes, he does. While I was in the jungle unconscious, I had a near-death experience. I met Jesus. It was the most unexplainable, powerful love. It was absolute love—I felt like I had come home."

"That's called the Lazarus Syndrome, when a person dies and comes back to life." His voice was still gravelly from the tubes that had been put down his throat during multiple surgeries to help him breathe, leaving his throat raw. "It's based on the story in the Bible of when Jesus resurrects his friend, Lazarus, back to life." Father Mike could see in Derek's face that there had been a profound change. His tattoos were gone. But he was still too weak for an in-depth conversation, and it hurt to talk.

"I'm amazed at how we can leave our physical body and its limitations behind." Derek moved around Father Mike's bed to fluff his pillow.

Father Mike could hear that Derek was surprised to learn he had a body made of spiritual substance. "Maybe you have learned something." Father Mike spoke slowly. "The church teaches that unlike the human body, our soul is the image of God. Only our soul can see God, it dwells between the flesh and the spirit. This is the Seventh Dimension."

Derek sat back down in the chair beside the bed. "I think I died and left my body. The sensations I experienced were sharper and more poignant than they ever were here on earth. I am still astonished how I felt so alive. I could see everything without even having to move my head. It was like I had a supernatural perception and awareness of everything around me. I could hear the thoughts of the people that I encountered, and they could hear mine."

His eyes grew distant. "It was mind-blowing, and hard to describe how totally consuming the whole experience was. I still had all my senses but so much more. I was endowed with a supernatural sense of touch and smell. Everything was now multiplied by an unexplainable amount.

He frowned. "I remember thinking, *how can I still have a body after shedding my physical body*? Immediately after leaving my physical body behind, I felt myself expand. It is hard to describe, but it is a feeling of unlimitedness. Like I was a part of eternity. I think what I had was a spiritual body. I could see that my spiritual body looked like my physical body except without pain and the tattoos. It felt separated and purified from earthly matter."

Father Mike spoke softly. "When your spirit connects to the spiritual realm of Heaven, it is like an electrical current reuniting with its origin."

The priest shifted in the bed. A grimace crossed his face. "We believe that when a person dies, his soul separates from his body. Our soul is who we are. We are composed of a physical body and an eternal soul. They are separated at death. The core of our being, the essence of ourselves, is a product of our choices and desires. This defines our character. Our spirit differs from our soul in that our spirit is always pointed toward and exists exclusively for God."

His voice had become raspy. Derek picked up the glass of water on his tray and put the straw to his lips. He took a painful sip and swallowed slowly.

"I hope you now realize that your inner possessions are what you collect on earth." Father Mike paused to take another sip. Then he continued, his voice a bare whisper. "Your habits and thoughts . . . feelings . . . beliefs and interests. Also, your skills, relationship ties, and memories all make up your soul, but your spirit belongs to God." He laid back exhausted from the effort and closed his one good eye.

Derek slipped quietly out of his room.

Father Mike was bedridden for weeks. On this sunny afternoon, Alejandro, one of his most devoted followers, had come to visit him.

Alejandro entered the small hospital room. Father Mike's one good eye lit up at the sight of his old friend. He had come to present him with a necklace made from a jaguar tooth. It symbolized honor and respect, a tribute from the villagers for his unwavering devotion to God.

Alejandro stood at the foot of the bed, unsure of what to say or do in the presence of such a revered figure, who had not only saved his life but now had given up his body to save another.

"You have brought me a precious gift, Alejandro," Father Mike said, his voice still raspy but filled with warmth. "I am grateful for your thoughtfulness."

Alejandro nodded, a lump forming in his throat. He had always admired Father Mike, and his unwavering faith and his dedication to helping those in need.

"I am sorry to see you in this condition, Father," Alejandro finally managed, his voice thick with emotion.

Father Mike smiled, his one eye filled with understanding. "Do not worry, my son. I am at peace. And I know that my work will continue through people like you."

Tears welled up in Alejandro's eyes as he reached out to touch the man's hand. He knew that Father Mike's words were true. His faith and wisdom legacy would live on in the hearts of those he had touched.

As he left the hospital, Alejandro could not help but feel a deep sense of gratitude for having known such a remarkable man. And he vowed to carry on his teachings and continue his work, fulfilling his duty to both the village in which he served and to God.

Derek realized that he had taken his inner possessions with him. He had experienced the death of his earthly body. When he moved from one life into the other, he retained everything he had seen, heard, read, learned, and thought in the world from his earliest infancy to the very end. This revelation made the material things in life a lot less important.

He slipped back into his hospital bed after one of his daily walks, pulling the light cover over his body. He lay back to ruminate on Father Mike's words. *Your body reflects your state of mind. Your body is an essential part of your nature. Your soul is essentially dependent on it. Your body is God's temple. God's spirit dwells in you.* How often had Father Mike told him these words: "You are what you think about." Now he was finally beginning to understand.

Derek waited until late in the afternoon to visit Father Mike. When he entered his room, he found Father Mike reading a Bible.

"They brought a Bible to me." He smiled, his one blue eye twinkling with obvious delight.

"That's great," Derek said with a stoic grin. "I can see it's helping your spirit."

Father Mike closed the bible and placed it on the overbed table. "How are you doing today?"

"Better. I had time to reflect on our conversation."

"That sounds positive." He motioned for Derek to have a seat.

"It is. Some of the pieces are starting to come together for me. After I died or came close to it from my reaction to the spider bite, I remember that when it first happened, I was drawn toward a black veil. I was in a similar state of mind that I had been on earth." Derek chewed the corner of his lip.

"You were still in the state of your external concerns," Father Mike said.

"At first, my thought patterns were like those of the man I had been on earth. Those deeper feelings and beliefs started to emerge and expand, then they pulled me toward the darkness. Before I was completely consumed by the black veil, I suddenly stopped. A hand reached for me, and as it pulled me out, I could feel all those negative feelings being vacuumed out of me. I watched them like a liquid stream sucked into the dark mire in front of me. My heavy weight disappeared, leaving me with my lighter spiritual body."

"You do understand that magic had nothing to do with this? There was no curse."

Derek nodded.

"Our Christian belief says our souls transition to a new dimension when we pass away from this earthly life," Father Mike continued. "Those who have accepted the faith and been reborn are said to enter the Sixth Dimension: Paradise. In this realm, the departed are rejuvenated in a celestial body and await the return of Christ during the rapture. During this event, they will leave their mortal bodies behind and take on immortal and incorruptible ones. These glorified bodies will then rule with Christ in the millennium and in the new Heaven and earth."

Father Mike paused to take another sip of water. "In the Seventh Dimension resides God, who reigns supreme over the universe with His boundless power and splendor. Heaven is His home and earth is merely a small part of His domain. One day, He will bring His kingdom to this world, uniting Heaven and earth in perfect harmony. The glory of God will fill every corner of the earth, and those with 'eternal life' within them will dwell in His presence for all eternity."

Derek looked down at the perfectly clean skin on his hands. There were no more tattoos over the top of his hands or up and down his fingers. "Yes. I understand that I have always been in control of what was happening to me. I kept looking to the outside world instead of looking into my inner being."

"Our body was given to us as a vessel, in the image of God." Father Mike ran his hand over the leather binding of the Bible. "Since Jesus was the last sacrifice, the Holy Spirit has filled us with the Truth. God is the divine and eternal life."

He picked up the Bible. "When you said you believed in Jesus, something took place inside you. Your spirit was born again. This has now resulted in an undeniable change in your inward being. By reaching out to the Holy Spirit, he has shown you with the removal of the tattoos that his salvation is real."

Derek had seen the changes. His appearance had gradually started to reflect his internal transformation. The ruling emotion he now held in his heart differed from the one that had lurked in the dark shadows of his mind. He appeared younger, and the deep frown lines had disappeared with the tattoos. His facial features seemed to reflect his positive thoughts and feelings—his new innermost self. They had begun to reflect what he truly now felt in his heart.

It was a powerful way to learn about his inner being. His focus and awareness were moving beyond his physical heredity and what had been displayed for the world to see upon his skin. He had let go of his earthly concerns and his true identity came into focus with new clarity. He now realized what he wanted and needed out of life. God's will for him.

It had been shown to him while in Heaven that the good spirits had loving faces with bright eyes reflecting the status of their soul; while the people on earth who were engaged in evil afflictions did not.

"This will help you to move forward." Father Mike adjusted his bed to sit up straighter. "You have been brought into a more refined state of mind by this experience. I can see it on your face."

Derek went to the mirror that hung over the sink. When he'd first looked in the mirror and laid eyes on his unmarked face, emotions overwhelmed him. Looking into the mirror was a jarring experience. His mind was accustomed to seeing a canvas of tattoos covering his face; the absence of them somehow had felt wrong. He stared deeply into his own eyes and immediately felt a sense of panic and unease wash over him. It was like his brain didn't recognize this person in the mirror as himself. It was disconcerting, and he almost felt as if the mirror was playing a cruel trick on him, creating an illusion that something had gone wrong with his brain.

He studied his face. His previous face had been shaped by his environment. Now, when he looked in the mirror, he was starting to grasp an understanding of his true identity. The person he had always meant to be. He was beginning to understand that losing everything—including his life—had brought out who he really was more than anything else he had ever experienced. It was still difficult to decipher who he might now become.

Father Mike watched him examine himself in the mirror. "I know that God's intent for you was to bring you into the deepest bliss in the highest Heaven to show you that you have autonomy over your life. You cannot pretend it is not wholly your responsibility anymore. The thoughts you have will impact the person you become. Your facial features will reflect your intentions and desires."

Derek ran the tips of his fingers across his cheek. He could still feel the vibrations of the remnants of the tattoos. The echoes of the symbols created by his past internal turbulence. He had experienced his vibration expand and contract. There was now a newfound freedom because he no longer had an emotional constriction bottled up inside.

"Your spiritual frequency is reflected in the levels of your love and wisdom." Father Mike said as he watched Derek examine himself. "Your lower ego thoughts and feelings resonate at a lower, denser frequency. The more loving and altruistic thoughts and feelings you have resonate at a much higher level."

Derek moved his head downward, his eyes locked on his reflection as he made a slight turn of the head. One tattoo still remained. He pulled his shirt open to reveal the heart on his chest. He was happy to see it. This was the symbol of his love for Kendal and God's love for him. He had felt welcomed with unconditional love and joy when he had been in Heaven, something he had only experienced with his grandmother as a child.

Derek turned from the mirror to face Father Mike. "I'm supposed to be here to *cheer you up*. Are you ready to go home?"

"Ready as I will ever be," he said, touching the bandage over his eye.

Derek was eager to return to Kendal. He sat patiently looking out his hospital room window, waiting for the release paperwork to be signed for him and Father Mike to check out.

He was a new man. It felt like his slate had been wiped clean. He now had to show Kendal.

Before he left home, he had reached his limit. His search for a solution had become paramount. Feelings of hopelessness and desperation over the tattoos had taken over his thought process. He was now earnestly sincere about making the long-needed changes in his personal life that he should have made long ago.

If he had only tuned into what Dr. Cole had been saying. He now understood that there was only so much pain a person could bear. He was returning home to make whatever changes were necessary to win his wife back and save his marriage. A tremendous amount of pain, anger, and bitterness had accumulated from his behavior. He prayed that he would not be met with resistance on the part of Kendal. She had seemed receptive when they had spoken on the phone. He had to reassure her that he was willing to make it right.

He was not the same man who had left her just a month before. The arguing, blame and finger-pointing would all stop. He now sat in a faraway hospital room at the point of tears. His anguish to make things right was palpable. He wanted her to have hope again too. He desperately needed to repair their marriage and their bond.

Unbeknownst to him, Kendal had gone through a transformation of her own. Their conversations on the phone had been positive. Before he left, their marriage had been at a point where it might have to be dissolved.

He had gone through a renewal process. He was now willing to work on himself and his relationship. He was willing to show her and engage with a restoration of his love. He was ready to invest some real effort and focus on his wife's emotional state. He would have to try to mend the painful feelings he had created with his hurtful behavior, rooted in his insecurities.

He wondered if he had pushed her too far by leaving. Would her love for him be the same? His love for her had been masked by his past, which had resulted in frustration and disappointment. Through his Heavenly journey he felt he had now been healed of those hurts. He yearned to make peace with his life and situation with Kendal. His emotions had been repaired, and his love for her had been replenished.

He understood that she might not trust him to engage in a restoration process unless he was able and willing to do some things that ran counterintuitive to his past way of thinking. He had been able to take an honest look at himself during his time in the jungle. He now was ready to make the changes. He had come to a clear understanding and acceptance of where his heart had been. Now he was ready to open up. He knew that he had to engage in the process of healing her heart and repairing their relationship.

This was his awakening.

Seek clarity each day.

This was Kendal's new mantra. *Seek clarity each day.*

The sun was beginning to rise, its orange light filtering through the massive curtains of the penthouse bedroom. As Kendal slowly opened her eyes, she felt a sense of calm wash over her.

Today was the day that Derek came home.

She had been mindful of the messages presented to her each day and looked for new insights as to how they would move forward in their marriage. Her thoughts often turned to Derek during the day. She wondered how he was doing. She remembered the odd silence between them before he had left. The words they had left unspoken.

The faint smell of coffee wafted through the air from the Keurig in the kitchen. A reminder that there was a whole new world waiting beyond the walls of this room.

The sun was rising higher in the sky, signaling a new day and with new opportunity. Kendal was ready to move on with her life. She now had a lot more to think about than just her and Derek. They had a baby on the way. She wanted to tell him as soon as possible—but she had elected not to share the news over the phone. She didn't want his memories of being told about having his first child to be negative.

And she wanted to tell him in person so she could see the look on his face. She would pay attention to any signals that came her way by his reaction. In truth, she wasn't sure he was ready for such a tremendous commitment. For her, there had been no choice. She had this new life growing inside her.

I'll tell him at the first opportunity, she told herself as she set out to pick him up from the airport. If a good opportunity didn't arise, then he'd find out once he got home. She'd already put a crib in the corner of their massive penthouse bedroom.

The bottom line is she wanted to announce her pregnancy in a way that would be fun. She wanted it to be something they would both enjoy and remember. She laughed aloud when she thought about how long it might take him to catch on. What would his first reaction be? Would he be in shock? She wanted to treasure the moment.

Kendal sat behind the wheel of the Bentley. She smiled as she thought about how excited he would be when he saw his car. Then she wondered how he would react to the crib in their room. She chuckled. After more than a week of talking on the phone, she was finally going to be with Derek in person so that she could tell him he was going to be a father. She had spent hours dreaming how he would react and what he would say. She could think only of his voice, his smell, his touch.

As she stepped off the escalator into the baggage area, she allowed herself to take a deep breath. She felt a strange sense of anticipation. She knew that their lives were about to change in ways they could never have imagined.

Father Mike slept for the whole flight. The trip had taken a lot out of him. Derek had given Father Mike the aisle seat to make it easier for him to get in and out. Derek sat next to the window, looking out to the clouds in the sky.

He was reminded of the people he had met in Heaven. They had shared the same thoughts and feelings. He felt in sync with their spiritual frequency. The feeling had been so strong that he could now only be around people he resonated with. God had warned us to distance ourselves from evil. He looked at Father Mike, asleep next to him. This was a person who would always be a part of his life. He was like a brother. No one had ever given so much to defend him—except maybe Kendal.

This was as close as he was going to get to evolving into the level of love that the angels live in. He had started to feel the result of being exposed to the deep knowledge of Heaven. The experience had fundamentally changed him.

"This is why many of us are called to the priesthood," Father Mike had told him.

He could sense a new beginning. This journey had brought him to a place where his mind and heart had been changed forever. The love of God and love of neighbor had carried him through.

Derek pushed Father Mike in a wheelchair down the ramp to exit the plane. His head was bandaged with his left eye covered. He was still unable to stand for very long. His abdominal wounds had been deep. Thanks to God, the vital organs had remained untouched.

Derek and Kendal locked their eyes as soon as he stepped into the terminal. He had not expected to see her at the gate. Fireworks went off inside his body. In this moment, nothing else mattered. He had not felt this connection with her for a long time. An intense electrical jolt shot through his body. It completely engulfed him.

Derek saw astonishment flash in her eyes when she realized she could see the man she once knew physically transformed back into his old self. His face was devoid of tattoos, sporting only a hint of stubble. His once bald scalp was now covered with thick dishwater-blond hair.

He started to cry and ran to embrace her. Tears streamed down both their faces. She was the last of his unmet needs. His subconscious immediately recognized that his life with Kendal would return the balance. He was ready to do everything he could to bring this woman back into his life.

Father Mike sat back in his wheelchair, watching the couple with pure joy in his heart.

Unbeknownst to him, Kendal had gone through a transformation of her own. Their conversations on the phone had been positive, encouraging, and comforting, but in person, their connection seemed to be even more profound. As they stood waiting for their luggage, they continued to kiss and hug each other. They both felt the same stir in their hearts. It was a feeling neither of them could quite explain, but it was there all the same. They were suddenly and irrevocably reconnected.

She slowly released Derek and bent down to hug Father Mike. "Thank you for bringing him back to me," she whispered in his ear. She kissed him on his cheek and turned back to Derek. "Let's go home."

Just as Kendal had expected, Derek was elated to see his Bentley. Some things would never change. He grabbed her and hugged her in his excitement, then put their bags in the trunk.

Father Mike asked, "I hate to ask you this, but can you take me back to the rectory?"

"No, no. I will be taking care of you." Derek said as he helped him into the backseat. "You're coming home with us until you are ready to return to work. Not before. I insist."

Kendal turned to face him from the front seat, "I will be taking care of *both* of you," she smiled, reaching out. Father Mike took her hand and gave it a weak squeeze. A single tear escaped his eye.

In awe, Derek climbed into the driver's seat and looked at her with admiration. It was like they were brought back together again for the first time. In her presence, he felt safe and secure. He had placed his faith in her, and it had paid off—he hadn't lost it all. He intended to be open and honest with her going forward.

His first realization of what he had done was when he lay on the ground paralyzed. He had sacrificed everything he had to keep on his quest to find answers.

She had accepted him with the tattoos. What else should have mattered? He'd worried about all the other people, but she should have been his priority, she should have come first. He prayed to God that this would be his second chance.

He connected with her on a heart level. He had implicit faith in her. She allowed him to experience life deeply instead of just letting it wash over him. If he had only been smarter about how he had been making his decisions, Father Mike would not have gone into the jungle and lost an eye. He knew when he was leaving that it would damage the relationship, but he had ignored Kendal's pleas.

His profound spiritual experience and the attack by the jaguar on Father Mike had led Derek to a mental and physical conversion. He interpreted his experience as a warning about unwise decisions and wrong behavior.

Thanks to Father Mike, he was granted the opportunity to turn his life around. When they were in the hospital, Father Mike explained to Derek what he believed the relationship for having Jericho tattooed on his back had been about. Father Mike knew that his grandmother had once read this passage to Derek, but he now had a deeper, more spiritual meaning that he relayed to him.

"I want to talk about one of Jesus's miracles," he said while lying in his hospital bed. With one eye covered, his other eye watered, and he would frequently wipe it. "It is so powerful. In Mark 10:46, it says they were leaving the city of Jericho . . . If you look at Luke's account, it says as he drew near to Jericho. So it would appear at first glance to be a contradiction. Mark says he was leaving Jericho, and Luke says he was coming to Jericho—so which is it?" He blinked and wiped his eye.

Derek shrugged. "I wouldn't know."

Father Mike continued. "Actually they are both right. During the first century, Jericho was divided into two different parts. Residential Jericho was set in one area, and Jericho's administrative area was about a mile and a half away. This is where King Herod had his palace.

"So, Mark tells the story from a Jewish perspective as Jesus is leaving Jericho. Luke, on the other hand, tells the story from a gentile perspective as he approaches Jericho; he is talking about administrative Jericho."

Derek felt a little confused as to where Father Mike was going with this, but he didn't want to show it since the priest was using energy he really did not have to explain this revelation to him.

"If you think about it, that makes sense because if you were blind, where would you want to be?" He didn't wait for Derek to answer. "You would want to be on the road between the two parts of the cities because that would be where the traffic is. The blind man has placed himself on a crossroads. You see, that is just the logistics of the miracle itself. Jesus is on his way to Jerusalem from Jericho, making His way for that last Passover feast. His final week before he is crucified.

"So, anyone else would be thinking about themselves, but Jesus takes the time to heal one more person with a physical malady. Jesus already knew; I mean, He is the son of God. He already knew what the man's problem was. But he still gave him the opportunity to identify it; Jesus asked him what do you want me to do for you? You see . . ."

Father Mike paused, wiped his eye, and gave a slight cough to clear his throat. "God wants to hear us. He already knows our problems and struggles but wants that level of communication with us, too. He wants us to vocalize it. Interact with Him. And Jesus gave the blind man that opportunity. This blind man somehow recognizes Jesus and calls Him the son of David . . . the King is coming! He cries out all the more loudly and identifies him as a descendant of David, attaching the title of King to Him. Jesus responded by healing him on His way to Jerusalem.

"I think this blind man, Bartimaeus, is a sort of hero in the Bible. This is a man who knew he had a problem, and there was only one person who could fix it—Jesus." Father Mike pushed the point home. "He was not going to let anything stand in his way. That is the approach we should take with our lives. Do you understand what I am telling you?"

Derek understood. He was starting to understand more of Father Mike's stories. The Bible would now be his blueprint for life. He had returned from an awful situation and was granted a second chance.

When they arrived at the penthouse, Derek drove his car up to the entrance. Kendal helped Father Mike out of the car. She led him directly to the spare room. He lay back on the bed, exhausted. She helped him take his shoes off.

"Get comfortable," she said with a smile. "Take a nap. I will have something for you to eat when you wake up." She covered him with the throw at the foot of the bed. Closed the curtains, then the door.

Derek came in with the bags.

"I put him in the room across from ours. I want to be able to check on him."

"That's a great idea." He sat the bags down inside the bedroom door and reached for her. They fell into an intimate kiss and immediately reconnected.

They lay in bed together in simple joy and pleasure. She rested her head on his chest. Her finger ran along the bright red heart with colorful blooms and green vines. The last tattoo that remained.

"I cannot believe it's really you back here with me," Kendal admitted. "It felt like you were gone forever."

He laughed. "What do you mean *really* me?"

"You know you disappeared on me," she scolded. "Now you're back with just this one tattoo. I didn't know if I would ever see you again, and tell you the truth, I had moments where I thought maybe I didn't *want* to see you again."

He gave a nervous laugh when something caught his eye in the corner of the room.

"What the heck is that?" His voice trailed off.

She sat up, watching his face. His eyes squinted as his forehead furled into a frown, trying to put the pieces together.

She felt a momentary spike of fear.

Then he turned and looked at her. The revelation registered across his face like the dawn of light first thing in the morning. He broke into a huge smile.

Derek grabbed her and rolled her onto her back.

He put his hand on her stomach. He could now feel the little pouch.

"It is true! Are we having a baby?" he said with a choked sob.

"Yes." Tears rolled down her face.

He started to kiss her. First her face, then her chest, finally making his way down to her stomach.

How could this be happening? Not only had he *not* lost her, but he had gained everything.

A week later, Father Mike returned home to the rectory. Derek and Kendal lay in bed for the first morning, entirely alone in the penthouse. Tyler had decided to take a trip back to Thailand. It was an excellent time to see family, and he wanted to give them time to reconnect.

It felt so good to be back in her arms. He had disrupted their relationship long enough over his obsession with tattoos.

"I'm not worried about when I die. I know that God promised me something far more," he confessed, "and he has already given me everything I could want in this life."

Kendal rolled over on her stomach and rested her arms on his chest to look him in the face.

"This feels like when we first spent time at your apartment." He reached out to tuck a strand of auburn hair behind one ear, his fingers gently brushing against her skin. "I felt like I had known you forever. Because of your faith in me, I could finally relax and breathe again. For a moment during that time, I was free of anxiety and panic attacks. Then . . . why I had allowed them to take back over again, I don't know. I had no direction, no compass. I have that now."

She had allowed him to enter her personal space when he felt broken, and he was grateful for that. He remembered how he had melted into her world. With the toss of her head and a knowing smile, she calmed his mind. He felt comfortable and secure around her. She had opened her heart and her home to him.

He lay dozing, reminiscing about the moment of that first kiss while standing on the beach. The feeling had radiated throughout his body and settled into his unloved heart. Lying next to her, he knew he had made the right choice. She was everything to him. Why had he not made her his priority instead of those darn tattoos?

As he lay dying in the rainforest, he had flashed back to all the significant and trivial events of his life. The brain, under stress, releases natural opiates that stop the pain and fear. A lack of oxygen disrupts the regular activity of the visual cortex.

Some of the revelations he experienced during his life review came from other people's perspectives. He was able to conclude the inadequacy in his life and see what changes were needed. When he was forced to take an honest look at his life, he understood that it had been crucial to his progress. He knew he would gradually be led toward the knowledge of truth and goodness as an acknowledgment and fulfillment of his nature.

He kissed Kendal on the forehead. "I learned from this experience that I can trust you and God. What is important to God ended up vastly different from what I had been taught as a child. He showed me all the hurtful things I had done, even the ones I did not know I had done. I could feel the person's hurt. God had stood by me lovingly, not judging me but letting me judge myself."

She gazed at him seriously. "Did this happen after the spider bit you and you almost died in the jungle?"

"Yes, I became aware of a bright Heavenly being. It felt like I was in God's presence. I no longer felt the pain. Kendal, I detached from my body and floated above. I could see myself lying on the ground."

She lifted onto her elbows. "You died?"

"Yes. I think so. If not, I was close. I could see Father Mike taking care of me. I felt blissful."

"It sounds like you had a near-death experience. I have seen a lot of reports about this."

"It felt like my soul had left my body. When that happened, all the pain disappeared. At first, it felt peaceful. I just kept floating up toward a light. But then I entered this dark place. It felt like I was being sucked into it. I did not have any control. I was really scared and alone. It was a bad feeling. It brought up all my feelings about having the tattoos."

Kendal laid her head on his chest.

"Then, suddenly, a hand reached for me and pulled me out, the bad feelings stopped, and I felt calm. It was like I just slipped into oblivion. Then, a warm light came and wrapped me like a blanket. I felt the overwhelming presence of the Divine. The only way I can explain it is everything had been stripped away. All my feelings, memories, everything. I felt like an empty vessel. But then I started to feel my consciousness expand. It was like there was no beginning or end. I have never felt anything like it before. I had this unlimited sense of power and love. I could hear and see Father Mike's prayers as they rose."

Her eyebrows rose. "Wow, what did that look like?"

"It was like little puffy clouds that smelled like roses. They would just float up past me. I could see they were coming from below, where he knelt, praying next to me. Like I said, it seemed I had unlimited powers. I could see and hear everything. Father Mike asked God to take this burden from me and give it to him. It's my fault that he had to fight that jaguar."

Derek choked back tears. "He risked his life for me. All because I could not figure out who I was."

Kendal eyes welled up. "Oh, Derek."

Derek lay quietly for a minute, thinking about the incredible sacrifice Father Mike had made for him. Then he continued. "I knew I had detached from all material possessions, and I could feel a greater good fill my soul. An undeniable love. When Father Mike was willing to sacrifice everything for me, I realized that was what Jesus had done for humanity. It is hard to describe.

"My mind felt invigorated. I had thought after thought in rapid succession. It is so indescribable to the natural mind. It took me backward—I saw everything that had ever happened. My whole earthly existence was placed before me in a panoramic view. I began to reexperience my entire life. It was a shameful disappointment. All I could feel was sadness."

"Oh no, that can't be true!" Kendal objected.

"At one point, I watched Father Mike take his crucifix off and put it around my neck." He cleared his throat, wiping his eyes. "I could see a white light coming through the trees. Then the bright light sucked me up into the color of the sky. It was a warm light. Then, out of nowhere, I started praising and worshiping God."

"That is beautiful," Kendal said, tears streaming down her face.

"I could hear Father Mike's prayers with mine. He asked God to give me peace, heal me, and repurpose me."

"Repurposed?" She frowned. "What does that mean?"

"I'm not sure, but maybe it was for me to have an opportunity to start over in a new way. I did not feel any judgment; I was wrapped in love and affection. Then I saw a man in a white robe and gold sash so bright I could not see his face. As he approached, I realized this man was my only way to Heaven. It was Jesus."

"You just gave me goosebumps. What a blessing to actually see Jesus."

"I asked Him, 'Why did this to happen to me?'"

"You said that to Him?" Kendal sat up next to him.

"He hugged me and said, 'Remember your prayer to me.' At first, I wasn't sure what that meant, but then I remembered praying with Father Mike. I had asked Jesus to come into my heart. I understood that he had now shown me the difference between going to Heaven and hell.

"Then I was back in my body. All the pain came back. It was terrible. I didn't want to come back, but then I thought of you." He put his hand under her chin, pulling her forward to kiss her passionately.

This is what Kendal had been waiting for. She wanted her Derek back.

After expressing their love, Derek fell asleep and began to dream.

Two spiritual angels from the Kingdom of Light were on each side of him. They came with a sweet smell that kept the evil spirits from coming near. The angels were there to help him into the Heavenly realm. He felt the coverings on his eyes roll back. He could now see a Heavenly-colored light way off in the distance.

Derek felt himself start to move closer. He became aware of his spiritual thoughts. His earthly weakness felt like a heavy bucket of cement. When he released it, he could become lighter and feel himself being escorted to a spiritual realm. Scenes of Paradise began to come into view. The profound state of joy he had felt when he was in Heaven seemed to again consume his spirit.

He began to learn about himself in a deeper understanding than he had ever had before. Each sensation was sharper than the next, more real than they had been on earth. He felt a sense of peace. Then, he began to understand what God had wanted for him.

He asked aloud, "What different choices should I have made?"

The answer came back in question form, "What have you learned?"

At that moment, he knew God had forgiven him, but he still had not forgiven himself for what he had done to Father Mike.

He woke for a minute. Kendal lay sleeping beside him. He began to think about the dream he had just had and what it meant. He thought, *Punishing myself will not improve things in His eyes. I need to accept His love and forgiveness*, as he dozed back off.

In a twilight dream, he thought that once he was able to accept God's love, it would become easier. His life review had been the first step toward change. It helped him sort out what thoughts and habits needed to be removed and what habits and attitudes he wanted to keep.

He then flashed to being in a garden on the penthouse roof. The night air was thick, full of the scents of trees and flowers like it had been in the jungle. He was aware of the distant laughter of children mingling with the chirping songs of the birds in the trees. He looked up at the stars that twinkled in the sky, strung together like diamonds in an endless web of light.

Kendal stood by his side, an unlikely pair with their height and build, him tall and broad, her petite and delicate. But as they gazed up at the sky together, he found solace in her familiar presence. She intertwined her fingers with his and they remained like that for what felt like an endless moment, until he eventually woke from his dream.

Kendal lay next to him. Still asleep.

"I love you," he whispered, brushing a strand of auburn hair from her brow. "I always have—since the moment I asked you to come into my office," he said softly, the words lingering in the air.

Her eyelids lifted slowly, and she gazed up at him. Her eyes shone with joy as she gave him an unfiltered, genuine smile. "I love you too," she said, her voice barely more than a whisper.

He squeezed her hand and brought it to his lips, kissing it gently before letting it go. He was no longer a captive to his past. He was free to heal, grow, and become the person he was meant to be.

She laughed softly and reached up, touching his face and running her fingers through his newly grown hair. He kissed her, and for now, they were as one.

Unbeknownst to him, Jesus continued to reappear in his dreams. He had come to the simple realization that we must confront our past demons. As he delved deeper into his subconscious, Derek would uncover the true meaning of life—emotional freedom.

ACKNOWLEDGMENTS

The 6th Heaven Journey

Dear Readers,

Embarking on an adventure through thick vegetation, rugged terrain, limited visibility, wildlife encounters, and humid conditions can be much like delving into the depths of your mind; yet every challenging trek offers its own rewards. I encourage you to make the effort. When you emerge on the other side, you'll find yourself a better person.

I am incredibly thankful for your purchase and the time you've taken to read my book. I hope it brought value and enjoyment to your life. If you find it worth sharing, please consider passing it along to your loved ones or leaving a review on a reputable site. Your feedback and support are invaluable as they allow me to pursue my passion. You can visit *the series page* to leave a review for others to see. Thank you again for your support and for being a reader of my work.

ABOUT THE AUTHOR

Writer, speaker, and certified life coach *Monica Broussard* is passionate about writing fiction that contains fantasy elements and keeps the reader intrigued about the lead character's motives. She also writes an occasional article for her hometown's magazine, *SeaCliff Living*. She belongs to American Christian Fiction Writers (ACFW) and enjoys attending national writers' conferences.

Born in North Carolina on a Marine Corps base, Monica now lives in "Surf City," Huntington Beach, California, with her husband of thirty-nine years. She has enjoyed various occupations, but her favorite job is the one she's doing now—writing.

The 6th Heaven is Book 3 in the *21 Tattoos* Series.